THE TINA PROJECT

Adam Grace

—————— ◆ ——————

A NOVEL

—————— ◆ ——————

ISBN   1-871217-54-7

cover photograph courtesy of
Patrick Black

published by
FAMILY PUBLICATIONS
6a King Street
Oxford OX2 6DF
www.familypublications.co.uk

printed in England

For Jean

"What experience and history teach is this – that people and governments never have learned anything from history, or acted on principles deduced from it."

– *GWF Hegel*

"There are powers at work in this country about which we have no knowledge."

– *Her Majesty Queen Elizabeth II*

Acknowledgements

Some authors acknowledge the contributions of their spouses almost as an afterthought, along the lines of "and last but not least, my wife, without whom this book would not have been written".

Not this author. Pride of place is reserved for my wife, my reality check, my oracle, who has never failed to enlighten me in areas of medical procedures, motherhood and morality whenever I have turned to her for help. Without her wise guidance this book may well have been written, but never published.

That it has been published is also due in no small part to the vision of Denis Riches, of Family Publications, for whom it represents a challenging venture into the unfamiliar territory of popular fiction. His confidence and enthusiasm have sustained me throughout the novel's later stages.

In addition, special tribute should be paid to Valerie Riches, whose remarkably prescient books, *Sex and Social Engineering* and *Sex Education or Indoctrination?* have proved authoritative and truly inspiring works of reference.

Among those who kindly read earlier drafts of my novel, I am particularly grateful to David O'Leary, who suggested improvements that have enhanced its appeal as a political thriller. Invaluable input and encouragement where also supplied by Professor Edward Hulmes, formerly of Harvard University.

In chapters dealing with the murky world of Freemasonry, I have relied heavily on Martin Short's illuminating classic, *Inside the Brotherhood* (published by Grafton) and on his expert advice on the several occasions when I have shamelessly picked his brains.

Nightly news bulletins from SPUC, the newsletters of Right to Life, information from the Royal College of Nursing and other helpful internet sources have also been instrumental in imparting (hopefully) an authentic flavour to my work. I am greatly indebted to them all.

Finally, sincere appreciation to my long-suffering 'technical adviser', Norman McLeod, for repeatedly rescuing me from a pathologically obdurate computer, and to my dear friend and fellow scribe, Bill Keenan, for his patient, if largely unrewarded, tuition in the beautiful game of snooker.

About the author

Adam Grace is a retired Fleet Street journalist. During a career spanning more than forty years, he has worked for local, regional and national newspapers, culminating in twenty years with *The Daily Telegaph*. His experience embraces news and sports reporting, feature writing and sub-editing, mainly during the old days of 'hot metal', which he maintains was a faster method of newspaper production than the new technology.

Adapting with some difficulty to computerisation, he now writes a weekly column for *The Universe* and divides his leisure time between his large family, including a great-grandson, and his addiction to snooker.

Although not the most accomplished cueist, he is confident he could bore for Great Britain on the subject of his exploits on the green baize, and his wife readily attests to their fast-acting, coma-inducing quality. She is trying to persuade him to market this talent in CD form as an infallible cure for insomnia.

The letter

THE letter lay unopened on the kitchen table. Going through his mail at breakfast, Edgar Brierley had left it until last because it looked boring. There had been more interesting things to read – an airmail letter from his son, Stanley, in Australia, and invitations to the Ladies' Night dinner (black tie) at a neighbouring Lodge for him and Janice.

A seed catalogue he had sent for had also arrived. The February snow was melting and spring was approaching. He had big plans for his miniature conservatory and the little patches of garden surrounding his bungalow. He poured some more coffee and picked up the last letter.

It looked ominously like a bill in its long buff envelope with a window through which he read: The Occupier, 23 Meadow Drive, Brawton. Inside was a printed notice from Brawton Borough Council. It informed him that the Council had received an application from International Pharmaceuticals Inc UK to develop the Meadow – a large expanse of uncultivated land at the junction of Meadow Drive and Station Road – for industrial use. Plans for the scheme were available for inspection at Brawton Town Hall. As his property adjoined The Meadow, he was invited to submit 'any comments and/or suggestions' within fourteen days.

Edgar was, to use his own expression, gobsmacked. He had lived in Meadow Drive ever since he and Janice were married thirty-five years ago. They had been lucky to find a home with such a pleasant outlook to the rear, the estate agent had told them. Stanley had been born there. And the stillborn daughter they never spoke about. Over the years they had grown to love the wild beauty of The Meadow with its tangled hawthorns, rhododendrons and copses of stately elms. It was unthinkable that it could now be ruined by a factory, which was surely what 'industrial use' meant.

Edgar scratched his bald head where it always itched at moments of stress. Because of an old head injury he sometimes found it hard to concentrate. He was re-reading the letter when his plump wife Janice came bustling in, carrying a pile of clothes for the washing machine.

"Take a look at that," he said. "Can you believe it?"

Out of breath, Janice pulled up a chair to the table, adjusted her spectacles and studied the official notice. When she looked up there was a glint in her eyes which her husband had grown to understand meant trouble. "You'll have to stop it, Edgar. There've been plans for our Meadow before and you've stopped them."

"Yes, but they've always been for houses. This is Big Business."

"What about your friends on the planning committee?"

Edgar sighed. "International Pharmaceuticals aren't your local house-builder. They're global, like Coca-Cola and McDonald's ..."

There was no disputing who wore the trousers in the Brierley household. Janice neatly folded the letter, replaced it in its buff envelope and slid it gently across the table to her husband. "There's no way we're going to put up with a chemical works at the bottom of our garden, Edgar. The health hazard for one thing. And the value of our bungalow – we'd never sell it." She pushed back her chair with a gesture of finality. "And anyway, I'm not moving." So that was that.

Edgar got the message. Janice suffered from angina. Stress got to her very easily, bringing on chest pains. These in turn caused more anxiety and the fear of another heart attack. She'd had one seven years ago. That had been touch and go. Moving house in her condition was not an option.

Why *should* they move? Janice was right. They had to fight back. He'd contact the local paper, organise a petition. The residents of Meadow Drive would all sign because they respected him. He was, after all, Chief Messenger on *The Announcer*. More to the point, he was also Master of Brawton Lodge, No 15392.

*   *   *

"For Howard Mitchell, the nightmare is just beginning."

It was a corny cliché, borrowed from some long-forgotten horror film. But journalists bound for home or the Press Club at the end of the evening shift invariably directed it at the wretch left manning the news desk as late duty reporter. It was part of the badinage you get in every national newspaper office, a sardonic parting shot from hacks stressed out after producing another 36-page issue of a broadsheet that had seen better days. It was all a joke, of course. Their mock warning never came true.

Except this time.

The reporters all took turns on the graveyard shift, as it was known. Tonight was Howard's turn. His only remaining colleague as the newsroom rapidly emptied was the late duty sub-editor, the veteran Bernard Baxter, on the subs' bench at the far end of the cavernous, open-plan office crammed with desks, computers and telephones. Bernard was already reclining in his chair with his feet on the desk. It would be a quiet night.

Only the final edition, earmarked for the Greater London area remained to be printed. The plates were ready to roll on the presses at 3 am – unless a major story broke in the meantime. The graveyard shift had strict instructions not to waken the editor, tucked up in bed at his Hampstead mansion, except in cases of terrorist atrocity or if the Queen died. Any other stories they could handle themselves.

Howard completed his routine 2 am calls to the police, fire and ambulance stations (all quiet, they reported) and had just returned to his desk with a plastic cup of coffee from the machine in the corner when his telephone rang. He picked it up. "News desk."

The caller was a man with a cultured but rather nervous voice. "Are you a reporter?"

Howard sipped his coffee. "Yes, my name's Howard Mitchell. Can I help you?"

There was a moment's silence. Then the voice said: "I've got a story for you. It's a true one."

Howard reached for his pen and notepad. "Can I ask who's calling?"

"No names, I'm afraid."

"Could you give me a rough idea what it's about?"

"Not on the phone, no."

"Would you care to send us an e-mail?"

"I'm sorry, nothing in writing either. I need to meet you somewhere. It's very important."

Howard tried one more ploy to open up his caller. "Where are you calling from, sir?"

There was irritation in the cultured tones. "Look, I'm offering you an exclusive. I need to talk to you … privately, in strict confidence."

At the word 'exclusive', Howard flicked open his desk diary. Genuine exclusives were few and far between. Circulation was falling steadily. The only time sales topped a million was when British suicide bombers hijacked the headlines. "How about tomorrow, sir? I'd be happy to call on you but if you won't tell me where you are perhaps you could come to our offices."

"Sorry, that's not possible. Listen, there's a small park round the corner from your building. I could meet you there tomorrow?"

"I know it. What time would be convenient?"

"Shall we say one o'clock?"

As he was on the late turn, Howard would not be awake before noon next day. "That's a bit early for me, sir. Could we make it two-ish, say two-thirty?"

"Very well. Two-thirty it is."

"Where will you be?"

"Walk through the park to the exit on the far side. Go through the gate. There's a side street. I'll be waiting in a taxi."

"How will I recognise you, sir?"

"I think I'll recognise *you* – from your picture in the paper. Good night, Mr Mitchell."

Strange cove, Howard thought. But you often encountered them on the graveyard shift. Full moon was the worst time. People would phone you in the middle of the night with wild theories about the international situation, politics, religion, police harassment, football referees, the end of the world…you name it.

Sometimes they were just desperately lonely and needed someone – anyone, even an *Announcer* hack – to talk to. He checked the paper's weather page. It wasn't the full moon that night. In fact, there was no moon at all. He finished his coffee and rang Norman on the switchboard. Could he trace that last call to the news desk? Norman tried. "No luck. Number withheld," he reported moments later.

All rather intriguing, Howard thought. Years of experience in dealing with cranks, weirdoes and extremists of every persuasion had bred in him a deeply cynical view of human nature, but there had been something genuine about this caller. Something he couldn't quite put his finger on.

For Howard Mitchell, the nightmare had just begun.

*　　　*　　　*

Sunshine and the cacophony of London's traffic combined to clear Howard's head as he strode through the lunch-hour crowds to meet his mystery caller. He had not slept well. He never did after a late turn. Barbara, his wife, had woken him at eleven before leaving for the hospital where she worked as a theatre nurse, but he'd gone back to sleep. If it hadn't been for the window cleaner scraping across his bedroom's leaded lights he might have missed the scoop of his career.

A cold breeze ruffled Howard's dark hair, prematurely greying at the temples, as he turned into the park entrance. Even though the sun was shining, it was still March and he realised he should have worn a topcoat over his smart blue worsted suit. Still, he would soon be back in the warmth of *The Announcer* office. This guy would probably be just another time-waster with some obscure axe to grind.

Rounding a bend in the path between beds of nodding daffodils he made for the far exit. It was almost two-thirty and the park was rapidly emptying as clerks and secretaries hurried back to their offices from their lunch break. As he spotted the taxi, its rear window was opened and a newspaper waved by a distinguished middle-aged gent wearing gold-rimmed spectacles and sensibly clad in a dark Crombie. Somehow, he didn't look like a time-waster. He looked more like a judge or a merchant banker.

"Good afternoon, Mr Mitchell," he called out and opened the door for the reporter to climb in.

"Good afternoon, sir." Howard said, sitting next to him and pulling the door closed.

The silver-haired man tapped on the driver's partition and the taxi moved off. Then he extended his hand and beamed at Howard. "Pleased to make your acquaintance. Do you have a Press card?"

The reporter showed him his *Announcer* ID, expecting some introduction from the man. "And you, sir. Might I have the pleasure?"

"Just call me William for the time being. You'll have to trust me."

Howard hesitated. The word 'exclusive' again crossed his mind. That, and his new friend's air of urbane assurance, formed a persuasive combination. "As you wish, but…"

"I'm just finishing *The Announcer* crossword. It seems to get easier every day. I suppose that's because you're going down market. There was just one clue I got stuck on: 'Lady not in the network'. Four letters, ending in D."

9

Cryptic crosswords were not Howard's forte. He regarded them as the ultimate waste of time. And time, as every journalist with an approaching deadline knew, was a merciless, uncompromising enemy. "Lady not in the network," he repeated, and thought for a bit.

"Four letters, ending in D," his companion repeated helpfully.

Try as he did, Howard could only think of the work piling up back at the news desk. He was supposed to phone his Met contact at 3.30 pm about the capital's latest crime figures. That was listed as a front-page story. Andrew Moran, the paper's news editor, would be growing more agitated by the minute. Howard had kept his boss informed about his whereabouts but that wouldn't stop him doing his old woman act. He wasn't called The Moron for nothing. "I give up," he said at length.

"Grid," exclaimed the elderly man triumphantly. "I must admit, it took me a while."

"Grid?" Howard said blankly. "How did you work that out?"

"The lady is Ingrid," the crossword genius explained. "Ingrid without the 'in' leaves you with 'grid'."

"Sorry if I appear stupid, but you've lost me…"

"Grid is a network. Take away the 'in' from Ingrid and…I'm sorry. You're a busy man. It's time we got down to business. Are you ready for a ride?"

"Where to?"

"You'll see."

As they drove past Victoria Station, Howard slyly switched on the state of the art, digital voice recorder in his jacket pocket. William, who kept glancing out of the rear window, didn't seem to notice. After a while, Howard said: "Silly question…where are we going?"

"South, dear boy."

"It's just that I need to update my news editor."

"Tell him you're going to be some time…"

Howard grinned. "You don't know my news editor."

"Tell him you're covering a story that'll double *The Announcer's* circulation. That should concentrate his mind."

When Howard relayed these comments on his mobile phone, he found they required no further embellishment. Andrew, in fact, calmed down very quickly and was almost polite. Someone else would talk to the

Met. No problem. "Stay in touch," he instructed tersely.

They trundled through the traffic in silence. The wind was getting up. Shoppers scurried along the pavements. Litter blew across the road. A large piece of waste paper flattened itself momentarily on the windscreen and the cabbie cursed loudly.

William relaxed a little. "You can't be too careful security-wise, as I'm sure you appreciate. Used to be safe to talk outdoors but now there are scanners and TV cameras everywhere...pick up what you're saying from half a mile away. Orwell was twenty years ahead of his time."

Howard checked the rear window. Traffic had eased off apart from two buses in traditional tandem. No-one seemed to be tailing them but you never could tell.

"I find a taxi's the best place for a private conversation these days. Just hire one at random. Drive around for a while...no tracking devices, no bugs...apart from your tape recorder of course, Mr Mitchell. Would you mind turning it off?"

Howard grinned, took out the voice recorder and switched it off. He produced a pen and a small notebook. "Am I allowed the odd shorthand note?"

William smiled and nodded. It was a genuine, engaging smile. He must be somewhere in his sixties, Howard estimated. But he wore his age well. The once blond, combed back hair, now turning silver-grey, was only slightly receding. The mature, clean-shaven features were still handsome. It was only the drawn and slightly watery blue eyes behind the expensive spectacles that suggested world-weariness, a profound sadness.

"How old are you, Mr Mitchell?"

"Thirty-eight."

"You won't remember the sixties then."

"No, the Beatles and England winning the World Cup... that's all I know about the sixties."

"They changed everything," William said simply. "The swinging sixties...the permissive society. People didn't realise it at the time but they were part of a massive social upheaval. Have you any children, Mr Mitchell?"

"Yes, two. A son aged eleven and a daughter aged seven."

"I have two sons and two daughters. Grown up, of course. Seven

11

grandchildren, one of whom…"

"Yes?"

"You'll see."

Howard didn't press the point. "What's your job, William?"

"Let's just call me a Whitehall whistle-blower."

The taxi stopped at a zebra crossing. Children were coming out of school, skipping across the road and laughing at the lollipop lady. William watched them thoughtfully.

"What sort of a future have those children got?" he said at length. "Your two children, Mr Mitchell…what does life hold in store for them?"

Howard thought about Christopher and Sally at their comfortable south London home. Barbara would soon be making their tea. Then it would be choir practice for Christopher and Brownies for Sally. What lay ahead for them? He hadn't given it much thought; they were still so young. Chris was always saying he wanted to be a footballer, but he'd grow out of that.

The one thing he hoped the boy wouldn't be when he grew up was a journalist. Far too stressful. Nothing but death, disaster and destruction. A 3-D job, they called it. And unless you were a named writer, the money was derisory. As for Sally, her mother hoped she'd go one better than herself and be a doctor. But when you came to think about it, all you really wanted for your children was for them to be happy.

He voiced the thought. "I just hope they'll be happy, I suppose… whatever careers they follow. No-one can see into the future."

"I wish I could have done, back in the sixties…if only I'd had the power I have now, I might have averted a tragedy. 'Liberating reforms' the government called their health and education policies. They gave us sex lessons, the Pill, the condom culture, legalised abortion. Morals went out of the window. Suddenly, we were all free to do our own thing, regardless of the consequences…because there wouldn't be any. The media called it a sexual revolution."

He glanced out of the window at the disappearing children and sighed. "None of us suspected the real name of the game."

"What was that?" Howard asked.

"State population control."

A special reason

The taxi had turned into the driveway of a shabby, single-storey building surrounded by a high fence, set back from the road. The place was badly neglected and in urgent need of a coat of paint. Some of its windows were cracked and boarded up. What once were rose beds were now tangled with weeds.

"We're here, Mr Mitchell," said William. "This is my granddaughter's nursery school. They hide it away from public gaze because it's designated a special school for children with learning difficulties."

The driver was told to wait and the two men approached the glass front door which was locked. William rang the bell. There was a long wait before a flustered young teacher appeared, carrying a large stack of books. She opened the door with difficulty.

"Good afternoon, Miss. I'm Rachel's grandfather and this is a friend of mine, Mr Mitchell. May we come in?"

"Of course, sir. Sorry about the wait but we're short staffed today. We are most days."

"That's quite all right," William said. Staff shortages were nothing new at special schools. Teacher training programmes were under-funded and salaries failed to match the demanding nature of the job. You needed teachers of a dedicated calibre to stay for more than a few months and there weren't many of them around.

The two men were led across a gloomy entrance hall that smelled faintly of carbolic and boiled cabbage, then down an uncarpeted corridor to the classrooms. "How's Rachel been today?" William asked.

The young woman's harassed expression broke into a smile. "Good as gold, as always. She's such a happy little soul, you know. She's been having a great time with her clay modelling project. Wait till you see what she's made."

As they opened the classroom door, a dozen little Down's Syndrome faces looked up expectantly from their workbenches. They all smiled. But none more happily than Rachel.

"Look Granddad," she shouted. "I made a boat."

Even Howard could tell that, for a six-year-old, the elegantly curved

13

boat, complete with a sail made from a tiny handkerchief, was a remarkably accurate scale model. Rachel might have learning difficulties but it seemed she also possessed rare artistic talent.

While William and the teacher fussed over their star pupil, Howard scribbled some notes on the deplorable state of the nursery school and its lack of resources. It would make a good inside page story, he thought, if hardly the exclusive William had promised. It had nothing to do with his enigmatic reference to population control. The journalist was still waiting for the whistle-blower to blow his whistle. He didn't have long to wait.

"Do you know what our enlightened, progressive Government wants to do with children like my granddaughter?" William asked as they settled in the taxi for the return journey.

"No."

"Kill them in their mothers' wombs."

The calm, matter-of-fact nature of the pronouncement struck Howard as incongruous. He wondered if he had heard correctly. "Sorry?" he said, startled.

"Kill them in their mothers' wombs. Abortion. They believe people like Rachel should never have been born."

Howard's knowledge of current embryo research was rather limited. He knew about the controversial 'screening out' of foetuses with severe genetic defects. There was an ongoing ethical debate about it. On balance, he could understand the compassionate motives of the scientists in seeking to spare a potential human being an unbearable quality of life. But he hadn't realised their plans extended as far as Down's Syndrome. The idea left him feeling uncomfortable.

William seemed to read his thoughts. He leaned forward and spoke very deliberately. "Disturbing, isn't it. But let me tell you something even more disturbing. It's not a new idea. It's been tried before. How's your European history?"

"Not up to much."

"Who were Hitler's first victims?"

"The Jews?"

"No. In the early 1930s, long before the Holocaust, the first victims of the Nazi death-camps were mentally handicapped children, including all those with Down's Syndrome. Their lives were deemed to be *Vernichtung lebensunwertes leben* – not worth living. Once the German people accepted the idea that some lives were not worth living, there was no stopping them."

"I do know the rest," Howard said. "The 'mercy killing' of deaf and disabled people…and the mass extermination of the Jewish race."

"Exactly, dear boy. So you see, once you start talking about screening out defective embryos because they might face a life not worth living … however compassionate and liberal your motives, you find yourself on a classic slippery slope. We've been there before. It all began with men in white coats. It ended with a madman in military uniform."

"And you think it could happen here?"

William sank back in his seat, removed his spectacles and pinched the bridge of his nose. Taking a chance, Howard furtively switched on the voice recorder in his pocket. Instinct told him the whistle was about to be blown. William didn't seem to notice.

"I think it entirely possible that it could happen here. But not for the same motives. Hitler and his henchmen were motivated by ethnic cleansing. It could happen here for a very different reason…money. For some years now, the Treasury has been concerned about the escalating cost of welfare benefits…job seeker's allowance, incapacity benefit, family income support, child benefit, legal aid, the state pension, you name it. I'm sure you know the annual bill for all these handouts."

Howard thought for a moment. "Roughly £100 billion, isn't it, all told?"

"The latest figure we have is £106 billion, including state pensions. The poor are bleeding the nation dry. I'm not exaggerating…we've exceeded our European Union welfare budget. The EU say there's a £10 billion black hole in the accounts. They've issued a directive telling us to close it or face sanctions. So we've decided drastic measures are the only remedy."

Howard was all ears. "Who's 'we'?"

William replaced his spectacles and looked over the top of them directly at the reporter. "This is strictly off the record, for guidance only. If you discover who I am, you can't quote me. Do you agree?"

"Agreed."

"A top-secret government committee is planning state population control, selectively aimed at the so-called underclass to stop them from breeding. Sounds far-fetched, I know, but I can assure you it's true. I sit on it myself. It's called the Tina Project."

"Why Tina?"

"There...is...no...alternative."

"Oh, I see." In common with most journalists, Howard had a low opinion of politicians. Nothing could surprise him when it came to their devious machinations. But this was something else. William had not been far off the mark when he said it would double *The Announcer's* circulation.

He managed to suppress a rising sense of excitement. "Who sits on this committee?"

William leaned forward again and lowered his voice. "There are eleven of us at present. More may be co-opted. We're all specialists in our respective fields. I represent the Treasury. There are three other first division civil servants from the Departments of Health, Education, and Work and Pensions, an MP, a baroness, two senior members of the medical profession, two representatives of the contraceptives industry – one condoms, the other pills – and one, er, reproductive and sexual health expert...an abortion provider, in other words."

Howard wrote it all down in his neat shorthand although the voice recorder in his jacket pocket would pick up the faintest whisper. "Are you what's known as a 'think-tank'?"

"Yes, except that officially we don't exist."

"Are you the chairman?"

"No, I'm the treasurer. The Pill man's the chairman ... a man called Marcus Quinn."

"How are you funded?"

"Jointly by the Government and the Pill man."

"How much?"

"Let's just say we are allowed a generous budget from both sources."

"Who does Tina report to – the Cabinet?"

"No, we report back to a man we simply refer to as the Director."

"Do you know his name?"

"No, only Quinn knows his name. He's the go-between. All the rest of us know is that he's a very big Mr Big indeed."

"Where do you meet – at the Commons?"

"Good gracious, no. Secret locations. Never the same one twice."

"How many meetings have you had?"

"Only three, so far. We're still at the exploratory stage."

Howard felt a sense of unreality as he asked: "What are the plans for stopping the underclass from breeding, William?"

The Whitehall whistle-blower closed his eyes and clasped his hands nervously. After several seconds, he said: "Nothing has been decided yet, you understand. Speculative proposals start with stepping up the sex education programme in primary schools."

"Even though people are saying sex education doesn't work…that teenage pregnancies keep going up?"

"The experts believe that's because the programme wasn't introduced early enough in the curriculum. We're going to begin the lessons at a younger age."

"How young?"

"The consensus seems to be at the age of five."

Howard's eyebrows rose a shade. "Isn't that a bit *too* young?"

"The sooner they start getting the contraception message, the more likely they are to be influenced by it…that's the theory, anyway."

"What if parents object?"

"They'll be over-ruled. Tina regards the family unit as the enemy. As the children get older, they'll be given condoms to play with…"

"Instead of toys?"

"As well as toys." William clearly felt uneasy about sex education in primary schools so he moved swiftly on to the secondaries. "Once they reach puberty and they become more sexually aware, they'll be provided with free condoms and pills."

"Including the morning-after pill?"

"Yes. And contraceptive jabs where necessary."

"Despite their side effects…they're banned in America, aren't they?"

"Some are…they can cause osteoporosis, bloating and fertility problems. Our medical profession is still divided over the side effects. On balance, they believe the risks are slight. In the context of population reduction they are regarded as well worth taking."

"What if all these measures fail and pregnancies keep rising?"

17

"Now we come to the second phase of the project – abortion. For a start, no more Down's Syndrome babies will be born. Once the condition is detected in a foetus, it will be terminated immediately, regardless of the mother's wishes."

"A life not worth living."

"Exactly. They're already discussing including other forms of handicap. It's the thin end of the wedge. They're following the Chinese policy of enforced abortions. So I want no further part of it. I'm sure you understand."

Howard remembered Rachel and her model yacht. "I understand, William."

"However, I still have to go through the motions. I can't quit now. I know too much."

"You mention China. Are they aiming for one-child families?"

"Absolutely, but only for unproductive members of society – the underclass. Single mothers on benefit are the main target. If they become pregnant with a second child, they'll be offered money to have an abortion – even if the foetus is healthy."

"How much?"

"The amount has yet to be decided. A termination grant of about £150 seems likely."

Howard shook his head in disbelief. Assuming this extraordinary story ever saw the light of day, he could already visualise the headline:

Is your child worth £150?

"What if they refuse?"

"We don't think many will…but, for those who do, subtle pressure will be applied. Social services will remind them they have powers to take children into care if they decide they're not being properly looked after. They'll also find themselves bottom of the list for free nursery school places. Life will become more difficult for them."

"Isn't it difficult enough already?"

"Precisely. That thought will no doubt exercise their minds. As their pregnancy progresses, a higher combined termination *and sterilisation* grant will be offered. We're thinking in terms of £300 – an attractive option to someone of restricted means."

"But I thought the object of the exercise was to save money, not hand it out."

"Yes, but it would be worth it in the long run, you see. A short-term investment with substantial long-term benefits. The number of welfare claimants would be progressively reduced with each generation."

"What if the woman still refuses?"

"She'll be breaking the law. Tina's not decided on the penalties yet. But they'll be exemplary."

"Cutting their benefit?"

"Worse than that."

The taxi rattled under a tunnel as a train rumbled overhead. The afternoon was fading and street lamps were lighting up. The wind had dropped but it had started to rain, keeping the cab's windscreen wipers busy. Howard took advantage of a pause in William's startling revelations to update the news desk on his movements. When he clicked off his mobile, the whistle-blower blew again for the second half.

"There's more, dear boy. The burden of the state pension is taking a crippling toll on the economy. People are living longer. They're upsetting all our actuaries' calculations. If life expectancy keeps on increasing we'll be staring bankruptcy in the face in twenty years. In the next week or so, the Government will announce new measures to raise the retirement age from sixty-five to seventy. Look out for it. And remember I gave you the tip."

"Thanks. So now we all have to work till we drop."

"Right, and for those who refuse to drop there's a bill going through the Lords at the moment, the Voluntary Euthanasia Bill…"

"I know. *The Announcer's* been taking a keen interest in it."

"But even if it's passed it won't go far enough. The committee feels that, sooner or later, legislation must be introduced to tackle the issue pragmatically. There seems little point in keeping a person alive when there is no realistic hope of survival. They argue that there comes a time when you have to balance compassion for geriatric patients with concern for the national interest."

Howard's eyebrows rose again. But he nodded. "As you say… pragmatic."

"So what the project embodies is a policy of *compulsory* euthanasia

19

once doctors are satisfied, in their clinical judgment, that it would be in the patients' best interests to end their suffering. There would be no lethal injections or anything like that – simply the withdrawal of food and water in the same way as the voluntary method."

"Except the patient would have no say in the matter?"

"Exactly."

"Sounds like murder to me."

"Absolutely not." The sardonic inflection said it all.

The taxi had slowed to a crawl as the early rush hour tightened its grip on the rainswept streets.

"Is that all then?" Howard felt it was more than enough to be going on with.

"Yes, I've spilled the beans. That's the Tina Project: a new, enlightened welfare strategy for the poor. From the cradle, if you escape the abortionists, to the grave – if bird flu or suicide bombers don't get you first."

"You really think it could be the 1930s all over again?"

"That's the obvious danger. Europe is involved again, you see, and history has a habit of repeating itself." The blue, world-weary eyes looked directly at Howard. "I've served under eight governments, Mr Mitchell. All have been doctrinaire and unscrupulous. But this lot are capable of anything."

"Not the Final Solution, surely?"

"Not yet."

"I can't believe today's medical profession…"

"Today's doctors are no angels, I'm sorry to say. They willingly collaborate in thousands of abortions every week … wholesale butchery whichever way you look at it. Some are performed on children of fourteen and fifteen – without their parents' knowledge. Your medical profession *already* withdraws feeding tubes from the dying – against the wishes of their relatives. They're allowed to do that *now*…in our so-called civilised society!"

"They have a code of ethics, the GMC guidelines."

"Of course, they have their ethics, their guidelines to protect them. They convince themselves they're acting out of compassion – but so did doctors of the Third Reich."

Howard grimaced. "Surely…in this day and age…"

"This day and age has given us Dr Shipman. He started by killing the terminally ill and look where it ended. He was a deranged maverick, I grant you. But all doctors play God to a greater or lesser degree. Only human nature after all…the power of life and death."

"I take your point."

"Tina has a strategy for enlisting the medical profession. They'll be told they're playing a vital role in an enlightened social project to help the deprived. GPs in places like Gateshead and Camberwell will be only too keen to take part."

"Are they target areas?"

"Provisionally. Other inner city areas are being considered – wherever – there'll be no shortage of men in white coats, believe me. As for a madman in military uniform…well, you're familiar with our great leaders, Mr Mitchell. What do you think?"

The taxi had stopped at traffic lights near Ludgate Circus. William leaned forward and opened the driver's partition. "I'll get out here, driver."

He opened the door and stepped nimbly out. "We'll meet again, dear boy," he said. "Put the cab on expenses."

Ambitions

It had been a low-scoring frame. It usually was when Edgar, the chief messenger, was playing. They'd cleared the reds and Edgar had potted the yellow. But it was a poor positional shot. The cue ball had finished up behind the brown. He'd snookered himself on the next ball, the green. Edgar grinned ruefully and scratched his noble extended brow, his "wide parting" as he liked to call it. How was he going to get out of this?

He chalked his cue and studied the angles. There was no straightforward escape shot. His opponent, Darren, a bright lad from dispatch with spiky hair that looked as if it had been styled by computerised equipment, offered a suggestion "Aim just past the middle pocket with plenty of right-hand side and come back round the table off four cushions."

Edgar laughed. "Who do you think I am – Howard Mitchell?"

Howard sometimes popped into the snooker room adjoining the staff restaurant on *The Announcer's* top floor for a quick frame on his supper break. He was the only journalist who did. Most of the others headed straight for the pub. They teased him that it was a sign of a mis-spent youth if you could play snooker, but he told them it was the sign of a mis-spent youth if you *couldn't*.

Edgar had two consuming ambitions in life. One was to grow prize-winning tomatoes and the other was to beat Howard at snooker. Crouching over his cue and doing his best to apply right-hand side (though he wasn't entirely sure how you went about it) Edgar sent the cue ball careering round the table in a blur of kinetic energy, before it disappeared into a corner pocket with a loud clunk. Serious snooker players like Edgar and Darren knew they shouldn't laugh at such times but it was difficult not to.

If only he could play like Howard.

*   *   *

Downstairs in the third floor newsroom Howard and Andrew Moran were listening to the voice recording of William's interview. Andrew prided himself on his dynamic, macho approach to his job. He knew he wasn't a gentleman and never pretended to be one. He had come up the hard way and was every bit as uncouth now as he was when a junior reporter with the *Croydon Advertiser*.

Unlike Howard, who was quite tall with a scholarly presence, Andrew was short, designer stubbled, overweight and possessed all the infectious charm of Sir Alan Sugar without the frills. Yet women, in their perverse, masochistic way, were attracted to him. Although shacked up with Britt, a Norwegian air stewardess, in his Holland Park pad, she was often abroad and there were rumours he was sniffing round Diane, the Editor's secretary. But you couldn't trust office gossip.

The news editor of *The Announcer* reclined in his executive swivel chair with his feet on the desk, while eating a banana. There was a breath of spring in the air and a window was partly open. When he finished his banana, he tossed the skin out of the window on to the crowded street below, although there was a waste bin alongside the desk.

Howard couldn't help wondering what readers of their up-market newspaper would have made of the scene. Despite its declining fortunes, the paper still commanded a distinctly blue chip readership – mainly socio-economic classes A, B and C1 – though most bought it for the crossword. If they gave it any thought at all, *Announcer* readers would probably have imagined the paper's news editor to be at least the product of a minor public school with a good Oxbridge degree. If they could have seen this curmudgeonly alumnus of Croydon Comprehensive with one A-level (biology) now biting into an apple, the core of which was destined for the same method of disposal, they would have been tempted to cancel the paper forthwith, crossword or no crossword.

After the apple core had duly prescribed its predictable parabola through the window and the recording finally came to an end, Andrew said: "Surely you don't expect me to believe this bullshit. Who is the guy anyway?"

"He says he's a senior civil servant at the Treasury."

"And you believe him?"

"Yes – gut instinct."

"It could be a trap. You wouldn't be the first to fall for some elaborate conspiracy theory cooked up by a rival paper. You know how many conspiracy theories are discredited? Ninety-five per cent."

"That leaves five per cent that are right."

"Not very good odds are they?"

"He's genuine."

"We'd better see the Editor."

*　　　*　　　*

If shaken by *The Announcer's* news editor, its readers' equilibrium would have been quickly restored on acquaintance with The Editor, the One to whom they addressed their letters of dismay at the erosion of standards in society, swearing on television and the unreliability of train timetables. The all-powerful One whose decision was always final. Unlike Andrew, Julian Geldard was a distinguished gentleman with impeccable credentials including an Oxford First and, perhaps more significantly, membership of the Jockey Club and the MCC.

Private boxes at Ascot, Goodwood, Lord's and the Royal Albert Hall were the particular preserves of this highborn aristocrat, a versatile and prolific author with several biographies of leading cricketers and politicians to his name. A devout Tory and monarchist – anathema to most of his staff – and with a deep distrust of the European Community, he nonetheless wrote immaculately impartial leading articles and often appeared on highbrow radio chat shows to offer listeners the benefit of his erudition on controversial issues. Slim and sprightly for his sixty-four years, with a ruddy complexion, shock of white fuzzy hair like a halo and dark bushy eyebrows, Julian effortlessly combined an informal manner with the gravitas of his exalted position. He was due for retirement at the end of the year. A knighthood was widely expected.

It was mid-afternoon, hours before the evening editorial conference, when the two newsmen knocked on the Editor's door and entered his imposing office, an oasis of tranquility in contrast to the bustling newsroom outside. Strong sunlight filtered through the half-drawn blinds and ranged across the deep blue carpet, the massive mahogany desk and book-lined walls complete with a clock, accurate to the second (you had to respect the enemy), and a large oil painting of His Lordship, *The Announcer's* distinguished proprietor. Just as you can detect the odour of sanctity in some churches (though by no means all), the atmosphere in this inner sanctum spoke of authority, probity and immutable moral rectitude.

"Howard's got a scoop, Julian," Andrew said, "but he can't make it stand up."

Julian stopped tapping at his keyboard, turned in his magisterial black leather chair and smiled. "How many of our stories do?" he asked sardonically. "Sit down and fire away."

They drew up smaller but comfortable chairs. Howard placed the voice recorder on the Editor's desk and switched it on. "It's quite long. I'll sub it if you like."

"No, let's hear it all."

Julian called the messengers on his internal phone. "Three cups of tea, please. No sugar." Then he buzzed his secretary in the adjoining office. "No more calls, Diane."

It didn't take long for Julian to get the picture. When Edgar came in with the tea, (it was always the head messenger who brought the Editor's tea) he motioned to Howard to switch off the recorder until he had left.

The three journalists heard it through to the end, Julian occasionally taking a shorthand note. Silence followed, broken only by the distant hum of the city traffic and a tiny clink of the china cup as Julian finished his tea, now quite cold. Andrew and Howard waited patiently for the Pronouncement.

"Intriguing. Do we know who he is, Howard?"

"No. He says he's with the Treasury. I think he's genuine."

"Fair enough. Are there any copies of this?"

"No."

"We need to get one – keep one in my safe, the other at the bank."

Andrew was incredulous. "You think there's something in it?"

"We need to find out, Andrew. He's talking about a £10 billion black hole in the national economy. That's a lot of money. Sounds like a good story. Have you checked out his retirement age tip-off with the Department for Work and Pensions?"

"Not yet. We've been very busy," Howard said. On *The Announcer*, that was a coded hint to the Editor that, strictly between gentlemen, your workload was intolerable.

Andrew remained unimpressed. "The guy sounds like bad news to me."

"You may be right," Julian said. "Let's judge him by results. If his tip comes good, we'll need to talk to him again…bring him in for a conference."

"I doubt if he'll come," said Howard.

"Then we'll go to him. In the meantime, we keep this story between the three of us. Not a word to anyone. Total secrecy. Understood?"

The two agreed and returned to their desks without an outward sign of anything unusual, which their pathologically curious colleagues were always on the lookout for. Although apparently concentrating on their flickering screens, they never missed a trick when it came to traffic in and out of the Editor's office. With the paper's circulation continuing to nosedive, several older members of staff had been paid off by way of early retirement. Redundancies were already on the cards. Who would be next?

Julian shut down his computer, stood up and stretched. He had known Howard long enough to trust his judgment implicitly. And the more he thought about the idea of the £10 billion black hole in the Government's crippling welfare budget, the more Tina made sense. If they were to cut the budget by say, a fifth, that would amount to a saving of about £20 billion – leaving a tidy surplus to fund more cluster bombs for their foreign wars.

He'd been around in newspapers long enough to recognise a potential scoop when he sniffed an unlikely story. Many of his previous triumphs had sounded as preposterous as Howard's offering in the early stages. Even as he placed the recording in the wall safe behind the picture of His Lordship, he was beginning to wonder if this extraordinary yet totally believable tale could finally provide him with his knighthood.

*   *   *

Barbara Mitchell finished loading the dishwasher, made herself a cup of tea and sat down, still in her uniform. It had been a hard day in theatre. A young man in a wetsuit had been brought in minus his right arm. The man had been scuba diving in a lake when he became entangled in a boat's propeller. His arm, which had been cleanly sliced off above the elbow, was recovered, packed in ice and flown to hospital by air ambulance.

The operation to reattach the limb using state of the art microsurgery was still going on when Barbara was relieved at the end of her shift seven hours later. It could continue for another seven. Every vein, every artery, every nerve cell had to be reconnected in a painstaking process calling for all the delicate skills of the surgeons and the diligence of the nursing staff.

Total concentration was demanded at every stage and Barbara, as anaesthetic nurse, had been responsible for monitoring the patient's blood pressure, pulse and respiration throughout. There were several anxious moments when she had to administer morphine injections as the man's condition fluctuated. The doses had to be precisely calculated, timed and logged. There could not be even the tiniest mistake.

The mental and physical pressures on the theatre team were enormous as they toiled in a hi-tech environment of cables, drips, cameras, computerised equipment and energy-sapping lighting. Mr Bowen, senior of the four operating surgeons, tried to relieve it by cracking jokes while he worked. He had experienced problems with the micro lenses on his headset. These were known as loops and one had somehow worked slightly loose. When a replacement set could not be found, the operation was delayed while a technician was called in to perform emergency repairs. "It's the pressure," Mr Bowen declared. "Even the loops are going loopy."

Barbara's recovery from her stressful day was not helped when Howard bounded in and, after kissing her head lightly and fussing over Oscar, the family's cross-bred collie, exclaimed: "I need to talk to you about sex."

She groaned. "Not now, darling. I'm worn out."

Howard grinned. "Relax, I don't mean a quickie. I meant sex education. What are Chris and Sally being taught at school? Where are they, by the way?"

"They're upstairs playing with their Lego. Is there a problem?"

"I hope not. It's just that I've received some rather disturbing information. It seems that kids of five are going to have sex lessons before they can read and write."

Barbara was surprised. "Five-year-olds?" she exclaimed. "That's the first I've heard of it. The school had better warn us. Sally's seven but she's far too young for that."

"Exactly. That's what bothers me."

"Where did you hear this?"

"Off the record. We're not sure yet but we think the Government are planning a new campaign. Sex education hasn't worked in secondary schools so they're lowering the age group to primaries. Brilliant idea."

"That's typical of this lot. They just can't admit they've got it wrong. I've said all along, the best form of sex education is the word: 'No'. Followed by three more: 'True love waits'. That's what I've told Chris and that's what I'll tell Sally. Pour me a whisky, love. Preferably in a clean glass."

Howard cast around the untidy kitchen. "That comes extra. Can't find one."

"They're all in the dishwasher."

Clouds of steam billowed from the machine, startling Oscar who had returned to his basket, and Howard hastily extracted a tumbler.

"Make it a stiff one."

"I thought you were too tired."

"You know what I mean."

They settled at the kitchen table with their drinks as the dishwasher resumed its low rumble. "True love waits...that's a bit old-fashioned, isn't it?" Howard asked.

"Maybe so...but it's still right. If someone really loves you, they'll wait until marriage before they have sex. We did."

Howard preferred not to go into that. "But kids these days are more or less told *not* to wait, aren't they? Everywhere you look, they're exposed to commercial pressure."

"That's where parents come in. It's up to us to counteract it...make sure they don't ruin their lives."

Howard remembered what William had said about Tina regarding families as the enemy. He thought he was beginning to understand.

"What's for dinner?" he asked, rummaging through the freezer.

So mote it be

Edgar was gobsmacked. He had collected thirty-four signatures from fellow residents of Meadow Drive on a petition protesting at the plans of International Pharmaceuticals Inc UK to develop The Meadow, and canvassed support from fellow Lodge members. He had tipped off the local paper, the *Brawton Bugle*, and they ran a front-page story headed RESIDENTS' FURY OVER £30M FACTORY PLAN. He had sent in his own letter of objection to Brawton Borough Council, well within the stipulated fourteen days. In this he had been careful to include the Masonic coded message that an IPI UK factory was not 'within their compass'. He'd even written to his Tory MP in similar terms but had not been favoured with a reply.

Despite all his strenuous campaigning, the Council's area planning committee decided to approve the scheme. Well, they would see about that. It still had to go before the full planning committee. They could veto it or there could be a call for an inquiry by the Planning Inspectorate. It was early days yet.

He changed into his best (only) lounge suit, a dark blue pin-stripe, packed his regalia in his battered black attaché case, kissed Janice and told her not to wait up. Then he climbed into his elderly bronze Proton saloon and set off for the Lodge meeting.

When he entered Brawton Masonic Temple, Edgar underwent a metamorphosis. He was no longer bald, unassuming Edgar Brierley, a 58-year-old nonentity who drove a clapped-out Proton. He was suddenly important. He was the Worshipful Master of his Lodge. True, he had waited thirty years for the honour – until everyone else had had a turn and there was only him left. But it had been worth the wait. Every one of the forty-two members deferred to him. All right, some were fish and chip shop proprietors, security guards, traffic wardens and Anglican clergymen. But others, incongruously, included solicitors, bank managers, council officials, high-ranking police officers and a crown court judge. Some of them drove Audis. Some even drove Jaguars.

All the aproned, bechained and bejewelled Lodge members stood respectfully as the Worshipful Master entered the windowless and sound-proofed temple. Edgar, grinning self-consciously, donned his own magnificent chain of office and white gloves, tapped his gavel, cleared his throat (a nervous mannerism), and declared the meeting open.

The chaplain, a local Church of England vicar who had swapped his cassock for a lambskin apron, intoned a prayer to an altogether different deity – the Great Architect of the Universe. He implored the Architect to look with favour on their fraternal gathering; that their noble precepts of Brotherly Love, Relief and Truth may be faithfully upheld; that their hands may be guided by Justice and their hearts expanded by Benevolence.

Thankfully, there were no ritual initiations or exaltations this time. There hadn't been any 'poor candidates in a state of darkness humbly soliciting admittance to the mysteries and privileges of Freemasonry' at Lodge 15392 for nearly a year. The last one had been old Sam Bates, a local publican, who in an attempt to calm his nerves before the initiation ceremony, fortified himself a shade too generously from his establishment's stock. The result had been unfortunate. Having been duly blindfolded and led round the Lodge by a hangman's noose, his left trouser leg and right sleeve rolled up and a dagger thrust to his bared breast, Sam stumbled and fell on his sword, so to speak.

Much to the consternation of the assembled Brothers, not least the Inner Lodge Guard leading him and the Deacons waving their wands over him, the poor candidate collapsed in a pool of blood on the recently-cleaned Lodge carpet. The dagger had missed his heart but penetrated his oesophagus; and the noose had almost strangled him as he fell. Sam was hauled off in an ambulance, not to the Royal Masonic Hospital since he wasn't a Mason yet, but to the rather less salubrious accident and emergency unit of Brawton Infirmary. Oddly enough, Sam seemed disinclined to reapply for membership when he'd recovered and the Masons themselves also neglected to pursue the matter. In the words of the Immediate Past Master: "So mote it be."

Edgar impatiently scanned the well-fed faces of the Brawton Brethren gathered in their shuttered secret enclave and noticed there were fewer of them than usual. When apologies for absence were read out, they included the names of all the council planning officials he wanted to speak to about IPI's intended vandalism of The Meadow. In fact, the only representative of Brawton's civic establishment in attendance was the Mayor, Arnold

Hicks, huddled in the darkness of a distant corner, apparently taking no interest in proceedings. Edgar had never seen eye to eye with Arnold, a sorter at the Royal Mail centre who knew how to open letters without leaving a trace. But he would need his support when he raised the matter under Any Other Business.

First, there were charitable matters to deal with – overdue funds finally received from the local Rotary Club for hire of the hall, authorisation of grants to Masons in Distress and their families, and token donations to profane (non-Masonic) benevolent organisations. The *Brawton Bugle* was promoting an appeal for £5,000 towards a body-scanner at the infirmary and it was felt that, although this was a non-Masonic charity, it would do no harm to make a donation. It might even raise the profile of the Brotherhood in the eyes of the community and you never knew when you might need *The Bugle*. After much discussion, the generous sum of £50 was agreed.

When it came to Any Other Business and Edgar raised the vexed question of The Meadow, Arnold was nowhere to be seen. The Worshipful Master made a carefully rehearsed and impassioned plea on the need to protect Brawton's dwindling green spaces but he sensed that, although they listened politely, environmental considerations weighed less heavily on the minds of the Brothers than a desire to adjourn to the bar. Some claimed that IPI's hi-tech manufacturing methods would ensure pollution would be minimal. The factory might even be a Good Thing by creating jobs in the area.

Edgar remembered seeing a similar suggestion in *The Bugle* recently and half regretted the £50 donation he had just authorised. It was clear that IPI's public relations people had been working overtime. Even the omnipotent Masonic influence, which Edgar had seen work wonders in the past and in which he had placed his child-like faith for decades, seemed to be wearing thin. The trouble was that few of the Lodge members lived near The Meadow. The problem was not in their back yard.

When the meeting ended he made for the bar, where most of the Lodge's real business was conducted. The police officers were busy comparing notes with the informers, mainly shopkeepers, solicitors, accountants and bank managers. Highly confidential details were exchanged on the business activities, bank balances and privates lives of people they suspected of offences or had crossed them in some way. It was part of what they called their 'noble cause'.

This highly ignoble activity involved 'leaning on' people when officers were convinced of their guilt but couldn't prove it. Their methods were many and varied, including illicit phone tapping, mail opening, entrapment and any other form of bloody-minded harassment to make life intolerable for their unfortunate enemies.

Nothing was too petty to fall into the noble cause category, even neighbours' disputes. If one of the neighbours involved was a Mason, woe betide the other. He would wake in the morning to find his tyres let down or slashed. Silent phone calls would be received late at night. If he went to the police, they would tell him to go ex-directory. It wouldn't help. After a week or so the calls would resume, when Masons at BT disclosed his new number. All this would exacerbate the dispute, as the victim would blame the hassles on his neighbour. It wouldn't be long before a 'For Sale' board appeared in his front garden.

Not all Freemasons subscribed to these nefarious activities, only those regarded as 'rogue elements'. It just so happened that Lodge 15392 contained more than its fair share of rogue elements. They liked to think that everything going on in Brawton was under their control. And they were very probably right.

That was why Edgar tracked down Arnold, propping up the bar with a couple of low-ranking CID bruisers, and demanded to know what was going on over The Meadow. Why had the Brothers in the Town Hall allowed the factory plan to go ahead when he, the Worshipful Master Himself, had opposed it? Such an occurrence was unheard of. It destroyed the very spirit of Freemasonry – mutual help and support between Brothers transcending all other interests even, on occasion, justice.

The CID drifted away at Edgar's approach, leaving Arnold, a wiry little man with a thin moustache and shifty eyes, looking uncomfortable. Edgar confessed himself mystified by the turn of events and asked why all the planning department officials had dodged the meeting. His Worship the Mayor did not know. He sympathised over Edgar's problem and promised his support. Other than that, there was not a lot he could do. He was sorry, he said, finishing his gin and edging towards the door, but his wife was ill and he had to be going.

The Lodge Master ordered a half of lager. A half was his limit as he couldn't tolerate alcohol since the head injury. He turned to Brother Cyril, his bank manager, always friendly and helpful in the past despite his esteemed customer's modest income and lowly credit status, but now strangely cool. He had to admit he supported the pharmaceuticals plant because it would bring jobs and increased prosperity to the town.

It got worse. Brother Theodore, Brawton's biggest estate agent, confirmed his worst fears that the development would decimate the value of his bungalow. The Lodge had seen-off house builders in the past, which was a pity because houses on The Meadow wouldn't have blighted the bungalows in the same way as a chemicals plant. Edgar was advised to move as soon as possible. But, of course, Janice had set her mind against that.

For once, the ever-cheerful Edgar lapsed into depression. His home of thirty-five years was about to be blighted and, despite their solemn, blood-curdling oaths of fraternity unto death, the Brethren were all deserting him. After all he had done for them, all their noble causes he had of course, supported, sometimes with deep misgivings. He downed his drink and packed his emblems of high office into the battered attaché case. As he slumped into his Proton and chugged slowly back to Meadow Drive, he felt like a king who was rapidly losing his kingdom.

Work till you drop

Howard placed his contacts book in his desk drawer and locked it. Like all the paper's reporters, he knew you couldn't keep contacts' identities in the computer system. The security simply wasn't there, despite all assurances to the contrary from management. Advice from his union, the National Union of Journalists, suggested there was no such thing as a secure computer. 'Someone somewhere' would always find a way of hacking into it. That was a risk you couldn't afford to take, bearing in mind the sensitive nature of many of his sources.

He had spent most of the afternoon sounding out contacts at the Department for Education and Skills over the suspected plan for primary school sex lessons without as much as a whisper, either on or off the record. On that subject they had taken a vow of silence. All they were interested in was where the leak had come from. On that, Howard remained equally tight-lipped.

You never stayed without work for long on *The Announcer* news desk. Within minutes, Andrew handed him a story that had been passed to him from the gossip column about one of *The Announcer's* favourite villains.

When it came to editorial policy, every national newspaper had its own trade-mark idiosyncrasy. *The Express* used to be obsessed with the British Empire until it fell into a state of terminal desuetude. *The Mail* had a problem with foreigners in general and asylum-seekers in particular. For *The Telegraph*, the BBC represented a subversive viper in our midst. *The Independent* could not abide the monarchy, and *The Gaydian*, as it was once known in Fleet Street, appealed to sandal-shod, organic lentil-eating free spirits, a significant proportion of them heterophobes.

The Times, once The Thunderer but more of a Whisperer since going tabloid, maintained a buttocks-licking relationship with the Establishment and *The Mirror* a similar obsession with the personal lives of TV celebrities. As they traded on nudity and crudity, the least said about the *Star* and the *Sun* the better.

In the case of *The Announcer*, its hobbyhorse was the trade union movement. His Lordship harboured an intense dislike of organised labour. It was a concept he regarded as unnatural, even ignoble. While he acknowledged that the worker was worthy of his hire, employers also had rights. He paid his staff generously. They owed him a debt of loyalty. They didn't need union protection. There was nothing to protect them against.

As for trade union leaders, they were all a bunch of parasites. Some of them lived almost as well as he did. He was particularly incensed when a lackey tipped him off about one union general secretary who had a habit of running up restaurant bills which His Lordship, out of a touching concern for that union's finances, considered excessive.

So it was that Howard was landed with a stringer's grubby exposé of the wretch in question. It seemed the profligate gentleman and six of his senior officials had stayed at an up-market south coast hotel for a night while on union business. Being hungry, they had the temerity to order dinner and the seven of them had run up a bill of £458.

The story was to cover the whole of an inside page, including pictures of the miscreant, the florid trappings of the hotel's restaurant and, in all its breathtaking horror, the itemised bill itself. Slowly, and growing increasingly hungry, Howard listed the dishes on his keyboard:

1 Ravioli	£ 6.00
1 Crab Cake	£ 6.00
1 May Salad	£ 6.00
1 Seafood	£ 6.00
3 Fritter	£ 18.00
3 Lamb	£ 81.00
1 Fillet of Beef	£ 27.00
1 Turbot	£ 27.00
1 Duck	£ 27.00
1 Cheese Restaurant ...	£ 10.00
1 Lemon Curd	£ 6.00
1 Chocolate Tart	£ 6.00
4 Chateau Tour St B 97 ...	£ 144.00
1 Sauvignon Trois Mouline ...	£ 18.00
2 Becks	£ 6.00
3 Still Water Large	£ 9.66
1 Pils	£ 4.00
Sub-total	£ 407.66
Service charge	£ 51.00
Total	£ 458.66

The moral of this story is that trade unionists aren't supposed to eat, Howard thought. The bill for each guest came to roughly £58 before the tip – hardly extravagance on a Sultan of Brunei scale. Unlike His Lordship, the diners were the elected leaders of thousands of colleagues. Where were they supposed to eat…Little Chef?

Howard waded through the stringer's disingenuous waffle and discovered that the arch gourmet had notified his union's finance department of the expense and had repaid the money within days. He was about to point out to the chief sub-editor that this rendered the whole grubby exercise a non-story when Andrew called over to him to check his PA. He switched to the Press Association file for their latest 'snap' and there it was:

GOVERNMENT RAISES RETIREMENT AGE TO SEVENTY

EU Directive prompts 'Human Rights' move

*   *   *

William's tip had come good sooner than expected. Of course, there had been rumours and speculation for months about plans to raise the retirement age but only William had provided the hard facts. Now they had real work to do. Andrew relieved Howard of the non-story and they cleared the decks for action. The reporter reached for his shorthand notebook, hauled out his contacts book again and launched an hour's telephonic interviewing.

As usual, government Press officers wanted to write the story for him. The European Union, they said, were anxious to protect human rights. As many people claimed their rights were being eroded by having to stop work at a statutory retirement age, the EU had decreed that all member states should abandon the principle altogether and allow people to work as long as they wished.

As a concession to those Little Englanders still clinging stubbornly to dwindling delusions of independence, the United Kingdom Government had decided instead to raise its retirement age from sixty-five to seventy for both men and women.

Off the record, the PR men admitted the European ruling was

remarkably convenient. It had reached our shores at a time when the Government was wrestling with an apparently intractable pensions crisis and would certainly come as a relief to the embattled Treasury. But, for guidance, they advised that this should not be the construction *The Announcer* placed on the story. The perception should be one of public-spirited politicians determined to enshrine the human rights of the nation's much-valued senior citizens.

Stuff that, thought Howard, as he wrote the new first edition splash, which eventually attracted the eight-column strapline:

Government's new idea to solve the pension crisis

followed by the banner headline:

WORK TILL YOU DROP

Then it was off to The Dog and Partridge, *The Announcer* staff's local, with Andrew for a noggin. Andrew was still deeply suspicious of William despite the handsome vindication of their new source's information. He kept banging on about the tip being the juicy bait in a devious trap by a rival paper, with William a plausible decoy. But he did tone the dire warnings down a bit when Howard insisted on buying the beers.

The news editor's lingering misgivings over the Whitehall 'mole' weakened further a few days later with a leak from another source at the Department of Health that the Government was to increase spending on sex education by £90 million. This was despite escalating teenage pregnancies and an unprecedented rise in the number of teenagers catching sexually-transmitted diseases. In response to news desk inquiries, the Department's PR lackeys expressed concern over teenage pregnancies and rising rates of STDs. A spokesman admitted that some infections had quadrupled in boys aged thirteen to nineteen and that three times as many girls were suffering from diseases that could make them infertile.

Latest figures showed the number of girls diagnosed with gonorrhea had more than doubled and cases of syphillis had risen by 374% in five years. New diagnoses of HIV were expected to reach 34,000 in the next two years.

But the Department's mouthpiece denied that the statistics showed a failure of the Government's sex education strategy. The real problem was that it was not being implemented early enough. Asked if that meant children of five would soon be given sex lessons, he declined to comment on or off the record. That could only mean one thing.

Andrew passed the story to Howard for a pull-together but before the reporter could switch on his terminal, his desk telephone rang. It was the commissionaire at the front entrance. There was a taxi waiting for him.

"I haven't ordered a taxi."

"The driver says to tell you Tina sent him."

"I'll be right down."

*   *   *

The old boy was as chirpy as ever as Howard squeezed himself into the back of the cab next to his companion's black briefcase. "Sorry about the mystery, Mr Mitchell, but I couldn't be seen in *The Announcer* building."

"I quite understand, William," Howard said. "Too down-market."

They both laughed and the taxi sped off towards the River.

"Not wired for sound again, are you?"

The editors had agreed that, as William had proved himself a reliable contact, the paper should respect his wishes over the voice recorder and rely on Howard's shorthand note. "No, sir. Frisk me if you like."

"I'll take your word for it. I see you went to town on the pensions story. How am I shaping as a whistle-blower?"

"No complaints so far, William. We're also working on your sex lessons info. The Department is keeping tight lipped on the five-year-olds angle."

"I expect they are. I suggest you ask them if they've hired a certain well-known film studio to produce sex education videos for infants' schools. I can assure you they have. Like to see one?"

It was the first Howard had heard of such videos. As contacts went, the man was almost too good to be true. An inner voice told him to be careful. It was Andrew's.

William unlocked the briefcase, took out a DVD and handed it to Howard. "You can keep that. It's a copy I've made."

"How many more are there?"

"There's going to be seven altogether…all for release when the time comes. All paid for by the taxpayer, of course."

After a time, the cab turned into Vauxhall Bridge Road.

"Where are we going?"

"Startimes Studios. I have to return the original, then they'll give me the second instalment."

The taxi drew up outside the glass and steel box headquarters of the famous film company and William nipped out smartly. "Wait here. You can be reading this." He handed Howard that day's *Announcer.* "Don't let anyone see you. I'll be right back."

Howard sat back and pretended to be reading a front page, most of which he had written the previous night. Moments later, his sprightly silver haired friend emerged through the swing doors clutching a small padded bag.

"Drive on," he instructed the driver as he resumed his seat. "It's not unlike the procedure at sex shops where you used to return one porn video and get another," he told the journalist. "Not that you'd know anything about that."

Howard folded the newspaper and grinned. "It's not something I do myself," he said.

"Nor do I, but I gather that was the drill."

"So what's next?"

"Back to the interface, dear boy. See what delights they've served up for the infants in Part Two. I'll make another copy and send it to you. Today's little jaunt was to prove that I'm kosher, for want of a better expression…just in case you think it's all some kind of bizarre trap."

"That thought has crossed certain minds in the office but not mine, William. I'm satisfied you're the genuine article. But if you want us to go public with this, won't that compromise you with the Tina Project? I mean, they're bound to suspect you."

"They won't know the leak's come from me. They've all seen the video. It could be any of them – or someone at Startimes, for that matter. No, I don't think they'll suspect me. But they'll tighten up on security."

"You should too, William. You're putting yourself at risk. I think you should talk to my editor about security. He can pull strings at top level."

"So can I, dear boy. But the marionettes don't always jump the way you want. No, I don't need *The Announcer's* protection, but thanks anyway."

39

Howard had been authorised to offer William a deal reflecting the importance of his information. "We know we can't put a value on your information but the paper's prepared to be generous…"

"I don't need money either, Mr Mitchell. I have enough. We all have our roles to play in life. I've just discovered what mine is."

They parted a short distance away from *The Announcer* building. "How can we contact you?" Howard asked, as he climbed out of the taxi.

"You can't, dear boy. I'll be in touch," William replied, and the cab sped away and was lost in the frenetic, anonymous London traffic.

Catch them young

A soothing female voice-over intoned: "Your penis or your clitoris sometimes grows hard and feels nice when you touch it..." and cartoon figures of a small boy and girl, hand in hand and both naked, danced across the screen, in a shower of tiny twinkling stars, accompanied by a happy musical box jingle.

Seated round the TV set in the Editor's office, Julian, Howard, Andrew, Irene Thomas, the paper's social affairs editor, and George Fergus, its education correspondent, watched in fascinated silence as the sex education video for infant schoolchildren progressed.

Hard-bitten journalists all, none could believe that five, six and seven-year-olds would soon be weaned off nursery rhymes on to close-up pictures of their genitalia and subtle hints about masturbation. References to love, marriage or morality were conspicuously absent.

"What's your view on this?" Julian asked each of them when the anodyne tones and musical box jingle subsided, the little stars faded and the screen went dark.

"Disturbing," said George Fergus. "I'm not sure if it's legal. Certainly, children of that age will not be ready for it."

"I'm not against sex education but I agree with George," Andrew said.

"Howard?"

"I don't think parents will go along with it. Barbara and I wouldn't."

"Irene?"

"Scary."

"Right. I'm bringing forward the conference so we can make an early start."

Diane was instructed to make the necessary calls and within minutes all department heads – news, sport, features, City, pictures, business, comment, parliamentary – were assembled for the editorial conference.

When Julian had brought everyone up to speed on the latest developments, he told them: "I think *The Announcer* should take a campaigning position on this issue. It's a calculated risk, I know. I'll set out my reasons for taking it in a leader article. Meanwhile, we're going to splash on the video story. Sex education doesn't work. So what do they do? Throw more money at it. Makes no sense. The gut feeling is that other forces must be at work here."

He gave no hint at what the other forces might be. At this stage, only Howard and Andrew were in on that one.

Turning to his news editor, Julian said: "Andrew, I want the reactions of primary school teachers, parents and church leaders. Talk to doctors, psychologists and lawyers as well. We need to know if the Government is breaking the law. And don't forget the sex education lobby. I want quotes from lefty MPs, people like that pony-tailed pagan…what's his name?

"Paul D'Arcy," Andrew said, busily taking notes.

"That's the chap. Gets on every progressive soap box." Then, to the pictures editor: "Aubrey…pix of teachers, parents, doctors, D'Arcy and the rest. Can you organise clips from the videos? Nothing too explicit, we don't want our readers choking on their breakfast kidneys and kedgeree."

Aubrey Vernon, an *Announcer* snapper from way back, laughed. "No problem, Julian. I'll bet Startimes will be glad of the publicity – the wrong kind as usual."

"Their TV pals might give us some of the same before long," Julian said. Then, turning to the sports editor: "Now, Reg…tell me about tonight's big match…"

*　　*　　*

Howard pressed the coffee-with-milk-and-sugar button on the vending machine and gingerly carried the scalding plastic cup back to his desk. It had been a gruelling round of phone calls, with the Department of Education expressing righteous indignation over the leak of their kindergarten sex lessons and more than usually defensive in their quotes. After reading up his copious notes and, for once well ahead of the first edition deadline, he started to type his copy for the front page lead story into the computer system:

By Howard Mitchell

Children as young as five are to be given televised sex lessons in a bid to halt escalating teenage pregnancies and sexually transmitted diseases.

The project, part of the Government's £90 million sex

education programme, is to be introduced in primary schools later this year, *The Announcer* has learned. It includes TV videos depicting nudity, masturbation, homosexuality and explicit scenes of sexual intercourse.

In the first of seven videos being offered to education authorities throughout the country, pictures of naked children are shown, with body parts including penis and clitoris labelled. The five-year-olds are told their genital areas "sometimes go hard and feel nice when you touch them".

A furious Education Department spokesman said those responsible for leaking information about the videos to the Press would be "traced and dealt with accordingly". Defending the film for five-year-olds, he claimed infants were likely to "respond more positively"if television were used rather than conventional teaching methods. Asked why references to love, morality and marriage had been omitted, he said they were considered "irrelevant in this day and age".

The controversial decision to lower the age for sex education to five was described by the Department as "part of an open and honest conversation to demystify sex". Children needed to be taught about sex and contraception at the earliest possible age, the spokesman said. Leaving it until later was no longer an option.

The scheme was welcomed by Planned Families, a known front organisation for the contraceptive industry, as a logical extension of the present sex education policy. Other supporters included Paul D'Arcy, the outspoken pagan MP and gay rights activist, who launched an impassioned attack on *The Announcer* and the "reactionary Press".

"What right have you and your backward-looking cronies to oppose such an enlightened project?" Mr D'Arcy asked. "Teaching children the facts of life can't be left to parents. They find it embarrassing. That breeds ignorance in children when they need to know about sex and how to avoid unwanted pregnancies."

"Tell them how to fit condoms and how to use them. The earlier the better. Habits begun in the classroom last a lifetime."

But critics maintained that classroom sex education had

already failed. A spokesman for Family & Youth Concern said that, despite sex lessons as part of the secondary school curriculum for over thirty years, Britain had the highest rate of teenage pregnancies in Europe. Sexually transmitted diseases had reached epidemic levels, with syphilis, once rare, increasing at a staggering rate.

Against this background, sex lessons in primary schools were "totally irresponsible", a spokesman said. They would compound the problem, predisposing infants to early sexual experiences by converting their innocent curiosity into prurience.

"The 1986 Education Act stipulates that sex education should teach about marriage, its importance for family life and the bringing up of children. By excluding such instruction this material is in breach of the Act."

Howard ended his report with an item disclosing that 25,000 free condoms had been distributed to 11-year-olds by a birth control pressure group using the internet. They were supplied by a major contraceptive manufacturer. The legal age for sex in Britain was sixteen.

TV SEX LESSONS FOR FIVE-YEAR-OLDS

Next day's *Announcer* carried Howard's splash beneath the banner headline; plus inside page coverage on the reaction nationwide, most of it unfavourable, to the controversial lessons.

There were cross-references to the verdicts of the specialist correspondents on inside pages and to Julian's leading article at the top of the Comment page. This was headed:

CATCH THEM YOUNG

Before they can barely read about the adventures of Postman Pat, five-year-olds are to be shown 'sex education' videos telling them it "feels nice" to play with their genitals. The videos, which make no mention of love, marriage or even basic human morality, have been produced by Startimes Studios, those guardians of the nation's moral standards. They are the government's ingenious solution to the problems of escalating teenage pregnancies and sexual diseases. *The Announcer* has seen the first of the videos and now alerts parents of primary school age children to its dehumanising character.

Sex education evangelists have never allowed evidence to distract them from following their religion. So it is no surprise that they are putting their faith in this latest form of indoctrination. What is surprising is that a government that claims to pride itself on pragmatism and evidence-based policies should fund it to the tune of £90 million.

The evidence which, inexplicably, they choose to ignore in this instance, is overwhelming. After thirty years of value-free, contraceptive-rich sex education in our schools, we have the highest rate of teenage pregnancies in Europe and sexual infections have reached a level at which genito-urinary clinics are unable to cope with demand.

These are not the claims of reactionary elements or pro-life lobbyists. Studies in the *British Medical Journal* and *The Journal of Clinical Epidemiology* have demonstrated conclusively that sex education fails to affect teenage pregnancy. Distinguished experts, including the Government's own adviser on sexual health, have warned that the country is facing a "public health crisis" over sexually transmitted infections.

What possible motives, other than monumental stupidity, can induce a government to ignore these eleventh-hour warnings? The only reasonable conclusion seems to be that other forces must be at work here. We do not know who or what these forces are. But we regard it as our duty to find out. The damage being caused to successive generations of our children demands it.

Touching nerves

A dripping Marcus C Quinn III hardly had time to say "Hello", on lifting the swimming pool extension phone at his Mayfair mansion, before an irascible voice inquired: "Have you seen today's *Announcer*?"

There was no need to ask: "Who is this?" He knew straight away who it was: one of the few Europeans he ever addressed as Sir.

"No sir. Not yet. It's ten before 8 am."

"I know what the bloody time is," snapped the voice. "What are we paying all these spin doctors for if they can't keep a rag like *The Announcer* off our backs?"

The chief executive of IPI reached for a towel. "What are they saying? Is it about the videos?"

"You bet it is. They're making trouble for us…hinting at sinister forces behind sex education…as if such a thing were remotely likely."

The American billionaire's little rat-trap of a mouth creased into a smirk amid the heavy jowls. "Perish the thought," he said.

"Exactly. Read it yourself. I'm worried they'll get wind of our other plans."

"With respect, sir, there's no danger of that. All our members are regularly briefed about security. The Tina Project remains strictly top secret. No journalist will ever get a sniff of it, I assure you."

"Well, you'd better be right."

"You can safely leave it to the team, sir. We'll nip it in the bud."

Quinn replaced the handset and watched Sandra, his favourite maid, swimming nude in the pool. He'd been married and divorced three times in the States. His ex-wives had all been gold-diggers, not to mention totally frigid. When it came to sex, as it rarely did, they'd expected him to take the necessary precautions.

He controlled a billion-dollar international corporation manufacturing and selling tons of contraceptive chemicals daily. So why wear a dodgy condom? Despite all the propaganda about 'safe sex', he didn't trust them. Never used 'em. The only really safe sex was the Pill and his company's latest long-lasting progestogen jab.

Sandra was a good girl. She knew better than to expect marriage.

She didn't hassle him over money, his halitosis or his habit of leaving the lavatory seat raised after use. She didn't mind his other women. She wasn't possessive. And she didn't lay down the law about rubbers. She had the jab every three months – he made sure of that. Too bad about side effects.

He admired the supple young body as she climbed out of the water and put on a robe.

"Do me a favour, honey," he said. "Go get me today's *Announcer*."

She trotted off obediently. Sandra was a good girl.

*   *   *

In the days that followed it was clear that *The Announcer* campaign, while touching nerves in some quarters, had captured the imagination of the paper's readers. Letters flooded in from anxious parents wanting to know if they could withdraw their children from the sex lessons. Many said they would do so anyway and face the consequences.

Some readers described sex education as the corruption of children for commercial gain. Others proposed a legal challenge to the lessons, which they claimed were a sophisticated form of child abuse. Many called for a national boycott of films and videos produced by Startimes. Family & Youth Concern invited signatures on a petition to the Prime Minister. Catholic Church leaders and Evangelical ministers added their protests. The Anglicans remained silent.

Well, not entirely silent. A certain bishop, noted for his unusual proclivities and universally described in the media as 'controversial', came out (to use the phrase loosely) in favour of the lessons. He was joined by members of the Gay Liberation movement, who condemned opponents as 'reactionary religious bigots' and, sure enough, 'homophobic'.

One of the letters in *The Announcer's* bulging mailbag was from the chief executive of a certain condom manufacturer. He was anxious to set the record straight regarding the 25,000 condoms his firm had supplied to 11-year-old children via an internet campaign.

He pointed out that, although the legal age at which young people could have sex in Britain was sixteen, there were no age restrictions on buying condoms. He continued, a trifle disingenuously Julian thought: "The campaign was not an encouragement to pre-teens to have sex but simply to show them how condoms worked. They were advised to practise by fitting one on a banana or blowing it up like a balloon."

Yes, but practise for what? Julian thought.

It seemed that the gentleman had been grievously distressed by suggestions that his reputable company had actually sold the condoms. They had, in fact, been donated.

"That makes it all right then," Julian observed as he approved the letter for publication. Hundreds of others, including e-mails and faxes, would have to be 'spiked', although he decided to use one from a remarkably percipient teenage girl in Edinburgh who wrote:

"Sex education of the kind described in your report has been banned in Scotland. It is unnatural and I hope it stays banned. Children should be taught self-respect not self-indulgence. I am sixteen and aware of all the pressures on today's teenagers to have pre-marital sex. I am proud to be a virgin and intend to remain one until I get married."

Self-respect not self-indulgence. Julian resolved to remember that line. Out of the mouths of babes…

*   *   *

'Steak and muchroom pie' read the menu in *The Announcer's* canteen. If you were management you called it the staff restaurant and sat in your exclusive enclave, partitioned off from the *hoi polloi*. Howard, who belonged to the latter, smiled as he read the menu and took a tray. It was a good job Mervyn's cooking was better than his spelling. The chef took a pride in the cuisine he served up every night to managers, executives, editors, printers, computer technicians, dispatch workers, drivers, sub-editors and reporters alike.

Tonight, in addition to the pie, there was braised steak and onions, one of his specials. Mervyn's braised steak could not be bettered by the Dorchester at ten times the price. Howard knew because he had sampled braised steak at the Dorchester more than once. The canteen assistant served him a generous portion of the culinary masterpiece with chips and the chef's unique brand of mushy sprouts (a delicacy in themselves; he couldn't stand *al dente*), and he carried his supper across the crowded canteen to a corner table.

Howard liked an occasional beer with the rest of the hacks and hackettes but, unusually for a journalist, he liked his food better. And at these subsidised prices it was a steal. Let the others shoot off to the pub. They didn't know what they were missing. If there was time, you could even fit in a frame of snooker before the second edition.

He was joined a few minutes later by Irene Thomas, the social affairs hackette, bearing a tray of salad and a bread roll.

"Hi," she said, pulling up a chair. Although she wouldn't see forty again, she wasn't bad looking. Bright and perky with a short, mid-blonde hairstyle, disarming blue eyes, trim figure. Must be all the salads.

"Hi," he said. "This is a rare pleasure."

Irene tried doggedly to spear a radish with her fork. "I'm on Channel 4 tomorrow and I need to pick your brains about sex education."

"The late chat show?"

"That's the one."

"Lamb to the slaughter. Rather you than me."

"Well, I'm not frightened of them. I've done it before…know what to expect. But I need all the info I can get on the health angle. You know, who picks up the pieces when sex education fails…you seem to know all about it."

"Perhaps I'm after your job," Howard joked.

Irene was not amused. What with all the talk about redundancies, everyone was getting nervous.

"Many a true word spoken in jest," she retorted. "Anyway, when I ask the health authorities about sex infections and treatment they clam up."

"That's because they're desperate." Howard had swotted up on sexual infections. "People are waiting three months for an appointment. They could be HIV positive all that time but they still have to wait…unless they go private. You can work out what that means in terms of health risks to the public.

"Three months before they're treated?"

"Longer in some parts of the country."

"Name one."

"London. Clinics bursting at the seams. They don't have the staff."

"It's a vicious circle isn't it. The more kids experiment with sex before they can cope with it, the greater the spread of disease."

"That's right. But don't blame the kids. They're taught that sleeping

49

around is the new cool. They've been brought up to believe the 'safe sex' message. It's a myth. I've been mugging up on the failure rate for condoms. Do you know what it is among teenagers?"

"No."

"Twenty-two per cent."

Irene stopped picking at her salad. "That's scandalous. The manufacturers should be sued."

"There's no legal redress, apparently. The makers say teenagers don't use them properly...that they're mostly drunk at the time. And anyway condoms don't give total protection – unlike the Pill. It's the Government's health propaganda that deceives people."

"Yet they carry on flogging the same dodgy message!"

"Incredible, isn't it. And it can only get worse. The NHS have got a real crisis on their hands but they won't admit it. Wait till panic sets in...it'll be contraceptive jabs for all, you'll see."

"So we're talking 'National Scandal' here?"

"Absolutely."

"Sources?"

"Unimpeachable."

"Castrate the lot of you, I say. That's the only answer!"

They both laughed. Howard pinched a bit of her bread roll and mopped up the last of his rich gravy.

"If you'll excuse me, Irene, I have a cue to chalk."

And he made for the snooker room.

The terrorist

The moment you stepped into the snooker room you could relax. All the intense pressures of the job, the office bitching and the tyranny of nightly deadlines simply slipped from your shoulders. It was almost physical. In the cavernous darkness, a soft pool of light illuminated the table, its contrasting coloured balls shining like jewels on an immaculate green baize lawn.

As a haven of peace and tranquility in a demented world, the snooker room had few equals. It reminded Howard of the Editor's office without its menacing clock. Its occupants may not have been the most skilful snooker players in the world but they went about the game in a calm, leisurely and thoughtful manner, in contrast to the frenetic pace dominating the rest of the building.

The snooker room also represented a microcosm of *Announcer* society. Here there was no segregation but a spirit of true equality. Managers played against messengers, van drivers with computer freaks. As Howard entered and quietly closed the door behind him, a four-hander was in progress involving two lads from dispatch and a couple of elderly printers, watched by Edgar Brierley, the head messenger, and other regulars.

One of the printers, Hughie, a short wiry fellow with a neat white moustache, was quite a good player and liked to boast about the time he played a frame against the Hurricane. Everyone looked up and said "Good evening" or "Hi, Howard" as the reporter took his seat among the spectators along a wall hung with cue cases. Word would soon get around that the star player had arrived and the room would fill up quickly.

While he waited for a game, Edgar was regaling the regulars with his favourite story – about the effect he had on airport metal detectors whenever he and Janice went on holiday. Most of them had heard the yarn before but the way it invariably reduced the teller to helpless mirth never failed to amuse them.

During a previous life as a motor mechanic, Edgar had been working under a car when it collapsed on top of him, trapping his head between the steel chassis and the concrete floor. After lying unconscious for half an hour, he was eventually taken to hospital with severe concussion and

51

several bones round his ear partially crushed. Surgery left him with a two-inch titanium plate in his skull, an enlarged inner ear cavity, chronic headaches and slightly impaired mental function.

Office associates sometimes teased him about being a sandwich short of a picnic or a sprout short of a Christmas dinner but that was far from true. Edgar could be a bit absent-minded. And occasionally rather childish. But his real friends knew he was no fool.

Apparently, it was the titanium implant that caused the world's major airports to grind to a halt whenever the Brierleys ventured abroad. It happened every time he passed through a metal detector. Bells would ring, buzzers buzz and bleepers bleep. Security guards would spring into action. Policemen would appear, guns at the ready. All hell would break loose. Oh, what fun.

Edgar had a doctor's note explaining his condition and he was supposed to show it to security staff beforehand. But he sometimes 'forgot' to do this, even when Janice reminded him – he was that absent-minded.

"They think I'm a terrorist," Edgar exclaimed, doubling up with laughter, his pink dome growing even pinker. His listeners fell about. No-one in their right mind could think Edgar was a terrorist.

"You should see their faces. They keep searching me but they can't find anything. Then I remember the note and the wife tells me off. But it's a great laugh." You could see that Edgar had fond memories of these incidents. For him they were the highlights of his holidays.

When the four-hander finished, Howard and Edgar found themselves teamed against Darren from dispatch and Eric, another printer. "Editorial versus the workers," Eric quipped. On these occasions, Edgar tended to undo all Howard's skilful safety play by missing a pot and leaving the other team 'on'. It was like playing three opponents. The challenge invariably brought out the best in his game.

Sometimes you find yourself trying to cue the white ball with your bridge hand held over intervening balls. This calls for a special bridging technique of raising the wrist and stretching the fingers. When Edgar faced such a shot, his cue waving all over the place, Howard tried to help him. It was then that he noticed the gold signet ring on the third finger of his partner's left hand. It was engraved with the symbol of two crossed compasses.

Howard knew what it represented and he was surprised that Edgar was prepared to advertise it. But he said nothing. Instead, he concentrated on his potting and won the game with a break of sixty-two, to the applause of spectators who recognised artistry when they saw it. But it made him a few minutes late in returning to his desk. (You were allowed one hour for supper break although everyone took longer, some one-and-a-half hours or more. In certain celebrated cases, one or two hadn't come back at all.)

When Howard returned to the newsroom, the acting chief sub-editor called him over to the news subs' back bench. He was a sarcastic young upstart, deputising for the chief sub and anxious to exploit his hour of power by demanding the second edition changes. All the subs knew there were rarely any second edition news changes, apart from the weather forecast update, which reached them direct from PA. Second edition changes were mainly for sport and the results of evening football matches. It was the third edition that carried all the news changes.

The reporter 'approached the bench', to use the sub-editors' whimsical jargon. "Rather a long break, wasn't it?" the acting CSE inquired.

Howard thought for a moment. "Sixty-two, actually. It should have been more but I missed an easy red."

For the wretched news subs, focusing intently on their screens but listening to every word, it was a moment to savour.

*   *   *

They brought extra chairs into the Editor's office to watch Irene's TV ordeal. In addition to Julian and Howard, there were George Fergus, Aubrey Vernon, Cyril Sharp, the aptly named night editor, and several news desk hacks and hackettes, including Kath Benson, Andrew's deputy. Andrew had been persuaded to stay late, thwarting his plan for a cosy drink with Diane. Even the paper's TV critic, a weirdo who wore a floppy bow tie, had been called in.

The chat show was hosted by a shifty-looking, hyperactive young man with a shaved head and a tuft of dark hair on his chin which gave him the appearance of a rather badly put-together police photo-fit. When the synthesized opening music faded, he excitedly introduced his guests as Baroness Gertrude Witherspoon; journalist Irene Thomas (there was no way Channel 4 would give *The Announcer* a plug), author Martin Pratt and

53

Paul D'Arcy, MP, the channel's resident male homosexual. It was a clash of ideologies in which the odds were stacked three-to-one in favour of the progressives. It should have been four-to-one but, due to an oversight, no lesbian had been included in the panel.

The subject was Sex Education: Is it Working? The Baroness, her grey hair knotted in a tight bun and peering over her rimless spectacles, started the ball rolling with a long-winded defence of primary school sex lessons. It was never too early to teach children about their genitals and the importance of contraception. Children had been kept in ignorance, their sexuality repressed, for too long. Old-fashioned ideas about chastity, modesty and religion were no longer relevant in today's society...etc, etc. It was the standard extrusion of a devout atheist and *Guardian* contributor.

The tuft let her ramble on in this vein for the best part of five minutes before turning to the foppish D'Arcy who, while caressing his expensively tinted coiffeur with his plump fingers, agreed with every word "the honourable Lady" had said. Now, there was a surprise.

If he could enlarge on her rational and clear-sighted arguments, it would be on behalf of those children confused about their sexual identity in forming relationships. Was enough emphasis being placed on teaching that 'gays' were normal people who just happened to prefer relationships with members of their own sex, he wondered. Perhaps in this crucial area, sex education might not be working as well as it should be.

Then the tousle-haired Pratt, almost as foppish but trying to convey an air of deep erudition, launched into an impenetrable dissertation on the subject of morality and how it was impinging on the vital development of "our young people" during their formative years. The upshot appeared to be that moral values and post-modern individualism were interchangeable.

While Channel 4's late night audience were trying to get their heads round that after staggering home from the pub, he added: "We are living in an enlightened, technologically advanced society...a sophisticated New Age. It calls for a New Morality."

Finally, Irene, the token dissident, was favoured with a few seconds. It was long enough for her to suggest that the New Morality was just another version of the Old Immorality. When it came to sex education, children needed to be taught self-respect, not self-indulgence. (She had been picking Julian's brains as well as Howard's).

Moving swiftly on from this uncomfortably contentious view, the tuft wanted to talk about sex education in Holland, which progressives never tired of holding up as a model for the rest of the world. Once again Her Ladyship waded in with a torrent of statistics. In the Netherlands, the pregnancy rate for girls aged between fifteen and nineteen was 8.1 per 1,000. In Britain, it was 62.6 per 1,000. That was because Dutch sex education was so thorough, she maintained. It started at a younger age, was explicit and continued throughout the school career.

Being a sexually liberated nation, Dutch parents were frank with their children in such matters so that, when children became sexually active, they were properly clued-up on how to avoid pregnancy. By contrast, sex education in Britain was patchy, started too late and was constrained by outdated ideas of modesty and the need to placate misguided moralists. Even with the Noble Lady's droning delivery, the argument sounded impressive.

Just when it seemed she would never actually pause for breath, she did. For a second, she looked round, beaming at the heads nodding approvingly. Seizing her chance, Irene dived in at the deep end. (She had done her homework on the Dutch question too). Wasn't it true, she asked demurely, that the eminent sociologist, Joost van Loon, had visited a wide range of schools in Holland – Catholic, Protestant, secular, middle class and deprived – and found that there was no standard model of sex education? Wasn't it also widely known that it did not begin at an earlier age than in Britain, nor was it more permissive?

The surrounding faces, shocked by the mention of such an authority as Dr Van Loon, were for once rendered speechless. Irene pressed home her advantage. Until recently, contraception had to be paid for in Dutch schools, unlike those in Britain where it was free – yet our teenage pregnancy was eight times higher.

Also, the family structure in Holland was more stable than ours, with half as many children born out of wedlock. There was a much lower divorce rate and one-parent families were a rarity. These were the real reasons for the difference between the two countries when it came to teenage pregnancy. What we needed to adopt was not Dutch sex education but Dutch family values.

She was about to launch into the scandalous failure rate of condoms when the tuft stopped her. Sensing that she had effectively hijacked the debate, he switched hurriedly to a fawning review of Pratt's latest impenetrable book, but the damage had been done. The programme had given out exactly the opposite message to the politically correct one the producers had intended.

Heads, including tuft's, would surely roll.

The pleasures of boating

"You were right, Mr Mitchell. I think Tina's on to me."

Howard and his distinguished Whitehall whistle-blower were again boosting the fortunes of the Hackney Carriage trade and, once again, William was preoccupied with the view from the cab's rear window.

"Do you think we're being tailed?" Howard asked.

William nodded. "Could be...or maybe I'm getting paranoid. It's a gut feeling. There was something wrong at the last meeting. Something you couldn't put your finger on. You don't spend thirty-five years as a Treasury civil servant without developing a sixth sense."

"Where was the meeting?"

"If I told you Lodge number 19145, would you be any the wiser?"

Howard thought for a moment. "Masons," he said brightly.

"Well done, dear boy. As I said before, Tina meets at a different location each time. The need for total privacy is paramount." William took another long look out of the rear window before continuing. "There is only one organisation left in this country that can guarantee absolute, cast-iron security and that's the Freemasons. Their lodges are completely sound-proofed, did you know?"

Howard shook his head. His knowledge of the clandestine fraternity was restricted to *Inside The Brotherhood*. He didn't think the book mentioned sound-proofed lodges.

"And they have their own security people...doormen outside and inside the doors."

"I thought lodges were for Masons only. You're not one are you?"

William laughed heartily. "Of course not. I left the Boy Scouts at the age of fifteen and never had any desire to join the grown-up version. No, it's just that certain members of Tina are also Brothers...so they get the rest of us in as sort of associate members. Grease a few palms, you know the sort of thing."

"What happened at the meeting?"

"Everything went smoothly. We drafted the necessary private member's bill – it's to be called the Health of the Nation Bill. Our provider of sexual health services waxed eloquently on the subject of 'termination grants' for single mothers and our chairman reminded us of the superiority of chemicals over condoms. He would, of course. He runs IPI. You know them, naturally."

"Sure, the world's largest contraceptive pill company. So they're muscling in on the act. Not surprising really. Tina must seem like a marketing miracle for them."

"Anyway, towards the end of the meeting, I got the distinct impression they were all keeping something from me. They were withholding an important detail, I could tell from the way they looked at me. They suspect me of the leaks, I'm convinced of it. So I've got to watch my step. We both have."

The taxi had pulled up on The Embankment, next to the jetty for the pleasure steamers. Bunting was strung between lampposts and billboards displaying the prices of various river cruises. The weather was warm for late spring and trippers were crowding the landing stages.

"Fancy a sail, Mr Mitchell? Down to Tower Bridge and back in time for tea?"

The whistle-blower was full of surprises. "Why not? It's years since I've been on one of these."

They waited in a queue for their tickets, their smart suits incongruous among the tourists' jeans and T-shirts emblazoned with such slogans as 'I'll do anything you want', 'Uncertainty rules – I think' and 'I'm proud of my Attitude Problem'. When it came to boarding the ancient, double-decker vessel, dressed overall with grubby bunting, William drew back. "Wait a moment. I want us to be the last on."

Only when the boatmen were about to cast off did the pair jump on board. Satisfied they were not being followed, they climbed the steps to the upper deck and sat down on the slatted wooden seats. The sun was shining and a light breeze blowing off the river.

"Ah, the pleasures of boating," William declared, leaning back and closing his eyes, as the steamer made its stately way downstream.

But he wasn't asleep. When the sun disappeared behind a bank of cloud, he opened his eyes and said: "There's been an important development." He looked round the upper deck where the teenage tourists were engaged in innocent horseplay before continuing. "By a roundabout process, I've discovered what they were keeping from me at the meeting. You'd better make a note of this."

Howard took out his pen and notebook.

"Tina's decided what to do with the women who refuse sterilisation." He lowered his voice and Howard had to bend forward to hear him. "Pressures will become less subtle. As the women will be breaking the law, the penalties must be seen to be a deterrent to others. First off, they'll be handed a stiff fine..."

"Which they can't pay, of course, as they're on benefit." Howard put in.

"Which it's unlikely they can pay. And it's equally unlikely they'll have enough possessions to sell. So, if they can't raise the money, the women will be sent to a special detention centre for a period – *with their children taken into care.* Special camps for dissidents – what does that remind you of?"

Howard's shorthand grew shaky. "You are *sure* about this, William?"

"Absolutely. Those provisions won't be mentioned as such in the parliamentary bill. They'll be added later by way of regulations, a ploy that's often used."

"Yes, I know: the devil's in the detail. The feminists will give you hell."

"Of course, there'll be demonstrations, petitions and the like...there always are when unpopular legislation is introduced. But it'll all die down. It always does."

Howard had covered many demos in his time. Nearly all had come to nothing. "I'm beginning to see what you mean about the slippery slope."

For a long time, the steamer surged on in silence broken only by the teenagers' high jinks. Then Howard said: "We're looking at a form of state terrorism here, William."

"Don't I know it!"

"You're taking a helluva risk telling me all this. I really think you should talk to Julian about security."

William gave a hollow laugh. "Don't worry about me, dear boy. Just look after yourself." He stood up and stretched, then leaned against the rail, the breeze ruffling his silver-grey hair.

The steamer was passing the Houses of Parliament and Howard wondered what steps could be taken to halt the Health of the Nation Bill by constitutional means. "Is there no way of stopping this thing in there?"

he asked, pointing across the river.

The older man turned to face him and smiled his disarming smile. "In a word: none. Once the powers that be decide to do something, they do it. Nothing stands in their way. Not Parliament. Not the Church. Not public protests. Only you – the Press – have a chance. Of course, the Bill has to go through the motions…consultation papers, advisory panels, First Reading – a mere formality, as you probably know. Then the Second Reading, when it's debated 'as a whole'. No amendments can be made. The MPs then vote for or against the Bill *in principle*. That's followed by the Standing Committee stage, when amendments can be tabled."

"It can be changed at that stage then…protest groups can be heard?"

"Yes, but by a Standing Committee that's overloaded with the Bill's supporters! You may not understand that the vote taken at the end of the debate usually determines the composition of the Standing Committee. MPs who voted against a government-supported bill – and rest assured, the Health of the Nation Bill will be government-supported – have little chance of a place on the committee."

"So it's a charade, basically?"

"Basically, that's what it is. I need hardly remind you that this Government enjoys a substantial majority, so you end up with a committee already heavily biased in favour of the legislation. Still with me?"

Howard nodded.

"The Bill then moves to the Report Stage where amendments are 'discussed' but, in this case, almost certainly thrown out. Then there's the Third Reading that normally comes immediately after the Report Stage. You can bet they won't be hanging about."

"Fast track legislation?"

"The faster the better. And the timing's perfect. Parliament is so preoccupied with anti-terrorist measures, a bill like this could go through on the nod."

"A good time to bury bad news, to quote the immortal phrase."

"Exactly. The devil has all the luck!"

"What about amendments at Third Reading?"

"Technically, they can be put forward but they're highly unlikely to be allowed. Usually only general statements about the Bill are permitted at Third Reading."

"Then it goes to their Lordships."

"Yes, the procedure in the Lords is almost the same…slightly different rules on amendments, but it's all academic. The Government will bin any changes they make."

"Suppose they were to lose the final vote…back-bench rebellion, that sort of thing?"

"Our great leaders still hold the ace. They could invoke the emergency powers they've held since the suicide bomb attacks. They may decide to bypass the parliamentary process and do that anyway. That would be the supreme irony, of course…using anti-terrorist measures to inflict state terrorism!"

Howard knew that deviousness was the currency of politics, but this…this was something else. "Whatever happened to democracy?" he asked, almost to himself.

William's lips tightened into a grim half-smile. "Democracy went out with the ancient Greeks, dear boy. As long as Tina plays her cards right, she's practically on the Statute Book already. Only one thing can stop her. That's why I'm talking to you."

They chatted about the power of the Press on their way back upstream. Many and varied were those with vested interests in curtailing it. Politicians, celebrities and certain members of the ruling class had joined forces in demanding anti-intrusion laws to protect their privacy, which usually meant their dark secrets.

Howard knew a government-sponsored privacy bill aimed at curtailing Press freedom would soon be debated in Parliament. Its timing, ahead of Tina, gave it a sinister significance but no self-respecting journalist would allow himself to be intimidated by politicians. The freedom of the Press was one of the few British traditions still envied by the rest of the world. There would always be journalists prepared to uphold it, even on pain of imprisonment.

William knew Howard was one of them. As the two men parted on The Embankment, he took the reporter's hand and shook it warmly. "It's up to you now, dear boy. Good luck. I have every confidence in you."

Howard thought it a little strange. They'd never shaken hands on parting before. He looked into the sad blue eyes and he knew it meant farewell.

Nothing but bad news

May did not so much creep up unnoticed on April as seize it by the scruff of the neck and batter it into submission. When the storms subsided they left a pink carpet of cherry blossom across the streets and neatly trimmed gardens of south London's suburbia. It was time Howard drove over to Cheam and visited his mother. He hadn't seen her since Easter, although they talked almost every week on the telephone. She understood that he worked unsocial hours, that he and his family lived several miles away and that when he did get some free time, Barbara was usually working so he had to supervise the children and the *au pair*.

Howard always phoned her in advance of a visit because, although still sprightly for her seventy years, she was profoundly deaf. She wore two hearing aids and could hear fairly well on the phone because it had a gadget to increase the volume, but you could knock on the door of her sheltered accommodation flat for hours without her knowing. Unannounced visitors usually had to call the warden to use her duplicate keys.

She had suffered progressive hearing loss for as long as Howard could remember. It had been mild at first but became more severe as he grew up and started dating girls. They both still laughed about the time when he introduced her to Barbara and said her parents owned a boarding house in Brighton. "Pardon," his mother had replied. "Did you say bawdy house?"

Armed with his customary bunch of flowers – sweet Williams, her favourites, and carnations this time – Howard climbed the stairs to her first floor flat. He lifted the knocker on her front door with its nameplate, Susan Mitchell, and rapped three times very loudly. It was their prearranged signal. His mother had seen his silver grey Rover saloon as he drove into the car park. She would be standing in the tiny hallway waiting for his knock.

"How are you, Mum?" he asked as he embraced his little old mother. Each time he visited her she seemed smaller and more frail. Her pale, lightly lined but still delicately beautiful face broke into a smile. He knew what she would say.

"Oh, I'm just the same, Howard. How are you?"

"I'm just the same, too." They both laughed. It was their shared catchphrase. He presented her with the bouquet, which she accepted with girlish delight.

"I'll put them in some water," she said, bustling across the minute lounge into the microscopic kitchen. "Sit down while I make a pot of tea."

Despite her high blood pressure and osteo-arthritis, his mother was always cheerful and childishly pleased to see him. She had put on her best floral dress for the occasion and had had her hair done, though perms never seemed to suit her. The unruly curls she had struggled all her life to control hadn't changed over the years. They were still a light, natural brown with hardly any grey. She never had it dyed. Didn't need to.

Howard relaxed on the two-seater chintz-covered sofa. Everything in the flat was just the same too. Afternoon sunshine filtered through the same crisp lace curtains. The same electric logs flickered in the hearth as they did in summer and winter. Grouped around the fireplace in their wooden surround were the same ornaments he remembered from earliest childhood...vases decorated with multi-coloured kingfishers and brass trinkets his father (a sea captain who died several years ago) had brought home from the sub-continent and beyond. There were small ceramic jugs, souvenirs from their holidays at Bognor, and a ship in a bottle they had bought in Ilfracombe.

There was the battered sideboard in which he'd kept his toys. A handle was missing from one of its drawers. It had been missing for over thirty years. In one corner stood the Victorian standard lamp with its green-fringed shade that had belonged to his grandmother. In another, his father's old bureau on which stood framed photographs of his parents' wedding, his own wedding to Barbara and smaller portraits of Christopher and Sally. On a small table next to the window were his father's naval binoculars. His mother liked to use them to watch the birds and squirrels in surrounding trees.

Out came the best china, daintily cut sandwiches – salmon and cucumber, potted beef and tomato – and chocolate biscuits in the old blue tin that brought back more memories. While his mother brewed the tea, she chatted animatedly. How were Barbara and the children? Where were they going on holiday this year?

He noticed that her movements were slower than usual and tried to sound her out about her arthritis but, unlike most sufferers from the complaint, she was reluctant to talk about it. "You're looking well," he fibbed. "I like your hairstyle."

"I had it done at Eugene's…you know, on the High Street. Went on Ring'n Ride. They're ever so good. They help you up the step on the bus and when you get off. They bring you back right to the door and help you up the stairs."

"It suits you in that style. Not a grey hair anywhere. I've got more grey hairs than you."

"Pardon."

He raised his voice slightly. There was a knack to it. If you shouted too loud, her hearing aids only distorted the sound. They were NHS aids. She wouldn't go private for a digital 'on principle'.

"I've got more grey hairs than you."

She adjusted one of her aids. "Sorry, Howard. I'm not tuned in properly."

"I said I've got more grey hairs than you." Sometimes the repetition wore you down and brought home the remark's banality.

She laughed. "I can't see any."

"Put your glasses on."

She put on her spectacles and made a show of closely inspecting his hair. "Not a one. You're in your prime. I wish I was your age again."

They drank their tea and talked for a while about the old days as they always did. His mother loved to reminisce about the war. She had been an infant when it started but had vivid memories of the air raids. "Nineteen-forty was the worst year. The Blitz. Every night they came over, the Germans. It was awful. The sirens would wake you in the middle of the night and you'd have to get up and run out to the shelter. When the all-clear sounded you'd come out and you'd find half the street had disappeared."

Howard had heard it all many times but he never tired of listening to her. It was history, after all. There weren't many people left who remembered the war. He had nothing but admiration for them and the way they survived the appalling hardships with such stoicism.

His mother poured more tea and sighed. "When I think of what my poor mother must have gone through. She was all alone, with me and my brothers. Your grandad was in the Army. He got wounded in Egypt. She must have been worried sick for us all – me and my brothers all huddled together in the shelter in our garden. Freezing cold it was too. We were in our nightclothes. All we had was a few blankets...and one candle.

"I can see it now...the condensation running down the corrugated iron...hearing the bombs going off all round you and the planes going over. You could tell which were the Germans and which were ours by their engines. The German bombers made a deep, throbbing sound...I'll never forget it...the sound of those engines, the fear they made you feel.

"Ours – the Spitfires and the Hurricanes – made a different sound. It was more of a steady drone. We all used to cheer when we heard them. They were heroes, all those boys in the Battle of Britain. Some were still in their teens, you know. They had hardly any training. Night after night they went up to defend us. Some of them got medals. They should all have got VCs."

She broke off her reverie and handed Howard the plate of sandwiches. "You're not eating, Howard. You must keep your strength up. That was another thing about the war...rationing. We were practically starving. One egg a week. One bit of cheese that big." (she formed her forefinger and thumb in a circle the size of a 2p piece). "No butter. Hardly any bread. No meat." She laughed. "How did we survive? People today don't know they're born. They expect counselling when they're thrown off Big Brother!"

Howard had to agree. "You were a tough lot," he shouted, and she laughed again.

"You're right. We're tougher than today's namby-pamby generation. You see them on the telly, twisting and jerking about...they call it dancing. A gust of wind would blow them over."

They both laughed. "You mustn't take any notice of me, Howard. I do go on. You must get sick of listening to me."

"Never," he assured her. "I'm just glad we don't have to go through what you did."

"You're a good boy, Howard. You've always been a good boy."

They polished off the chocolate biscuits and then it was time to watch the News.

"It's nothing but bad news," his mother grumbled. "You don't want to watch it do you?"

Howard reminded her that news was his business so they watched it in silence. It was the usual stuff: Israeli tanks mowing down stone-throwing children, terrorist alert in Leeds, more nations trying to get into the EC while we were trying to get out, Cabinet split over the euro, a new bird flu outbreak on the way, flooding in the south-west and, finally, elderly driver dies as car leaves M25.

*　　　*　　　*

On the drive home, Howard tuned in to the news on the radio. It was compulsive. The job never left you. Nothing new had happened in the thirty minutes since he'd said goodbye to his mother and promised to phone her next week. He was about to switch off when the announcer in another bulletin said they'd just heard that the driver killed in the motorway crash was a senior Treasury civil servant. His name was being withheld until next-of-kin had been informed.

Howard mentally checked out a list of Treasury contacts. Suddenly his grip tightened on the steering wheel and he began to feel slight pressure in his stomach that had nothing to do with the seatbelt. He slowed down and reached carefully for his mobile. When he got through to the news desk, Kath Benson answered.

"Hi Kath, it's Howard. Do we know the name of the motorway civil servant?"

"Yes, it's Sir William Greaves, a senior economics adviser to the Treasury. We're dusting off his obit."

Howard felt the pressure tighten and his throat had gone dry. He knew it was William, his Whitehall whistle-blower. His mind went back to the Embankment only a week earlier. They had shaken hands and Howard had realised it meant good-bye. But not like this...

"Are you still there?" Kath wanted to know.

"Yes," he managed to say. "Where did it happen?"

News desk had checked with the police Press Office minutes earlier. "Just before the Redhill turn-off, Junction Eight. A snapper's on his way. I've phoned our local man."

"I'm not far away," he told her. "I'll cover it." The story was much too important for a stringer. "Cheers."

He pulled into a lay-by and extracted a roadmap from the debris in the glove compartment. Then he phoned Barbara. He'd be late again.

"Tell me about it," she said wearily, although what she meant was "Don't tell me about it." She'd have to take Chris to choir practice, even though she was whacked. That would mean Sally would have to go with them because Yvette, their French *au pair*, had been given the night off. Barbara might be able to organise a lift home for Chris from other parents. With luck, Howard's dinner would be in the microwave.

"Sorry, darling," he said. "This is the big one."

"How many times have I heard that?"

"I'll make it up to you tonight."

"Promises…I won't wait up."

He sped off south on the A217 towards the M25.

The dark green Mercedes S-class limousine (what was left of it) lay on its side in a ditch beyond the hard shoulder. There were skid marks across two lanes where it had careered off the motorway. Both lanes had been coned-off for a time while traffic police officers marked them with chalk and photographed them. They had since been reopened but traffic was still trundling past at walking pace.

Two police motorway patrol cars, their blue lights flashing in the encircling dusk, stood guard at the scene while the yellow-jacketed crew of a tow truck struggled to raise the wrecked vehicle. No other media had arrived yet.

Howard showed the patrolmen his Press card and asked a sergeant what had happened. It was a miracle that other vehicles had not been involved, the officer told him. The Merc had been in the fast lane and could have caused a disaster. They'd taken witness statements from several drivers of cars and trucks. All said they didn't think the Merc driver, a silver-haired gent, had collapsed at the wheel. He'd suffered multiple injuries but had still been alive when the ambulance took him away. No-one else was in the car.

They dropped down the grassy embankment into the ditch. It was certainly a spectacular write-off. The front and back ends of the luxury saloon had been concertinaed by the impact so it looked about three-quarters of its original length. The fire brigade had sprayed the wreckage with foam. There had been no fire but there was still a strong smell of petrol. Howard was reminded of a similar spectacle involving a mangled Mercedes in a Paris underpass a few years before, which had plunged the world's media into a frenzy of unresolved speculation.

The sergeant pointed to the tyres. Three were inflated but the front offside was flat and half-torn away from its rim. "Classic blowout," he said. "He was probably doing about seventy. At that speed you don't have much chance of controlling it. He may have tried and over-corrected."

"Can you tell if the tyre's defective?" Howard asked.

"It's not defective in itself. But someone's *made* it defective."

The remark, delivered with complete certainty, hit Howard like a punch in the solar plexus. He caught his breath. "How can you tell?"

The sergeant pointed to a neat triangular hole about a quarter of an inch wide in the tyre wall. "It's been got at," he said cheerfully. "Vandalised."

"You mean it's been cut deliberately?"

"S'right. Very nasty, specially on the front wheels. When you're doing over sixty the tyre heats up. The lining expands through the hole and then bursts. Result: bang! And it leaves no trace, as you can see."

"That's terrible. Are you quite sure?"

"Absolutely. Seen it before, several times. The people who do it are sub-human…don't give a damn how many innocents get hurt. This could have caused a massive pile-up."

Howard closely inspected the tiny clean triangle and realised it represented crucially important evidence. There was still no sign of the other journos. By the time his paper's snapper reached the scene, the wrecked car might have been removed. "I'll be right back," he said, clambering up the embankment. He hurried to his parked car and rummaged through the glove compartment again, this time for his digital camera.

On his return, the sergeant was directing the salvage crew, who were securing a large hook to the roof of the Mercedes. Howard took two close-up pictures of the tyre and its hole, one with flash as the light was growing dim.

"Can you tell me your name, sergeant?" he asked.

"Certainly, sir. Sergeant Peter Scott. Number 472. Traffic Division."

At that moment, the officer's lapel radio crackled into life. There was another emergency further up the road. "Got to be off now," he told Howard. "We're all finished here."

That was handy, Howard thought. With any luck, the rest of the newshounds would miss the sabotage angle.

"A grim business, sergeant," he said as they turned to leave. "Who could possibly do such a thing?"

"Mostly kids…or else someone didn't like him."

Returning to the Rover, Howard extracted his laptop from the boot and filed an on-the-spot report of the accident for the first edition. He confined himself to the basic facts; time and place of the crash, victim's identity, no other vehicles involved, police still investigating, too early to establish the cause. The desk would already be working on the PA versions, complete with background on William.

What he did tell them, which nobody else could, was that a police source said foul play could not be ruled out. That disclosure alone, and Howard's picture of the burst tyre, would guarantee him a byline on the front-page story, however many hacks might have worked on it.

*　　　*　　　*

Now that the World Snooker Championship had finished on the telly, Edgar was left with a feeling of desolation to compound the deep sense of grievance over the looming threat to The Meadow. The snooker had taken his mind off his anxieties. Now, they returned to haunt him as he set off on one of his favourite walks through the pristine green wilderness with its lush carpet of bluebells.

Perhaps this would be the last year he would see The Meadow in all its spring glory. Next year the elms, the hawthorns and the rhododendrons might be chopped down, the wildflowers crudely uprooted by the bulldozers, the birds that dined regularly at his bird-table driven from their nests, the squirrels and rabbits robbed of their natural habitat.

The little hollow that only he knew was the secret home of rare wild primroses would be flattened, desecrated. All this vandalism just for a bloody chemicals factory. And he, Edgar Brierley, Worshipful Master of Lodge 15392, who very rarely swore, was powerless to prevent it.

Or was he? There could be other forms of resistance. He lengthened his stride. The battle was not over yet.

For the time being, he sought refuge in another distraction. Returning from his walk, he set to work installing this year's tomato plants in the tiny conservatory at the side of his bungalow. There was only room for six plants and he had chosen them carefully at the garden centre. Two Moneymaker, two Shirley and two Gardener's Delight, plus three growbags for the long window boxes.

Lovingly, he transferred the spindly seedlings from their plastic pots to their new places in the sun – two plants in each box, not three as some gardeners preferred. Give the roots space to spread. That was one secret of success. Another was never to use the same compost two years running. It was worth buying new growbags each year, you got a far superior crop. As long as you remembered regular watering and feeding, of course. As he worked, he whistled under his breath but all the time he was thinking: bloody factory...bloody factory.

He was watering the new plantation when Janice returned in the Proton from the Co-op supermarket, breathlessly laden with bogofs and a huge bag of repeat prescription medication for her angina and other ailments. Her shipping order, she called it. There were four drugs for her blood pressure, two for oesophagitis, two for osteoporosis, one for cholesterol, one diuretic, one angina spray, one pain-killer, one laxative and, of course, her daily soluble aspirin to thin the blood and protect against another heart attack.

Then there were the one-a-day cod liver oil and garlic capsules, plus her multi-vitamins. All the chemists and assistants at the pharmacy counter knew her. They could spot her approaching in the crowded store while she was still a hundred yards away. It was their standing joke that she was keeping them in business.

Edgar put the kettle on and helped her with the bags. "Guess who I saw at the Co-op," she said as they replenished the fridge with twin packs of bacon, cheese and fruit trifles.

"Lord Lucan."

"Gloria Hicks, Arnie Hicks's wife. You know, the mayor. He's one of your friends isn't he?"

A good question, Edgar thought. "Oh, yes. How are they both?"

"They're fine. Off to Biarritz next month. And they've bought a new car...a Lexus, I think she said."

"A Lexus? Well I'm gobsmacked!" How could Arnold Hicks afford a Lexus on a postman's wages? That was another good question.

*   *   *

The funeral was a low-key affair. The 12th century Norman church nestling in a fold of the Downs, surrounded by wisteria-covered stone cottages, was packed. William's two sons and two daughters and their families sat in the front pews with his widow, Lady Greaves, a brave, upright figure all in black, her composed features barely visible behind a black veil.

William's grandchildren were all there, including Rachel. Among the other mourners Howard recognised several familiar faces: well-known bankers, a few MPs, senior civil servants and the odd TV financial pundit. Howard sat in a rear pew, with the rest of the media, among the cables for the TV cameras.

The wheezy organ struck up with *Now thank we all our God* and the congregation, led by a small choir, joined in weakly. Then the vicar, in a glowing eulogy, paid tribute to a lifetime of public service, recalling William's former role as a guiding light in the world of politics and finance.

When he came to the love and affection in which he was held by his dear family and his generosity as a father, grandfather and charitable benefactor, there were suppressed sobs from some of the teenaged grandchildren.

William's elder son, Dominic, bespectacled with a full head of greying hair like his dad's only darker, read a poem which he said was his father's favourite. It was by Arthur Hugh Clough and it ran as follows:

> Say not the struggle naught availeth,
>> The labour and the wounds are vain,
> The enemy faints not, nor faileth,
>> And as things have been, things remain.
>
> If hopes were dupes, fears may be liars;
>> It may be, in yon smoke concealed,
> Your comrades chase e'en now the fliers,
>> And, but for you, possess the field.

For while the tired waves, vainly breaking,
    Seem here no painful inch to gain,
Far back through creeks and inlets making
    Comes silent, flooding in, the main.

And not by eastern windows only,
    When daylight comes, comes in the light,
In front the sun climbs slow, how slowly,
    But westward, look, the land is bright.

Howard was not familiar with the poem. He found it strangely moving and uncannily apposite. Then they all sang *He who would valiant be* (a fitting choice, Howard thought, especially when they reached the line: Gainst all disaster) and the dark oak coffin, bearing a single wreath of red roses, was carried slowly out of the ancient chancel into the bright May sunshine.

When Sir William had been lowered to his well-earned rest in the immaculately kept graveyard, the final prayers said and the dust sprinkled on the coffin, Howard noticed from the dates on the gleaming nameplate that he had been exactly seventy; no age at all these days, he thought.

A cold breeze had sprung up and, one by one, the mourners began to drift away to their waiting cars. Howard had almost reached his car when he felt a light tap on his shoulder. He turned to face Dominic Greaves.

"Excuse me, I'm Dominic. Are you Howard Mitchell, from *The Announcer?*"

"Yes, that's right. I'm truly sorry about your father. He was the same age as my mother."

"Thank you, Mr Mitchell. It's hit us all very hard. Especially the suspicion of foul play. When we read your report and saw the picture of the burst tyre, we asked the police if we could see my father's car. Mother insisted on seeing it. They took us to a compound and showed us the wreckage. The tyre had come off the rim but there was no hole in it. Are you sure there was a hole, Mr Mitchell? Your picture wasn't very clear."

"I know what I saw, Mr Greaves. A police sergeant pointed it out."

"That's very strange. We don't know what to think. It's all so distressing."

Howard thought fast. They'd changed the tyre. Destroyed the evidence. Dominic would never believe it. Nor his mother. This probably wasn't the best time to try to convince them. "All I can say at this stage is there are reasonable grounds for suspicion. I expect there'll be an inquest. I'll keep you posted."

"Thank you. We'd be very grateful. Dad did tell me about you. He said he had very important business to discuss with you."

"That's true," Howard replied cautiously. He didn't know how much Dominic knew about his father's affairs. "I did meet your father. He took me to see Rachel."

Dominic seemed taken aback. "Oh, I see."

"In strict confidence, of course. He had good reasons. He needed to prove a point."

"What point was that, if I may ask?"

"I'm sorry, Mr Greaves, I can't tell you. I have the greatest respect for your father and I hope to carry on where he left off. I hope nothing but good will come of it."

"Well, I hope so too. We take *The Announcer* at the Hall, so I'll be keeping my eye on it. Sorry I can't invite you to our home, by the way, but mother's insisting on privacy. She asks the Press to respect her wishes."

"I understand. I have to get back to the office anyway."

"Dominic," a voice called from the group winding towards the waiting limousines.

"Coming," he called back. "Oh, I almost forgot, Mr Mitchell. Dad asked me to give you this...if anything should..." His voiced trailed off and he handed the reporter a white envelope bearing the words: 'Strictly private. To be opened only by Mr Howard Mitchell, of *The Announcer* newspaper, in the event of my death.'

A fine broad stairway

Howard could feel the envelope burning a hole in his pocket as he eased himself behind the wheel of the Rover. Through an instinct he couldn't fully explain, he pressed the central locking button and the doors snapped shut. Then he carefully opened the envelope. It contained two typewritten sheets of paper. The letter read:

Dear Howard,

I have taken the precaution of recording these few notes in case, by some mischance, I should become the victim of an 'accident'.

As I told you when we met, Tina's plans are well advanced to inflict the so-called Health of the Nation Bill on the unsuspecting citizens of this country; and that only the Press stands in the way. As you and your admirable newspaper prepare to do battle, you will need to know the identities of Tina's key players. They are:

Marcus Quinn, chairman; Baroness Witherspoon; Justine Harvey-Ozgood, and Paul D'Arcy MP. At the last count, there were six other members – the condom man who never says a word, two doctors and the three departmental civil servants. They are minor players at this stage. It is likely that many more prominent supporters of eugenics and population control will be co-opted before a definitive policy document can be drawn up for approval at a plenary session.

For the necessary background on state population control, I suggest that you research the following:

Brock Chisholm; Thomas Malthus; Charles Darwin, Frances Galton; Mary Calderone; Margaret Sanger; Marie Stopes; IPPF, FPA, the Sexual Law Reform Society and the British Euthanasia Society.

Some study of the present demographical situation in China may also be helpful.

Now for what you and your colleagues call the 'crunch'. I believe I have identified the Director of Tina's great and far-sighted enterprise. But as I am only 90 per cent sure of my facts, I dare not name him. The matter is too sensitive for premature and possibly misleading disclosure.

Suffice it to say that the gentleman in question is a committed eugenicist of the highest standing in the international community. When you discover his name, as I am sure you will, given your tenacity and ingenuity, you will understand my problem.

You have rightly acknowledged that we are dealing with state terrorism. Tina's methods may be more subtle than those of the suicide bombers but the end result is the same – mass murder. And the casualty toll of abortion and euthanasia is infinitely greater. Abortion alone has claimed over six million souls in the UK since it became legal. Six million!

Tina's terrorists believe, with good cause, that they are untouchable. Their cast-iron security makes them virtually impregnable. But I firmly believe the power of the Press is stronger. I know you will regard this mission as a challenge and I have every confidence in your ability to accomplish it.

In the end, truth will out!

I leave you with this quotation from Winston Churchill:

"I have watched this famous island descending incontinently, fecklessly, the stairway which leads to a dark gulf. It is a fine broad stairway at the beginning, but after a bit the carpet ends. A little further on there are only flagstones, and a little further on still these break beneath your feet."

Think about it, dear boy. Haven't we already reached the flagstones?

Yours ever

William

(Sir William Greaves)

Howard read the letter through a second time before taking his mobile from his pocket. He thought about phoning Andrew. Instead he called Julian on his direct line.

The oil painting of His Lordship was swinging away from the wall when Howard arrived. Julian had already opened the safe behind it. He was in his shirtsleeves and had lost his usual urbane manner. The dark, piercing eyes looked anxious beneath their bushy brows. "Have you copied it?" was the first question he asked.

"No, I came straight here." Howard took the envelope out of his breast pocket and handed it to Julian.

The Editor adjusted his spectacles and scrutinised the letter. "A voice from the grave," he said quietly, almost to himself. "Let's get it photo-copied."

Curious eyes followed the pair as they strode to the office copier. It wasn't often you saw Julian doing a messenger's job. A reporter, yes. But not the Editor. Glancing nervously around them as the copier hissed and squeaked, they took two copies of the letter and hurried back to the inner sanctum. Julian placed the original in the safe behind His Lordship's portrait and locked it. He placed one copy in his briefcase and locked that also.

"That's for the bank. First thing tomorrow. I'll take it myself." He handed Howard the remaining copy. "You take that. Keep it locked in your drawer. Let Andrew see it when he comes in tomorrow but keep it in your possession…OK?"

"OK."

They sat at the Editor's massive desk, half-covered in proofs of early features pages, and pored over Howard's copy of the letter in detail. "He knew they'd make it look like an accident – Tina, whoever they are," Julian said. "They must have been following him …realised he was defecting."

Howard thought of the funeral hymn, *He who would valiant be.* "He was a brave man. When the tyre blew he managed to steer clear of everything else." That reminded him of what Dominic Greaves told him about the tyre and he relayed it to Julian,

"They don't hang about, do they? Contact their Press office. Find the car. We need to get to the bottom of this."

"Right, Julian." The reporter got up to go.

"Just a minute, Howard. I've been thinking. I'm going to take you off general reporting. You'll be seconded exclusively to this investigation.

I'll tell Andrew. Ideally, we'd have a team working on it but you know the score." (It had been several months since the last suicide bombs but the Met and the Press were still on high level terrorist alert.) So for the time being it's your baby...are you comfortable with that?"

"Fine by me. It may not be too comfortable."

"That's what I mean. Things could get hairy from now on."

Howard shrugged his broad shoulders and his boyish face took on the grin of a seasoned campaigner. "I've been there, Julian,"

"I know. Good man."

*   *   *

Howard was back in the office next morning bright and early. Well, early. First things first. Check the law's Press office. Yes, they remembered the car. It had gone to the scrapyard and been crushed.

What already? Yes already. Was there anything else? Well, yes. Could they ask Sgt Peter Scott, No 472, Traffic Division, to contact *The Announcer* urgently?

There was a long pause. Then: "Sorry, there's no Sgt Peter Scott, No 472, in the Traffic Division."

"But I spoke to him."

"You must be mistaken."

Howard couldn't believe it. "No way. I've written his details in my notebook. They'll be shown to the inquest."

"There won't be an inquest."

"Really...who says so?"

"The coroner's officer. Inquests are held only when the coroner is informed there's reason to suspect a violent or unnatural death, sudden death cause unknown, or a death in prison."

"You can't get more violent that death in a car crash, can you?"

"But in this case the cause was known – it was a tyre blowout."

"There were suspicions of foul play, as reported in *The Announcer.*"

One stonewalling answer followed another. "Police investigations indicated no evidence of foul play."

"I personally took photographs of a hole cut in the tyre."

"We have no record of any holes in the tyres. The coroner has ruled that the investigation is now closed."

Howard controlled himself with an effort. All coroners were deadlegs. This, as far as he was concerned, was an infallible law of journalism. He'd lost count of the number of perverse inquest verdicts he'd reported over the years…misadventure when it was obviously an accident, lawful killing when it was anything but lawful.

The phenomenon was something you learned along with basic rules like the importance of spelling people's names correctly, that mendacity is the currency of politics and that wherever there is no justice in the world there is always violence.

On a personal level, dodgy coroners were as inevitable as the infallible metaphysical law that whatever theatre, concert hall or cinema he entered, there would always be somebody in the seat behind suffering from the advanced stages of tuberculosis. Or the likelihood that in every restaurant throughout the entire space-time continuum, there is a woman laughing hysterically.

He conceded that, somewhere in the universe, it might be possible to find a coroner who was as thick as only one short plank, but that would probably be due to a timber shortage caused by excessive deforestation on that particular planet.

As to why coroners should be so universally afflicted, Howard found metaphysics less helpful. In discussions with fellow hacks, the theory seemed to be that congenital mental retardation was the inevitable consequence of inbreeding among the legal and medical professions. The kindest solution to the problem was to promote the more severe cases sideways to coroners' courts, thus sparing individual practices the disastrous consequences of their actions. In the old days you might have sent them to Australia or had them committed to an institution. Nowadays, you made them coroners.

Well, at least we all know where we stand, he thought as he slammed the phone down. They certainly didn't hang about. They'd disposed of all the evidence, 'lost' Sgt Scott and an obliging, half-witted coroner had closed the case all in little more than a week. They obviously had plenty to hide.

News desk would follow it up. The paper would campaign for an inquest. Dominic Greaves would be advised to take legal action demanding one, if he hadn't done so already. Then they'd find Sgt Scott, wherever he'd been hidden, and they'd have a heart-to-heart.

Meanwhile, Howard had his own investigation to pursue. There was the little matter of tracing the origins of state population control, as William suggested. As a learning curve it was still a stubbornly straight line. Everyone knew about Hitler's approach to the subject – a process of ethnic cleansing involving sterilisation and euthanasia, leading ultimately to the gas chambers. Could people still believe in population control after that? Had history taught them nothing? According to William, the answers were Yes to the first question and No to the second.

It was time for some research. He checked the letter again. Brock Chisholm. Who was he? In his early days as a junior reporter, Howard would have gone tramping round the library searching through reference books and encyclopaedias. All you did now was click on the right places on the internet and there was the learned gentleman's biography.

Brock Chisholm was an eminent Canadian doctor born in 1896. He served in the First World War and won the Military Cross. He received his degree of doctor of medicine from the University of Toronto in 1924 and later worked in several British hospitals. After the Second World War, during which he held high office in the Canadian Department of National Defence, he became the first Director-General of the World Health Organisation. By the time he left it, in 1953, the WHO had 83 member states.

Nothing sinister in any of this, Howard thought. Then he noticed that in 1958 Dr Chisholm had written a book entitled *Can People Learn to Learn*, in which he set out his idea of world government. That sounded promising. But although he tried every conceivable website, he could find no trace of this book. So it was back to tramping round the library. Louise, the sad faced but ever-helpful librarian, had not heard of the book but unearthed a dusty tome on the World Health Organisation, which expanded on the views of its first Director-General.

He was a secular Humanist who believed the main barrier to a civilised world was the concept of right and wrong. He had no time for codes of belief (except Humanism, apparently), fixed rules or dogmatism. Children should be freed from national, religious and other cultural prejudices inflicted on them by their parents, whom he saw as 'suppressors of their better nature'. Classroom sex education should be introduced, eliminating 'the ways of elders' *by force if necessary*.

Howard began to take a less rosy view of the eminent doctor, which was not improved by the information that this early pioneer of sex education believed those who opposed him were neurotic, selfish or mentally ill.

Next up on William's list was Thomas Malthus. This time the internet was a mine of information. The Rev Thomas Malthus (1766-1834), a historian, economist and Anglican clergyman, turned out to be a distinctly nasty piece of work. In his *Essay on the Principle of Population*, published in 1798, he forecast that increases in population would eventually diminish the ability of the world to feed itself.

His final solution to this problem when sexual abstinence, fewer children and other factors were found wanting, was *the possible deliberate annihilation* of the world's least productive and most defenceless citizens.

There was a lot more on Malthus but Howard felt he had seen enough. The reverend gentleman was an obvious example of the extremes to which fanatics can be driven by ideology. Hitler was another. So far, he had researched two enthusiasts of state population control and it was significant that both of them advocated violence as part of their philosophies.

Charles Darwin (1809-1882) next. Howard recalled from his school days that Darwin wrote *The Origin of the Species*, which became the bible of naturalists and evolutionists throughout the world. He also knew he had written *The Descent of Man*, in which he claimed the human species was closest in ancestry to African anthropoid apes. As he trawled the net, he realised there was a lot he didn't know about the great man. It seemed he had adopted a Malthusian bias in his theory of evolution by means of natural selection. His "Malthusian error", according to Prof Daniel P Todes, of Baltimore, was to emphasise the evolutionary role of overpopulation.

Darwin believed that civilised societies weakened themselves by misplaced compassion. "With savages, the weak in mind and body are soon eliminated," he wrote. "We civilised men, on the other hand, build asylums for the imbecile, the maimed and the sick; we institute poor laws; and our medical men exert their utmost skill to save the life of everyone to the last moment…Thus the weak members of civilised societies propagate their kind…this must be highly injurious to the race of man."

Although Darwin did not seem to be actively advocating the mass extermination of sections of his fellow humans, Howard rated him on a par with Chisholm and Malthus in terms of breathtaking arrogance.

And so to Frances Galton (1822-1911) a cousin of Darwin. Galton, a geneticist and psychologist, was the founder of eugenics. This 'science' of controlled breeding asserted that certain people are of a superior strain and that the human race could be improved by breeding selectively from them. The main problem for eugenicists was that 'inferior' strains would insist on breeding and damaging the racial stock. Most inconsiderate. What could be done to stop them, short of actually killing them? Galton's successors came up with an ingenious answer: birth control. We're getting somewhere, thought Howard. He took a break and a sweet, milky coffee from the machine to help dissipate the bad taste in his mouth.

Birth control was where Dr Marie Stopes (1880-1958) came in. It turned out that she was another charmer. A proto-feminist and member of an affluent Edinburgh family, she married Reginald Gates in 1911. The marriage was annulled due to non-consummation five years later. It would be incorrect to describe the distinguished doctor as infertile, however. Her progeny spread across thirty-eight countries (mainly Third World) in the form of the Marie Stopes International Global Partnership. This offered sexual and reproductive health services including contraception, sterilisation and abortion.

Among her books was *Radiant Motherhood*, published in 1920, in which she wrote: "Society allows the diseased, the racially negligent, the thriftless, the careless, the feeble minded, the very lowest and worst members of the community, to produce innumerable tens of thousands of stunted, warped, inferior infants…a large proportion of these are doomed from their very physical inheritance to be at best but partly self-supporting, and thus to drain the resources of those classes above them who have a sense of responsibility. The better classes, freed from the cost of institutions, hospitals, prisons and so on, principally filled by the inferior racial stock, would be able to afford to enlarge their own families."

The great social reformer had an answer to this pressing problem: "The sterilisation of those totally unfit for parenthood to be made an immediate possibility, indeed made compulsory." (Stop the poor from breeding, in William's words).

Stopes had an American friend, Margaret Sanger (1883-1966) a nurse who was married to an architect. They had three children. Initially motivated by compassion for the poor women she treated in the Lower East Side of New York, she seemed to have become influenced by Stopes's vision of racial purity during a visit to England. She founded the Planned Parenthood Federation of America and coined the slogan 'Birth Control to Create a Race of Thoroughbreds'.

She drew up a 'Plan for Peace' which included the recommendation: "To apply a stern and rigid policy of sterilisation and segregation to that grade of population whose progeny is already tainted, or whose inheritance is such that objectionable traits may be transmitted to offspring."

Twenty years later, Sanger inaugurated the International Planned Parenthood Federation, whose eight founding bodies included the British Family Planning Association. The same year, 1952, saw the creation of the Population Council in America. It was founded by John D Rockefeller III. State population control was in business. Big business.

Next on William's list was Mary Calderone (1904-1998) another American visionary in the field of social engineering by means of classroom sex education. A mother of three children, she became executive director of SIECUS, the Sex Information and Education Council of the United States, an organisation dedicated to bringing about a humanist revolution. Calderone supported theories put forward by Rudolph Dreikus, a humanist luminary of the day, which included 'liberating children from their families' and 'abolishing the family as we know it'.

Howard recalled what William had told him about the apologists of sex education having hang-ups over families. He had clearly done his homework. When you added up the views of all the weirdoes he had researched so far you couldn't avoid the suspicion of a planned international attack on the family unit and even on the value of human life.

On checking out the Sexual Law Reform Society, Howard discovered that among its erudite dissertations was a document entitled: Report of Working Party on the Law in Relation to Sexual Behaviour, published in 1974. This sounded like the sort of turgid government extrusions he had to decipher and translate into readable English almost every day of his working life. The longer and more important sounding the title, the more impenetrable the contents. Howard had to dig deep into the portentous waffle to discover its hidden gems. It was worth the effort.

Among its sexually liberating reforms, the society was calling for the age of consent to be reduced to fourteen, *including consent to incest*, the fear of which was regarded as 'irrational'. For all its specious academic language, it sounded to Howard horribly like child abuse.

He swallowed another mouthful of sweet coffee. It did nothing to take away the nasty taste. Perhaps the FPA would ameliorate matters. In his mind, the organisation had always represented a pillar of respectability in British society. He and Barbara subscribed to its philosophy of planned families, with every child a wanted child. So it came as something of a shock to learn that, as recently as 1978, the FPA had been involved in the promotion of a book by Jane Cousins,the former secretary of the Sexual Law Reform Society, called *Make it Happy*. This publication gave information on oral and anal intercourse, group sex, communal masturbation, incest and sexual contact with animals short of actual coupling. It suggested that those who opposed such activities were 'old fashioned' and 'killjoys'.

Next time we find ourselves in bed together, if such a happy event should ever occur again, Howard thought, I'll tell Barbara I'm really an old-fashioned killjoy. He visualised the scene and grinned at her predictable reaction. It brought a moment of light relief to his increasingly grim task. But only a moment. Then it was back to the FPA. It had apparently promoted another book, this time published by the National Secular Society, which suggested oral and anal intercourse as acceptable methods of contraception.

On and on it went. The Health Education Authority, the Brook Advisory Centres…all in receipt of taxpayers' money, all bitterly opposed to conventional morality and parental influence over children's lives. Howard believed he detected a sense of desperation behind the proselytising. Could it be that these sad control freaks had so little love and sexual fulfilment in their own lives that they were driven to inflict their hang-ups on others? Were they really all depraved – or just deprived?

As he reached the end of the repressed social engineers, he stretched back in his swivel chair, feet on the desk and closed his eyes. Now he knew how a weevil felt after it had chomped its way through a rotten apple. Distinctly queasy. He ran through the named individuals in his mind and realised they all had several things in common besides being seriously deluded. They all came from privileged backgrounds. They shared the overbearing arrogance of dangerous despots. And they were all rich.

All he had to do to fulfil William's mission was track down their modern counterparts and their mysterious Mr Big. Someone so important that he would not believe it. That was all.

*   *   *

"Asleep on the job again." It was Andrew. Like all news editors, he had a laugh-a-minute sense of humour.

Howard sat upright. "Asleep but still writing," he replied. "Has Julian told you the glad tidings?"

"Yes, but not how to run the desk without you. Look at today's news list." He handed *The Announcer's* new investigative reporter a printout of the bizarre happenings in the outside world. Howard glanced at it:

Prince breaks elbow in fall from horse, he read. "At least he now knows his arse from his elbow."

Andrew, a staunch royalist, was not amused.

"Sorry, couldn't resist that." Howard scanned the rest of the news list: Terror suspects held at Gatwick…Cabinet minister in sex romp scandal… Company boss flees with millions…Freed killer strikes again…Injured burglar sues for damages…Bird flu pandemic feared…Woman, 102, dies after eviction from care home…Soap star faces drugs charge…Bondage and orgies sex lessons for kids…

"I'll have a look at that one if you like," Howard said. "Sounds like our friends the sex education freaks."

"That's big of you." Andrew also had a devastating line in sarcasm.

"Don't mention it. How many words?"

"Six hundred."

Howard called up the agency copy. It was a straightforward tarting-up job. And it tied in neatly with his current research. A new sex education handbook being distributed to schools nationwide contained descriptions of multiple-partner sessions, sado-masochism, bondage, wife-swapping and homosexual role-playing. There were quotes from shocked parents, teachers and a paedophile survivors' group concerned that it could represent a sophisticated form of child abuse.

The handbook's publisher, described as an 'independent provider of health education services', defended the bizarre material. He said it was 'madness' to oppose sex education in schools. Howard had to laugh. The real madness, of course, was to promote promiscuous behaviour among schoolchildren at a time when sexual infections were rocketing. But that was comment, so did not qualify for inclusion in his news story.

Rewriting this particular story, albeit in dignified *Announcer* style, had not helped to relieve the lingering nasty taste in Howard's mouth. The day was becoming hot and humid. It was also lunchtime – time for a beer in the Dog and Partridge.

He never bothered with the lift. It was usually out of order anyway. Running up and down the stairs was the only form of exercise he took. That and snooker. People said you couldn't call snooker exercise but he told them you could walk miles round a full-size table in the course of a few frames.

On the way down he met Edgar, the chief messenger, on his way up. He looked depressed. Not like him. Maybe the old head injury was playing up. "Hi, Edgar. How about a frame tonight?"

Edgar just grunted and carried on up the stairs. He seemed even further away than usual, in a world of his own.

The smell of men

Life as we know it in the Dog and Partridge had changed little since the days of Dickens. The ancient inn with its low beamed ceilings, uneven floors, leaded lights and original open fireplace was still the spiritual home of dedicated drinkers from *The Announcer* and surrounding office blocks. The barmaids were still pert and pretty but now more feisty than blousy, and the landlord more smarmy than ruddy. But the main attraction by far, apart from the keg beer, was the absence of deafening rock music. It was possible to hold an intelligent conversation with someone without screaming into their ear.

The place was packed, as usual. It now served food, to use the word loosely. The jars of pickled eggs had been replaced by sandwiches, pies, pasties and mysterious concoctions of flavoured noodles you could heat up in a microwave.

Howard contented himself with a pint of best bitter. As he surveyed the heaving mass of humanity troughing out on their pies and pints, he spotted a familiar figure in a shabby beige sports jacket and crumpled grey slacks slumped half asleep at a tiny corner table. It was Bernard Baxter, the late sub. He fought his way over. "Hi, Bernard, you're up early."

Bernard, an ageing Liverpudlian with receding grey hair and thick spectacles that gave him a permanently startled appearance, roused himself. "Hello Howard. Yep, it's a bugger. The chief sub's put me on early home copy – straight after a late turn. He's not human."

"Have you had any sleep?"

"Couple of hours in the library. Hardly worth going home. You have to turn round and come straight back."

"What are you drinking?"

"Thanks but I'm making this last," indicating his gin and tonic. "Don't want to go in drunk at three in the afternoon. Mind you, I have seen it happen – at *The Gaydian*, you know."

Howard never did know the full story of Bernard's departure from his previous employment. There were several versions, some more lurid than others. This seemed a good time to learn the truth. "That wasn't why they slung you out, was it?" he asked, pulling up a stool.

Bernard took a sip of his gin and T and laughed heartily. He was a good-natured chap who shook when he laughed. "No, it wasn't the demon drink. But it's a cracking yarn. I still dine out on the strength of it. What happened was this. I was subbing a story about a queer theatre director who had 'come out', as they say. Well, it was some big deal...he was making a right song and dance about it."

"As they do."

"Exactly. He must have had a few because he started to go into graphic detail about what turned him on. It was the exquisite beauty of the naked male form, the hairy chests, the sweat and the sheer smell of, well...men!"

Bernard shook with suppressed mirth. "That's what the shirt-lifter said: 'The sheer smell of, well...men'!"

Howard had to laugh. It was a combination of Bernard's Scouse accent and his robust sense of humour. He took a swig of his pint. "Go on."

"Well, you know how you sometimes toy with things on your screen... just for fun...like we do with messages to each other...strictly not for publication..."

"Yes."

"I couldn't resist playing around with what the guy had said. So I altered it to 'The sheer smell of, well...shit'."

Both hacks fell about. "Just to see what it looked like, you understand," Bernard spluttered. "I was going to change it back."

"Let me guess," Howard said, regaining a straight face. "You never did."

"You're spoiling it, Howard. What happened next was the fire alarm went off. They were always having fire drills. Never any fire. Anyway, off we all marched to our assembly points..."

"And when you got back to your terminal you carried on subbing?"

"That's right. I forgot to change it back. The chief sub flagged me another story so I just wrapped it up. Being *The Gaydian* – you know what plonkers they are – nobody spotted it all night. It ran through all four editions."

"Wish I'd seen it."

"There was hell to pay. Switchboards jammed. Half the readership

87

must've phoned in. Up before the Editor and two side-kicks next day as if it were a capital offence. Murder they could have forgiven but not homophobia. That's what they called it."

"But of course."

"I apologised. It had been a mistake, a foolish thing to do and I was sorry. Didn't make a blind bit of difference. They were determined to label me homophobic. I told them there was no way I feared homosexuals. It was the gay lads who were *heterophobic*...afraid of heterosexual relationships. Of course, that only made matters worse. I got the boot. Three months' wages in lieu. Black bin liner. Escorted out by security."

"Great story," Howard said, regarding his colleague with new respect. "Where did you go?"

"Straight to the pub."

"I mean after."

"Two weeks later I was working for *The Announcer*. Best move I ever made."

*   *   *

The letter lay unopened on the kitchen table. It was addressed to Mr and Mrs E Brierley, 23 Meadow Drive, Brawton. Janice noticed it when she came out of the shower, still drying her damp grey hair on a towel. It was probably more junk mail, she thought. First things first. She prepared her usual morning filter coffee and glanced at their free copy of *The Announcer* her husband always brought home in the early hours.

It was much the same every day. Always a war or a strike somewhere. She blamed men. Women could run things much better. No sooner had this thought occurred than another one, that of Margaret Thatcher, instantly dispelled it, so she fished her spectacles out of her handbag on the dresser and opened the letter.

She wished she hadn't. It wasn't junk mail in the accepted sense although by the time she finished reading it, that seemed a pretty accurate description. It was from International Pharmaceuticals Inc UK, and signed with a squiggle by someone in the absence of its chief executive. Headed with the words 'Without prejudice' it said IPI had been distressed to learn of the Brierleys' opposition to their proposed 'development' site.

It had come to their attention that the couple felt it would adversely affect their amenity and the Company was anxious to correct this entirely unwarranted misconception. During construction work, intrusion and disruption would be kept to a minimum. Once in operation, the development would be fully landscaped and all discharges completely controlled by means of the latest technology. There would be absolutely no pollution.

The Company took its social responsibilities very seriously. It was proud of its hard-earned reputation for openness, integrity and the highest standards of environmental protection. It operated a policy of the fullest co-operation with local authorities and of enlightened human relations in every sphere of its international operation.

In the unlikely event of the couple being unable to accept the Company's assurances on its site development, however, it was prepared to consider offering them the market value of their property should they decide to 'relocate'. Accordingly, as a gesture of goodwill and entirely without prejudice, the Company was prepared to purchase the Brierley's bungalow for the sum of £75,000, subject to vacant possession within a period of three months.

Janice felt an angina attack coming on. She had taken all her morning medication . . . the soluble aspirin, the isosorbide mononitrate, nifedipine, nicorandil, losartan, simvastatin and her esomeprazole, but the pain was starting to tighten in her chest. She dropped the towel and reached into her handbag for the emergency glyceryl trinitrate spray. Two squirts under the tongue and the pain usually eased. This time though, in her agitation, the spray missed its target and landed on her bottom lip.

She tried again. You weren't supposed to use the spray more than twice at a time but the pain and shortness of breath were getting worse. She managed to direct it accurately and the crisis gradually passed. For good measure, she took two of her strong painkillers with a glass of milk.

By the time Edgar started frying his full English, she had almost recovered. Her panic had been replaced by mounting indignation and a barely controlled anger. "Read that," she said, pushing the letter across the table to her husband.

Edgar was not at his best in the mornings. Indeed, there were few times these days when he was ever at his best. Following the habits of a lifetime, he concentrated on cracking his egg so the yolk didn't run. If the yolk broke during this delicate operation it was a sure sign it would be one of those days.

"Read it," Janice ordered, her voice several decibels louder.

The yolk broke. He sat down with a loud sigh and took the letter. As he read, his brow furrowed and he scratched his head at the side, where the ginger-grey tufts met the 'wide parting'. He was gobsmacked. "I can't believe this," he said, shaking his head repeatedly.

"Neither can I. Seventy-five thousand for our bungalow. It's worth at least twice that. The Simmonds at No 31 sold theirs for a hundred and eighty thousand. She told me on my Avon round."

"That was last year. The market's changed."

"Not that much. It's an insult. They're just adding insult to injury."

"What they're trying to tell us is how much the bungalow will be worth once they build the factory."

"I thought you were going to stop them."

"I'm trying to. It's not settled yet. IPI are jumping the gun. The plan still has to be approved by the full planning committee." He didn't say it but in his heart of hearts he knew approval would be a formality. This was one planning application no-one was going to stop, not even the Masons.

"Well, you'd better come up with something because I am not moving. This has been my home for thirty-five years. I'm not going to be pushed around by a bunch of foreign shysters."

"You're talking about a multi-national corporation, one of the biggest in the world."

"I don't care who they are. I'll leave my home when I'm good and ready – not when they say so."

Edgar folded the letter thoughtfully. "This is only their first offer. If we ignore it, they'll increase it."

"Whatever they offer, I'm not moving. It's as simple as that. You're always telling me about your powerful friends, Edgar. Surely they can help us now."

Her husband thought about his 'friends' on the planning committee. He tried to switch on his cheery grin but his heart wasn't in it. It was at times like this when you found out who your friends were.

*   *   *

Towards the end of June, a week of showers and thunderstorms freshened up the chaotic streets of London after a long and oppressive heat-wave. The see-through T-shirts, bare midriffs and miniskirts that had dangerously distracted drivers were now shrouded by macs and umbrellas. The muggers, dips and drug pushers who always came out with the sun, retreated to their bolt-holes and the young bobbies, patrolling in pairs, could concentrate once more on chatting up spy camera operators on their radios. Rain was always the best policeman.

The rain also seemed to have cooled the ardour of sex industry acolytes in the Departments of Health and Education. Lengthening queues at genito-urinary clinics throughout the country signalled a startling change in the official attitude to the upsurge in sexual infections. For the first time, the Commons Health Committee was prepared to acknowledge that they faced a 'crisis'.

In *The Announcer* newsroom, Andrew studied the Committee's report on the nation's sexual health as it reached his screen from the Press Association. The MPs declared themselves "appalled by the crisis". They added: "We do not use the word 'crisis' lightly. In this case it is appropriate." The cross-party Committee blamed lack of political will, failure by NHS bodies to recognise the scale of the problem, and lack of money to deal with it. They urged the Government to set aside an extra £30 million for sexual health.

They also called for the urgent introduction of national screening for chlamydia, a disease that affected one in ten sexually active young people. As many sufferers did not know they were infected, they needed to be seen by a doctor within forty-eight hours rather than the usual six-to-eight weeks. Hundreds, if not thousands, of potentially infected people, some HIV-positive, were walking around unaware of their condition due to lack of resources to treat them. It was a formula for disaster.

The Committee acknowledged that syphilis rates had increased by 1,000 per cent and rates for chlamydia and gonorrhoea had doubled. It confirmed over 6,500 new cases of HIV infection – an increase of 25 per cent – in the past year. Most were homosexuals. Millions of pounds more of government money was needed for effective HIV prevention.

Andrew wondered whether such prevention would include warnings that homosexual practices were a health risk, in the same way that millions of pounds had been poured into warnings about cigarette smoking. Somehow, he doubted it.

Howard would have been the ideal man to rewrite this story but he was now employed on the Editor's top-secret assignment. As he had not been replaced, the paper's reporting strength was severely depleted. Some thoughtless hacks had even gone away on holiday. The story would have to take its chance with the news subs as it stood.

Choral discord

"I don't want to go to choir practice. I want to play football." Christopher was having his usual pre-choir tantrum.

Howard was having none of it. "Why do you want to play football? It's not even the football season."

"Well, cricket then."

"I thought you didn't like cricket."

"I like it better than singing."

"You're a very good singer, Chris. The choirmaster at St Peter's told me."

"He's tone deaf."

Howard had to smile. The things children would say. "What is it you don't like about choir practice?"

"There's only three other boys besides me. The rest are all girls."

It seemed Chris was a budding male chauvinist. "What's wrong with that?"

"They're always giggling all the time and messing about. They can't even sing properly." Then after further thought, he added: "And they won't join our union."

"Your union...what's that?" The mind boggled.

"Well, you know when we sing at weddings and stuff and they give us £5...well, we don't think it's enough. So me and the other boys are forming a union. If they don't pay us more we're going to go on strike, and let the girls sing and it'll be horrible."

With a supreme effort, Howard managed not to burst out laughing. His son was serious. They were standing at the threshold of a new age in industrial relations...the birth of the NUC, the National Union of Choirboys. Or, to be politically correct, the National Union of Choristers. It was a moment calling for due solemnity.

"Whose idea was this?"

"Darren's."

Ah, so Darren would be shop steward and general secretary. "How old is Darren?"

"He's ten."

Howard simply couldn't resist the headline potential: 'Ten-year-old to lead new trade union'. Still keeping a straight face, he advised the young revolutionary about the methods adopted by unscrupulous employers to crush such forms of industrial rebellion. Short of calling in the troops, St Peter's would merely recruit more non-union labour. He refrained from describing them as blacklegs because Chris would probably apply the label to the girls in his choir. That would upset them, as they would be sure to take it literally.

If necessary, he added, the employers would 'lock out' Darren and his fellow malcontents.

Chris was unfazed by this dire warning. "I wouldn't care," he said. "Then I could play football instead."

His father thought for a moment. "I'll tell you what: next time you sing at a wedding, I'll give you another £5 on top of your choir fee. How does that sound?"

"Okay, I s'pose."

"Right, if you'll get ready now, I'll drive you to church and bring you back. Your Mum's very tired tonight."

"And can we go to McDonald's after?"

He didn't know about Darren but his son would make a perfect union negotiator. Either that or a member of ACAS.

"Go on then."

Chris ran off to get washed. A settlement had been reached.

*   *   *

Even on his night off, his research into population control and the machinations of Tina were never far from Howard's mind. As he and Chris sat munching their burgers and fries in McDonald's, he thought about the enormity of his task. On the drive home he thought about it. When he finally put his feet up in the lounge, scotch and ginger in hand, he was still thinking about it. It was becoming a bitch of an assignment, and he'd only just started.

The large room with its inglenook fireplace, beige fitted carpet and regency style three-piece suite in blue and gold always had a soothing effect on him. It was illuminated by a blue-shaded, art deco standard lamp between well-stocked bookshelves and the velvet-draped french windows. In a corner stood the Bluthner baby grand they had bought when he joined *The Announcer*. He didn't play himself but Barbara could tackle anything from Chopin to Fats Waller, note perfect.

She was watching TV. Some fatuous American sitcom based on characters suffering varying degrees of neurosis. "How did it go – the choir practice?" she asked. "Did they all turn up?"

Howard switched off from work for a moment. "Yes, I think so. I met Chris's friend, Darren. He's a lad destined for great things." He related the story of the inchoate trade union, much to Barbara's amusement.

"Not all sweet singing in the choir, it seems," she laughed.

"Make a great story for the tabloids."

"Where did you go while they practised? Let me guess…the Church Inn?"

"Well, it *is* next door."

"I might have known." The elegantly arched eyebrows that enchanted Howard when they first met, rose a shade higher in mock reproach. The luminous green eyes which had beguiled him as they danced under the flashing lights of the Students' Union disco teased him again now in the glow from the standard lamp. Then she'd been wearing a skimpy mini-dress that left little to his vivid imagination. Now she wore her shapeless blue uniform and she still looked sensational. She could look sensational in a boiler suit.

He knocked back his scotch and poured them both another from the drinks trolley. It was, after all, one of the rare evenings when they were at home together. Thoughts of work were relegated to the back burner.

Opportunity taken at the flood…

*　　　*　　　*

Later, as she slept with her fair hair draped across his shoulder and her soft breast nuzzling his side, Howard realised that a packet of condoms remained unopened in his bedside drawer. The population controllers would not approve. It didn't worry him in the slightest.

He was drifting deliciously away when something else did. The bedside telephone rang. He turned over and picked up the receiver. "Hello."

There was silence, followed a few seconds later by a click and the line went dead. He checked his miniature alarm clock. It was 2.50 am.

95

Wearily, he dialled 1471 although he knew what the disembodied voice would say.

"You were called, today, at 02.50. The caller withheld their number."

Barbara had not stirred. Careful not to wake her, he gently lifted her arm and eased himself out of bed. The night was cooler after one of the hottest days of the year but it was still humid. He put on his pyjama trousers and slippers, and switched off the bedroom telephone extension. Then he tiptoed downstairs and diverted incoming calls to the answer-phone before helping himself to a nightcap. Oscar, curled up in his basket, opened one eye and quickly closed it again.

On the way back to bed, Howard looked in on the children's rooms. Christopher had thrown off his duvet and lay sleeping at an angle across his bed. But Sally was still cosily tucked up, her fair hair on the pillow matching her teddy bear's. He smiled to himself. How angelic they looked when asleep. Pity their haloes sometimes slipped when awake.

He climbed back into bed next to Barbara but sleep would not come. The mystery call had restored his assignment to the front burner. It had to be connected, even though his acquaintance with Tina had barely begun. They were making sure they got in the first blow. It was a warning shot across the bows.

*　　　*　　　*

Howard got his first break a few days later. Driving to work early, tuned in as always to BBC news, he heard the newsreader say the European Parliament had voted to compel all member states of the European Union to support the United Nations programme of population control.

This would involve aid of £350 million to the United Nations Population Fund, to replace funding withdrawn by America in protest at the agency's support for coercive abortion and sterilisation in China.

An EU spokesman said the European aid would be used to promote reproductive and sexual health throughout the world but particularly in those areas unable to sustain current levels of population growth.

The newsreader continued: "The move was welcomed in some quarters. Mr Paul D'Arcy, MP, the pagan and gay rights activist, praised it as a far-sighted development in the ongoing struggle to limit world population to sustainable levels."

But other politicians and church leaders condemned it. A spokesman for the charity, LIFE, said the UN's support for China's compulsory one-child policy was unacceptable. Chinese women were being dragged from their homes by soldiers and forced to submit to brutal abortions and sterilisation, in clear breach of their fundamental human rights. The European move would lead to widespread abortions throughout the Third World.

And that's just for starters, Howard thought. How long before it reached the Second and then the First World? Only recently, the prospect of compulsory abortions and internment camps for women who refused sterilisation seemed unthinkable in Britain. Not any more.

He parked the Rover in *The Announcer's* secure underground car park and bounded up the stairs past advertising and marketing staff beginning another day's losing battle against the paper's downwardly spiralling circulation. Every promotional gimmick management dreamed up to attract more readers kept backfiring. Their latest wheeze had been to sign a former sporting champion to write a weekly column but as this weirdo was widely regarded as the world's worst sportsperson, the exercise proved spectacularly counter-productive.

Howard wondered how many other graduates of the prestigious Ian Paisley Charm Academy might yet be hired to alienate the paper's loyal core readership. The possibilities were endless. Still, that was management's problem. He had his own.

First a call to the coffee machine, then a check on his e-mails. The usual junk, plus confirmation from his travel agents of the family's summer holiday. They were off to Mijas, on the Costa del Sol, in August. If you wanted sun, and who didn't, it had to be the Costa. If you got sick of the sangria you could always nip across to Gibraltar for a pint of the real thing.

There was one e-mail from Dominic Greaves, asking for any news on the missing police sergeant. He had to reply that so far they'd drawn a blank. He seemed to have been spirited off the face of the earth but *The Announcer* was still on the case. He asked Dominic to update him on moves for an inquest and signed off with the opening line from Arthur Hugh Clough's inspiring poem: 'Say not the struggle naught availeth…'

The poem encouraged Howard in his exhaustive research into the ultimate method of population control – abortion. He switched to the internet and called up UNFPA, the United Nations Population Fund with a budget approaching $500 million. While the UN agency disclaimed any part in the abortion industry, it was known to funnel money and equipment to non-governmental organisations heavily involved in it.

For the past twenty years, it had played a major role in providing funds for China's social engineering policy, knowing it was based on coercive abortion. On a visit to Beijing its executive director, Thoraya Obaid, praised this policy, saying China had "scored a remarkable achievement in population control".

Digging further, Howard found that UNFPA had also funded the International Planned Parenthood Federation, which advocated the circumvention or, when necessary, outright breaking of national abortion laws. Other supporters included organisations ranging from the sinister to the eccentric. One South American film producer calling himself William Tell offered land to peasant men who would have vasectomies as part of a crusade against 'the tyranny of fertility'.

Humming the stirring strains of the *William Tell Overture*, Howard ploughed on. Such lunatic fringe groups seemed to have taken their cue from his old friend Margaret Sanger, founder of International Planned Parenthood Federation, who was on record calling for 'the extermination of human weeds, the cessation of charity, the segregation of morons, misfits and the maladjusted...and the sterilisation of genetically inferior races'.

In the magazine *Birth Control Review*, she had openly supported the infanticide programme promoted by Nazi Germany and publicly championed Hitler's goal of white supremacy. She organised her 'Negro Project', a programme designed to eliminate members of what she believed to be an inferior race, and looked forward "to seeing humanity free some day of the tyranny of Christianity".

Howard's labyrinthine research led him to a quote by Ismael Hermandez, executive director of the Fort Myers African and Caribbean American Centre, who said: "In the past racists snatched black babies from their mothers' arms and sold them into slavery. Today, they snatch them from their mothers' wombs and throw them into the garbage."

As recently as 2003, the New Jersey Supreme Court upheld a law depriving women of benefits if they had additional children while receiving public assistance. Marie Tasy, of Right to Life New Jersey, said statistics showed abortions increased under the inhuman law. It sent "a terrible message that the poor woman and her children are not valued by society".

Howard was startled to realise that a precedent already existed for Tina's oppressive measures. The same terrible message was about to be inflicted on Britain, with the same terrible results.

Suddenly overcome with a feeling of intense depression, Howard decided to wrap it up. He clicked on the 'print' icon and signalled to Edgar, stationed nearby at the office printer, for a hard copy.

"What's that about sexual health?" Andrew wanted to know, his unprepossessing stubbled face leering over Howard's shoulder "Do I detect a high prurience rating?"

"Get back to the *Sun*, Andrew. This is serious stuff."

The news editor flopped in his executive chair, lumped his size ten loafers on his desk and did just that. After an inordinate length of time studying page three, he flipped through the rest of the rag in seconds. "Something's gone wrong," he said, tossing the dross aside. "There's several pages without the word 'sex' in the headline."

Howard was still reflecting on the depressing implications of what he had just written. "Do you realise it's only a matter of time before population control hits us in this country."

Ever ready for an argument, Andrew pitched in with: "You don't seriously believe all that sinister Tina stuff do you?"

"I'm keeping an open mind. But William's not been wrong so far."

"Have you found any corroborating evidence for this population control horror?"

"No direct evidence…yet. But there's plenty of circumstantial."

"In what way?" Andrew could be deliberately obtuse.

"Come on, Andrew. You know why they put up the retirement age… because they can't afford to pay the pensions! Look at this month's figures for welfare benefit – up again on last month. Teenage pregnancies still rising – more mouths to feed. Sooner or later the government has to call it a day. Tina's the obvious solution, like it or not."

"But the birthrate's falling, old boy. Women are being urged to have more babies, not fewer."

"Yes, but not *underclass* women! They just breed more benefit claimants!"

"So Tina's targeting single mums?"

"That's right...and geriatrics, the weakest elements in society. People who don't have the muscle to kick up a fuss."

"But you can't prove there's a co-ordinated campaign, can you?"

"Not at this stage but all the signs are there...fanatical sex education, the condom culture, the abortion craze, the sudden euthanasia propaganda... all happening at once. Are you saying it's coincidence?"

"Probably."

"It's *too much* of a coincidence. It has all the hallmarks of an organised strategy – that's much more plausible."

"All conspiracy theories are plausible. It doesn't mean they're convincing."

"William's convinced me, Andrew. And the more I think about it, the more I believe there's a hidden political agenda behind it all."

"Not another conspiracy theory, surely," Andrew scoffed.

"Think about it...if you could stop the poor from breeding...there'd be a fantastic political spin-off. By reducing their numbers, you could say you were cutting poverty at a stroke. Plenty of politicians have promised to do that but they've never delivered."

"Hmm..." the sceptical news editor seemed almost persuaded. "I take on board what you say. You may have a point."

Praise indeed, Howard thought. He pressed home his advantage. "So they're starting by eliminating large families, and by that I mean those with more than two children."

"Suits me. I don't have any kids. How many have you got, Howard?"

"Two point four." He didn't know how right he was.

"See what I mean. It's people like me who keep the birthrate steady. We have to compensate for randy buggers like you."

Howard resisted the temptation to reply that it was family men like him who had to compensate for selfish sods like Andrew, to perpetuate the species and produce the next generation of taxpayers. The man, however unlovely, was still technically his office superior.

His printout was a long time arriving. Edgar, also on the early turn, was busy making the morning tea, still brewed in the huge brown teapot that had survived from the paper's hot metal days. Then there had been twenty editorial messengers. Now, since the new technology, there were only three, working different shifts. They were all middle aged, with Edgar the oldest. He was, as some hacks unkindly described him, slow but unsure. But he didn't miss much. When he finally handed Howard the printout, he gave him a broad, knowing wink.

The bottom line

Justine Harvey-Ozgood, mid-forties, overweight, divorced, feminist, B-list television celebrity, *Guardian* columnist and passionate crusader for all things progressive, was concentrating on the bottom line of her numerous interests. Times were growing hard at her Options 4 Today chain of abortion clinics or, as she preferred to describe them, providers of sexual and reproductive health services. She was becoming increasingly concerned at the steady decline in demand for what her charitable trust's literature delicately called 'terminations'.

Business had been booming for years as a result of the sexual revolution. There was money in misery if you knew how to go about it. She'd read somewhere that the Planned Parenthood Federation of America had made a profit of $36.6 million on a quarter of a million surgical abortions in the previous year.

But lately the misguided propaganda of the pro-lifers had begun to make an impact on unfortunate women facing unplanned pregnancies. Times were changing. There seemed to be more young women pushing prams in the streets – single mothers, no doubt. Didn't they know about contraception? Weren't there enough mouths to feed in our overcrowded world without adding more?

And these irresponsible young mothers invariably looked so happy, thought the poor, childless Justine, for whom love was nothing more than an indecent four-letter word. Well, they would see about that when Tina took over. Pregnant underclass women who exceeded their quotas of children would soon be lined up outside her clinics for state-funded abortions. Until that blessed day dawned, however, immediate steps needed to be taken to maintain at least a degree of profitability. She scanned her clinics' scale of fees and sighed. There was only one thing for it – they would have to be increased.

With the cost of living forever rising, the cost of killing needed to keep pace. Not that she accepted the word 'killing'. The word was 'terminating'. In any discussion of semantics, she would point out that you could not kill something that wasn't alive. It was the mother who was alive and she had exercised her fundamental human right...her right to choose. At this moment, however, Justine was more concerned about her own human right to choose a Christian Dior creation she had her eye on in Harrods' sale. It had been reduced from £7,000 to £4,950. A modest increase in fees would help defray the indulgence.

If a client wanted a termination badly enough she could surely afford to pay more than £440 – the going rate for a surgical abortion up to fourteen weeks. She decided to increase the fee to £500, or rather £495. Women liked prices with a nine in them rather than round numbers. For a moment she toyed with a fee of £499 but then thought better of it. After all, this wasn't Tesco's. It was a respectable provider of sexual and reproductive health services.

* * *

Of all the gardens in Meadow Drive, No 23's looked the loveliest. A combination of hot July sun and Edgar's diligent watering in the early hours of the morning after work (he had been mistaken for a burglar more than once) had rewarded him with a stunning display. The tiny patches of impeccably trimmed lawn were surrounded by vivid scarlet peonies and geraniums, pink and gold fuschias and marigolds, against a backdrop of elegant blue lupins and delphiniums.

Bees buzzed, butterflies fluttered and a soft, musky scent wafted towards Edgar's nostrils as he leant on his spade and surveyed his masterpiece. He felt utterly dejected.

IPI had increased their offer for his bungalow following his indignant rejection of the insulting £75,000. It now stood at an equally derisory £90,000 and was, the company insisted, their final offer. He realised it was all a cynical joke but there was nothing he could do about it. From informal soundings he had made among local Brothers, they were equally impotent – a truly unprecedented situation in the affairs of the Antient Order.

There was something rotten in the state of Brawton and he had a shrewd idea what it was. On her rounds as an Avon lady, Janice gathered items of intelligence hidden even from the all-seeing eye of Lodge 15392. In addition to the Mayor driving round in a new Lexus, there were rumours that certain senior planning officers had also acquired new cars, including top-of-the-range Jaguars.

With the crucial meeting of the planning committee only a week away, several councillors had suddenly taken off on expensive package holidays to such exotic locations as the Seychelles and Hawaii. There was talk of mysterious flight and hotel upgrades. One known opponent of the IPI factory had sailed off with his wife on a Caribbean cruise as occupants of an upper deck suite, no less.

Doubting that they had all struck lucky on the Lottery, Edgar had contacted the *Brawton Bugle*. He alerted them to the gross dereliction of civic duty at a time when the future of the town's environment lay in the balance. Oddly, this obvious front page lead story hadn't even merited a paragraph on an inside page.

They'd come crawling to him for quotes after next week's council meeting. If the decision went against him, as he was sure it would, he and his Meadow Drive neighbours planned a spectacular demo on the Town Hall steps. While stopping short of self-immolation, Edgar intended to make sure he set The Meadow issue well and truly alight.

*   *   *

Howard was about to shut down his terminal and see if the canteen's lunchtime menu matched its gourmet suppers when a message from the paper's Parliamentary staff flashed on to his screen:

Second reading for Euthanasia Bill

Witherspoon's Bill to legalise euthanasia for the terminally ill given unopposed second reading in House of Lords today.

William had said Tina included euthanasia among the methods of population control. Andrew might still not believe it but it seemed that all the forces William had warned against were moving into place ready for a combined assault, like an invisible army mobilising for war. Now the euthanasia enthusiasts were suddenly emerging from the woodwork. The culture of death was definitely on the march. It couldn't all be coincidence.

Andrew wanted more evidence but the evidence unfolding daily before their eyes clearly vindicated the integrity of William's impeccable information.

Howard reflected on the news editors' mistrust of conspiracy theories throughout lunch in the canteen (a shrivelled, almost cold *coq au vin* with flaccid chips which he judged far inferior to Mervyn's night shift cuisine). His boss was right about 95 per cent of such theories being unsustainable, of course. But that left a tantalising five per cent. You couldn't ignore it simply because it was a small number.

He tried a pudding. Steamed jam roll and custard. Solid as a snooker ball. He looked at his watch. There was time for a frame.

Howard had learned his snooker during his student days in the eighties, when the game was at the peak of its TV popularity. And he had learned it the hard way. On lecture-free days, he gravitated towards the local billiards hall and quickly fell victim to a sharp-eyed hustler. While relieving Howard of a sizeable portion of his grant, the hustler taught him a technique which most amateur players fail to master in a lifetime. It had been expensive tuition but worth every penny.

The room was empty except for Edgar when Howard entered. "Set 'em up, Edgar," he called, switching on the light over the table. The head messenger racked up the balls and Howard broke off. Aim for the penultimate red ball at the back of the triangle (not the end red, as some will tell you) with a touch of right-hand side and you'll thread the cue ball back between pink and blue into baulk. Without that touch of side, the cue ball will strike the blue on its way back and you could be in trouble.

Edgar knew what to expect – the perfect break-off shot. He was no longer fazed by his tutor's immaculate safety play. He had devised his own game plan – if in doubt, lash out. He smashed the cue ball into the pack of reds, scattering them kicking, kissing and careering in all directions. There was always a chance a red would drop into a pocket. When the kissing had to stop and none did, Howard proceeded to make a break of thirty-five and the frame was effectively over.

As there was no-one waiting for the table, he offered Edgar a few tips on his stance and cueing action. He knew he'd never cure the bad habits of a lifetime but there were some areas in which a modest improvement could yield dramatic results. The main one, the one which so many beginners failed to understand, was that you had to hold the cue lightly. It wasn't a spade or a pitchfork, it was a precision instrument.

"Let the cue do the work," he instructed, and Edgar was listening.

They practised cue ball control by running the spots. This involves clearing the table of all balls except the white, which you place on the brown spot and roll towards the top cushion over the blue, pink and black spots. If it returns to you over those spots without any deviation you know you're striking the cue ball correctly. It's much more difficult than it sounds. You have to strike the exact centre of the cue ball, otherwise you'll inadvertently impart 'side' which will throw the ball off course.

Edgar was keen to learn and practised the stroke repeatedly, once or twice getting it right which pleased him mightily. During the instruction, which also involved straightening out Edgar's bridge, Howard couldn't help noticing the ring again with its crossed square and compasses and his journalistic curiosity got the better of him.

"I thought Masons were a secret society," he said when Edgar paused to chalk his cue.

"They are," his pupil replied.

"Then how come you're wearing the ring?"

"I don't mind people knowing. I'm proud of it." At least he had been until recently.

"They're pretty powerful people, I understand," Howard prompted.

"You'd be surprised."

Nothing surprised Howard any more. He persevered: "I know police and judges are in it. Not many journalists, I don't think...?"

Edgar took another shot at running the spots. The cue ball returned wildly off course. He straightened up and fixed Howard with the standard Masonic stare. "It's no good, Howard. Our secrets are our secrets. They'll never be revealed to the profane – to outsiders."

Howard understood. He knew all about the ritual bloodletting threatened against members of the Brotherhood who betrayed its precious secrets.

Edgar valued his expert tuition very highly, however, and didn't want to seem ungrateful. He was not as slow as people thought. He had read all the printouts of the journalist's recent work and realised that he and the reporter could have a common enemy, albeit for vastly different reasons: International Pharmaceuticals Inc UK.

Perhaps the time would come when they could join forces to their mutual benefit. After all, he had lost confidence in the Lodge. He needed to let Howard know that he was not alone in his crusade. So he took his chalk and wrote very lightly in spidery letters on the table's green baize cushion:

I P I U K

When he had made sure Howard had seen the message, he rubbed it off with his hand. Then he did what Masons do when they're trying to tell you something. He tapped the side of his nose with his forefinger and gave a knowing wink.

You could almost have called it conspiratorial.

Save money, not the patient

Back at the interface, Howard discovered a plethora of information on euthanasia. The pros were led by the British Euthanasia Society, of which the formidable Baroness Witherspoon was the 'chair'. Reading through their promotional material, you had to admit that their aim of trying to alleviate suffering was an admirable one. They were campaigning for the rights of terminally ill people to end their lives with medical assistance rather than prolong their suffering.

They had introduced 'living wills' which patients could sign in advance and which absolved doctors from any legal consequences of their actions. This process was described as assisted dying and was based on the principle of patient autonomy, i.e., the patient making decisions not the doctor.

Living wills would be important in cases of serious stroke or severe dementia when sufferers were unable to communicate. If they had opted not to be resuscitated, tube-fed or kept alive on a life-support system, medical staff would be legally obliged to respect their wishes. The euthanasia society's living will documents were described as pro-choice – they could not be used to actively end life but to refuse or request life-prolonging medical treatment.

It all seemed entirely reasonable, Howard felt. Then he spotted the catch. Although refusals of treatment were legally binding on doctors, *requests for treatment were not*. Doctors would use such requests 'for guidance' but they were not legally binding. So much for choice, then. Patient autonomy seemed to apply only if you wanted to die. Where did it leave the vast majority of people with impairment who wanted to live? Opponents of living wills quoted the case of an elderly man who showed signs of recovery from a stroke who had his hydration stopped by doctors. He clung to life for ten days without fluid.

In another case, an elderly woman who suffered a fractured skull and brain damage was put on an intravenous drip, which came out of its own accord. It was not reinserted. "It took seven agonising days for her to die of dehydration." The most common form of living will authorised this form of death from lack of fluid. Many signatories would not realise what could happen to them.

While euthanasia supporters were clearly motivated by humane instincts, the consequences of their proposals might cause more suffering than they relieved. There were horrific anecdotes from Holland where euthanasia was legal. Some patients, it was claimed, had been killed even after withdrawing their consent.

But what concerned opponents of euthanasia most of all were its long-term implications, notably its potential for abuse. Article 2 of the European Convention on Human Rights, now part of British law, laid down that everyone had the right to life. Once you started tampering with the law you were on dangerous ground, they pointed out. Where would it lead? By way of an answer they cited Nazi Germany in the 1930s. That nightmare had started equally innocuously and look how it finished. If Tina had her way and made euthanasia compulsory, the same virus would spread to Britain.

Howard unlocked his desk drawer and took out his copy of William's letter from its hiding place between copies of the *Journalist* magazine. Something about a stairway. Ah yes…the stairway leading to a dark gulf, Churchill's quotation:

"It is a fine broad stairway at the beginning, but after a bit the carpet ends. A little further on there are only flagstones, and a little further on still these break beneath your feet."

State terrorism was what lurked in the dark gulf. And, yes, we'd already reached the flagstones.

*   *   *

One of Barbara's many talents was the ability to transform basic dishes into delicacies by means of closely guarded secret recipes. So when Howard phoned home to ask what was for dinner and she told him corned beef hash – her speciality – any thoughts of deviations via the Dog and Partridge after work disappeared immediately.

They ate on the pine table in the kitchen, except for Sundays when the traditional roast was served in the rosewood dining room on Barbara's best Spode. Yes, traditional Sunday lunch with the family…'in this day and age'. How Andrew and his fellow bachelors in *The Announcer* newsroom would sneer. Which bothered him not at all. Jealousy, he knew, took many forms.

When the four of them had polished off the culinary masterpiece, watched enviously by Oscar who had devoured his own portion in seconds, it was time for Chris to do his homework and Sally her piano practice.

As Howard helped Barbara to stack the dishwasher, he told her about his research into the complex question of euthanasia. What were her views as a nurse on the subject?

"I've worked for fifteen years in hospitals and I've seen many people in pain," she told him. "I've heard patients cry 'Let me die' in childbirth but the moment the baby's arrived they're glad to be alive. Should we have taken them at their word and helped them die? Of course not. We know they'll change their minds so we give them pain relief."

Howard was doubtful. "Sometimes that doesn't work. The mercy killers say it's more compassionate to end suffering – by withdrawing food and fluids."

"Death by thirst and starvation…with the teeth sticking to the inside of the mouth, and the patient gasping for water…how compassionate is that?"

"Not very, I agree. But they say it's preferable to intolerable pain."

"Pain is pain, Howard. It hasn't got any worse over the last fifteen years. It's stayed the same. But pain relief has got a lot better. We can relieve pain now, however acute. We know what we're doing – just like you do in your job."

"So there's no need for euthanasia?"

"None at all. It's all about bed availability. Palliative care for a dying patient costs money, it blocks a bed that someone else could have."

"The management needs to save money, not the patient?"

"Exactly. The answer isn't to kill off the patients. It's to build more hospitals."

"Obvious really."

"Yes, but that costs money. And money is all politicians understand."

"Tell me about it."

*   *   *

It was one of those July evenings that refuse to cool down after a sultry day. The air was still heavy and humid as if a storm was approaching. Which, in every sense, it was. Slowly, a little unsteadily, a small group

110

of perspiring residents of Meadow Drive climbed the steps of Brawton Town Hall, led by the dapper figure of Edgar, carrying a home-made placard reading: 'Say *No* to Meadow vandalism'.

He had grown attached to the placard. Janice had helped him make it out of white cardboard packaging from her Avon products, fixed with twine and strong glue to a broken curtain pole from the garage. Using a felt tip pen, they wrote the slogan in block capitals, going over each letter several times. It had taken hours. By the time they had finished they were quite proud of their handiwork.

Wilting in the enervating heat, the demonstrators had first refreshed themselves in the Brewer's Arms next door to the Town Hall. Although this had been strictly in the interests of hydration, it was noticeable that their initial morose mood had now grown more buoyant. Their leader, having unwisely exceeded his usual limit of a single glass of lager, was the most relaxed of all. The forthcoming challenge no longer seemed a lost cause. He was confident of leading his men to victory.

Janice had thought about coming but the heat always affected her breathing and the slightest excitement could bring on an angina attack. So she decided against. It was just as well.

Right-thinking people

Brawton Town Council's planning and highways committee held its meetings in the Town Hall's main committee room, a spacious chamber with a high, ornate Victorian ceiling in keeping with the rest of the building's architecture. As Edgar and his neighbours were ushered noisily into the public seats, they were surprised to find so few councillors gathered to decide the crucial issue of The Meadow's future.

They knew the area committee had already granted outline planning permission for IPI's factory but many, including Edgar, had made strenuous attempts to rally councillors to their cause when it came to the crunch. Some had promised support but now that the all-powerful committee was assembled and battle lines drawn, none of them could be seen. Edgar, who had been made to leave his placard outside the room, found his worst fears rapidly returning. What they were about to witness was an elaborate charade.

Several tedious measures for improved street lighting and drainage were debated by councillors, seated at the long table covered with a blue cloth and complete with jugs of water and glasses. Despite the prosaic nature of the subjects, most of the speakers clearly fancied themselves as orators while blissfully unaware that nobody else did. At a smaller, plain table reserved for the Press, a young reporter from the *Bugle* yawned and doodled in his notebook. Edgar had tipped off the nationals and local TV stations but no other representatives of the media seemed to have turned up.

Finally, the main business of the evening was reached. The chair, as he was known, a well-padded version of one, intoned: "An application by International Pharmaceuticals Incorporated UK for planning permission to develop that area within the town's precincts abutting Meadow Drive and Station Road, known as The Meadow, for industrial purposes."

The chief planning officer, a member of Edgar's lodge who had been unable to attend recent fraternal gatherings "due to pressure of work", glanced nervously towards the protesters before proposing that planning permission for the IPI factory be approved.

While he accepted that the scheme had met with opposition in certain quarters, IPI's architects had convinced his officers that the development would cause minimal environmental impact. There would be no tall chimneys, emissions would be fully controlled by sophisticated, computerised equipment and a generous budget had been set aside for large-scale landscaping of the site. This landscaping would preserve several of The Meadow's elms since the company was mindful of the trees' ecological importance in the face of Dutch elm disease.

This gesture was just one example of IPI's outstanding reputation in the field of conservation and community relations. The company was as proud of its 'social profile' as it was of its record for providing employment opportunities in deprived areas. As an organisation of 'international repute', it had satisfied the council's officers that any intrusion into local residents' amenity would be more than compensated by the increased prosperity it would bring to Brawton.

At the end of the day, economic arguments had to take precedence over minority interests. IPI was prepared to invest over £30 million in the development. It was an investment in the town's long-term prosperity. It would create hundreds of jobs, both short and long-term, in an area long regarded as an unemployment black spot. There would be employment opportunities for skilled and unskilled workers, with an emphasis on jobless young people in the town, which had long been a matter of concern.

The proposed development was one which should concentrate the hearts and minds of all right-thinking citizens who put the interests of the community first and as such he recommended it to the meeting.

It had been a rousing and eloquent appeal to the community spirit of the burghers of Brawton. Had it gone on much longer, you could have visualised the raising of the Union Jack to the strains of *Land of Hope and Glory*. The well-padded chair looked around for objectors. But the reference to 'right-thinking people' was still ringing in the councillors' ears and there seemed a certain reluctance to be regarded as 'wrong-thinking'.

Then one elderly lady, in a floral dress and redolent of lavender, did sound a dissident note. She had listened carefully to the argument in favour of the factory but, as a member of the Green party, her priority had to be what was acceptable to the natural environment. The unpleasant smell of a chemical works was clearly not acceptable. It would pollute an area of natural if somewhat untamed beauty and the home of much rare

113

flora and fauna. She felt the issue was too important for the Council to decide. There should be an inquiry into the proposal by the Office of the Deputy Prime Minister.

This suggestion brought loud applause and stamping from the public seats. Edgar bravely shouted: "No Meadow vandalism!" The chant was taken up by the other residents and proceedings were halted. The chairman called for order and informed the protesters that he had the power to expel them if they continued to disrupt the meeting

When the disturbance subsided, the Meadow contingent's champion suddenly changed tack completely. However, she declared, the importance of creating jobs in the town had not been lost on her. You had to be reasonable and she was willing to compromise. If, and she repeated if, a factory had to be built on the site, why not one that gave off pleasant smells rather than unpleasant ones – why not one that manufactured soaps and perfumes, for example?

More uproar from the public benches. There were cries of "No... no..." and the chant "No Meadow vandalism" echoed once more round the chamber's ornate ceiling.

The chair spoke quietly into a mobile phone and almost immediately two substantial members of Brawton constabulary strode into the chamber. They were not heavy about it. They were not exactly gentle either. Firmly, and in one or two cases slightly more persuasively, they led the sheepish demonstrators out of the room, down the marble staircase and out on to the Town Hall steps. As demos went, this was not going to overthrow the Constitution. There would be no need for riot gear, dogs or water cannon.

The forlorn knot of agitators, now completely subdued and sober apart from Edgar, was allowed to wait on the steps for the outcome of the vote. Spots of rain were falling as the threatened storm finally broke but they did not have long to wait. On a show of hands, the amendment to seek an inquiry was defeated and full planning permission for the IPI development granted, in each case by an emphatic majority.

It had all been a foregone conclusion, the rebels told each other. It was institutionalised vandalism, that's what it was. Edgar was the last to leave, having been handed his placard by one of the police officers. In a final gesture of defiance, he turned on the top step and, swaying slightly, waved it at the constables, shouting: "No Meadow vandalism". This time, the reaction of the officers was not so restrained. They both grabbed him and told him to shut up or else he would be arrested. At this, Edgar's few remaining followers melted into the gloom.

In the scuffle that followed, his placard was broken and fell splintered on the rain-spattered stonework. There was a flash of light, not lightning but from a camera. The Press had finally arrived. But Edgar no longer cared. The sight of the broken placard, so lovingly created by him and Janice, seemed to symbolise their hopes for the future – shattered beyond repair.

It was more than he could bear. "You can't do this," he cried bitterly. "Lodge 15392."

The non-Masonic officers were unimpressed. "Move along now, sir," said one. "We don't want to arrest you. Your wife will be waiting at home."

A better-case scenario

As part of *The Announcer's* new crusade on state population control, Julian had taken a number of radical decisions on editorial policy. He cut back on stories about the royal family and other celebrity tittle-tattle. Trade union trashing, BBC bashing and stories about illegal immigration also felt the pinch. His Lordship wouldn't notice, at least not for a time since he rarely read the paper. As a field sports enthusiast, he spent most of his life giving foxes, fish and birds a hard time. His idea of a sporting contest was to pit a heavily armed, 15-stone man against a defenceless 3lb bird. It was 'sport' in which there could be only one winner.

The Editor had discussed the change in editorial policy at senior management level and, while there was scepticism in some quarters, there was general agreement that drastic measures were necessary. For the first time in the paper's recent history, circulation had fallen below a million and advertising revenue had reached a level where a further increase in the cover price had to be contemplated. If implemented, circulation would be sure to fall again. It was the law of diminishing returns. Wholesale staff redundancies would then be inevitable. That was the grim, worst case scenario.

Julian had a better-case scenario. Over his several decades in Fleet Street, he had developed an unerring instinct for detecting potential social upheavals. The trend towards liberalisation in all walks of life – some of it good but much of it disastrous – had become inexorable. It was borne on a wave of fanaticism that gave no thought for the consequences. There was almost a Gadarene quality about it. Sooner or later it would run out of steam and teeter over a cliff. Julian intended that, when it did, *The Announcer* would be on hand to administer the final push.

State population control had been tried before, he reflected. It had started in the same innocuous manner and finished in the worst case scenario of all – the Holocaust. It was the vital duty of the media in general and *The Announcer* in particular to prevent it ever happening again. Howard's daily confidential updates on his research were suggesting the unthinkable – that it *could* happen again; that an insidious culture of death was beginning to take hold on the national psyche. Julian's objective overview of developments in Parliament and elsewhere on abortion, euthanasia and sex education confirmed the message. There was no mistaking which way the wind was blowing.

One story to which Julian gave front-page treatment was:

Europe votes for abortion

by Irene Thomas, Health Correspondent

The European Parliament yesterday legalised abortion in all EU countries. MEPs in Strasbourg voted by 280 to 240, with 28 abstentions, to adopt a report entitled 'Sexual and Reproductive Health and Rights', promoted by Belgian women's rights groups.

They issued a directive that "in order to safeguard women's reproductive health and rights, abortion should be made legal, safe and accessible to all."

Sources revealed that EU officials in Brussels had already earmarked £74 million to be spent on "reproductive and sexual health planning", of which abortion was the main component.

The bombshell had a particular effect in Ireland where abortion is illegal. An Irish government source said they would disregard the directive, as they did not consider it binding on member states.

The ruling also applied to prospective EU members, raising the scenario that countries such as Turkey would be forced to compromise their no-abortion policies in the hope of hastening their entry into the European Union.

A spokeswoman for UNFPA welcomed the decision as "a logical development in an enlightened policy of upholding women's rights across Europe". If member states chose not to accept this policy they should be subjected to economic sanctions.

The MP, Mr Paul D'Arcy, took the punishment theme further, saying dissenting countries should be expelled from the EU. Such nations were invariably dominated by outdated, backward-looking religious elements. The sooner forward-looking secular paganism was adopted throughout the European Union the better.

The Pro-Life Alliance said: "This is a sad day for all those who seek a Europe based on respect for human rights, ethics and democracy." It would inevitably lead to abortion on demand. While women's rights were now widely recognised, those of the unborn child were consistently ignored.

There were more quotes from both sides, disillusionment from pro-life, jubilation from anti-life.

The Editor was particularly interested in Irene's follow-up story next day. It had not made the front page because there had been another major terrorist alert in London. It was a four-paragraph item, tucked away on Page 7. As he read it, the sinister scenario prophesied in William's letter – ensconced in the wall safe but engraved in his mind – grew ever more persuasive.

'EU spy unit' targets Pro-Life Movement

Organisers of the Pro-Life Alliance in Britain say they are being spied on by a top-secret intelligence unit in Brussels set up to monitor members of pro-life organisations across Europe. They claim the unit came into being following the recent decision by the European Parliament to legalise abortion throughout the continent. There are reports of members' homes being photographed, telephones tapped and letters opened.

"Big Brother is finally watching us now," an Alliance official said. "This is one of the most dangerous trends we have faced. We are being treated as the enemy of freedom and human rights. These sinister people are the prophets of a post-Christian Europe. Anyone who disagrees with them is a threat."

Another said: "It smacks of dictatorship. History shows that any society relying on secret police is up to no good. The abortionists are part of a culture of death we have seen before in Europe. This time round they call it reproductive and sexual health planning. It's abortion with a new sanitised image."

An EU spokesman denied any spying operation. The Brussels unit had been established merely to monitor the output of pro-life groups, which he believed to be misleading. He blamed the reports on "hysteria" inspired by "well-funded pro-life groups in America".

Julian read the story again. Of all the recent developments in their campaign, this was the most disturbing. The spooks were coming out of the woodwork. And they were not British spooks. You knew where you stood with British spooks.

The EU spokesman's disingenuous disclaimer was merely par for the course. The intelligence unit's activities as described by its pro-life victims tied in neatly with William's 'accident'. European secret police were not like their British counterparts. Their culture was based on crude, Mafia-style methods. They would think nothing of it.

Irene's story was an important breakthrough. They were in a whole new ball game. He sent her an electronic message of congratulation and flagged the story to Howard, just in case he hadn't seen it. Five minutes later, back came his investigative reporter's message: "Alors…they won't spook *The Announcer!*"

A woman's right to choose

Howard was checking the latest Test match score on PA when Andrew told him Reuters had an important news flash. He switched over and read:

> The two women whose cases were largely responsible for the legalisation of abortion in the US, Sandra Cano, "Mary Doe" of Doe v. Bolton, and Norma McCorvey, "Jane Roe" of Roe v. Wade, are asking the Supreme Court to reverse the rulings of thirty years ago. Both women regret their part in the abortion law and see their return to the Supreme Court as representing women harmed by it.

Another page-one story in the making, he thought. He'd deal with it later when the agency's fuller version came through. Right now he was supposed to be researching the ownership of abortion clinics in Britain and having a hard time. So it was off to the library where Louise could run rings round the internet.

After much diligent searching, the sad-faced librarian came up with three main operators. All were companies described as not-for-profit charitable trusts. As they checked through the interminable lists of trustees looking for recognisable names, Howard struck gold. Listed as chief executive of a group called Options 4 Today Ltd was none other than Justine Harvey-Ozgood, author, TV personality and relentless campaigner for women's rights. She made no secret of her commercial activity. Everything was above board although Howard noticed there were no up to date company accounts.

Louise explained that, for technical reasons, Options 4 Today Ltd did not need to produce up to date accounts. To Howard's suspicious mind this seemed like a useful device to conceal profits but Louise again put him in the picture. Charitable trusts were not allowed to make a profit but they were allowed to show a surplus.

Sweet charity!

They called up Options 4 Today's website on the library computer. No mention of the formidable feminist. Just the usual script about women's rights to choose reproductive and sexual health services.

"Hah," Louise exclaimed. "The way they dress it up! Why don't they just call it abortion and have done with it? Because they know it's wrong, that's why."

Startled by her outburst, Howard pointed to the clinic's slogan: "The fundamental human right to have children by choice, not chance."

"That's all very well," Louise said sadly. "My daughter had a choice five years ago. She chose an abortion and she's never been the same since."

Howard murmured sympathetically.

"Clinical depression. In and out of psychiatric hospitals. It's destroying the whole family. Women only learn the truth about abortion when it's too late."

*　　　*　　　*

Although an unashamed self-publicist, Justine Harvey-Ozgood drew the line at giving interviews to newspapers like *The Announcer* so Howard had to work out a strategy for approaching her. He decided to say he was working on a women's interest feature for the paper's Saturday Magazine whose editor, Fiona Templeton, a niece of His Lordship, was rumoured to be a 'close friend' of Justine's. Fiona was a lesbian, something which His Lordship found acutely embarrassing. Although he imagined it was a family secret, it was known to everyone on *The Announcer* payroll from the Editor down to humblest machine room greaser.

Howard cleared his plan with Fiona first, saying that if the interview appeared in *The Announcer's* news pages, it would also be offered to the Magazine as a simultaneous feature, complete with pictures to suit its quasi-artistic and vacuous coverage of the upper class social whirl. He would take a snapper with him, one who fancied himself as a photographic Rembrandt not a newshound. So there was no question of any deception.

Much to his surprise, Ms Harvey-Ozgood agreed almost at once to his request for an interview when he phoned her at her St John's Wood flat. She was in a good mood. She had been to Harrods and purchased the Christian Dior outfit she'd set her heart on. It had been a rare bargain. There was just one caveat: under no circumstances would she answer any questions about her sexual orientation.

The picture desk was stretched; they gave him Barry, a young art school graduate with a wispy beard and a baseball cap. It didn't matter. This assignment was about something more important than capturing a subject's character or lack of it on film. They took a cab and Howard tested his voice recorder with a few pleasantries to his young colleague.

Barry, unlike most members of his species, remained uncommunicative, engrossed with the light meters and state-of-the-art Nikons draped round his shoulders. Only when the conversation turned to West Ham United did he suddenly acquire the garrulousness of his trade.

It was another warm and sunny day but the red-brick block had a dingy, uncared-for look about it, despite the £1 million price tags of its dwellings. They took the lift to the second floor and were greeted by the famous columnist, her ample figure clad informally in ill-fitting jeans and an embroidered lilac top. They were ushered through a musty hallway into a large lounge, leading off into a study complete with computer, filing cabinets and overflowing bookshelves.

The flat was functional rather than comfortable and the décor slightly dated. It had the same uncared-for appearance as the building. Justine had several other homes after all. This was just her London pad.

Barry was granted permission to prowl in time-honoured fashion, checking the light and snapping items of interest, which seemed few and far between. There were no flowers, no ornaments, no framed photos of children. But on one of the bookshelves stood a photograph of Justine and Fiona Templeton exchanging meaningful, some might have said libidinous, glances.

"Why should a paper like *The Announcer* be interested in me?" Justine asked, as they seated themselves on opposite leather armchairs.

Howard took the voice recorder out of his pocket and placed it on a glass and steel coffee table between them. "For the record, if that's OK? Or I can take a shorthand note."

"That's fine."

"May I call you Justine?"

"Why not, Howard? Everyone else does."

"The *Announcer* Magazine is running a series on the lifestyles of celebrities and it was felt that a profile of yourself and your home life would work well in that context."

Justine laughed, tossing back her short dark hair. Permanently forty-something, she had a boyish face with a prominent nose, double chin despite a facelift and rimless spectacles framing small dark eyes. There was a hardness about the eyes but she was not unattractive when she laughed. It made her look younger. "I'm flattered that you regard me as a celebrity. Fiona is a friend of mine and she's never called me that before."

"This isn't your main home, of course?"

"No, I only stay here when I'm in town to see my editor or my agent, or doing TV appearances. My main home is in the Cotswolds, as I'm sure you know…"

Howard smiled. "Plus a house in the Bahamas, a villa in Tuscany…"

"You've been doing your homework. Yes, I own several properties. I acquired most of them in a divorce settlement when my former husband, Donald Ozgood, and I split up."

They chatted inconsequentially about her privileged childhood, her Cheltenham Ladies College education and her early years in her father's merchant bank after graduating in history at Cambridge. Then turning to family life, Howard asked: "Was it a conscious decision not to have children or was that a disappointment?"

"Very much a conscious decision," she answered briskly. "Family life and politics simply don't mix. Children can be very demanding. They put too much of a strain on you if you're serious about pursuing a career. That's why so many professionals' marriages break up."

"But you had no children – yet still got divorced."

"That was because Donald wanted kids and I didn't. He desperately wanted a family. I couldn't understand it. I thought it was women who wanted children."

Howard decided to come to the point. "Can I ask how you came to be involved in the abortion business?" he asked abruptly.

She studied her plump fingers and manicured, clear-varnished nails before fixing him with her hard-faced stare.

"It's not about money."

Howard managed to keep a straight face.

"As I've said many times in my column, women have a basic human right to make decisions about their own bodies. Not long ago, if they had an unwanted pregnancy, they were obliged to go to back-street

123

abortionists. Some of them died as a result. That can't be acceptable in a so-called compassionate society."

"I quite agree."

"A pregnant woman must be allowed to decide whether to give birth or not. If she chooses not to, then she should receive proper professional help. That's what we do in our clinics."

"For those who can afford the fees."

"We offer credit facilities for those who can't. We regard it as our duty to uphold women's fundamental human right of choice."

"Doesn't the baby also have a fundamental right to life?"

"It's not a baby. It's a foetus. It's not a *viable* person. It can't survive independently."

"Your opponents say it's an unborn child and it's wrong to kill it."

"You can't kill something that's not alive."

"How do you define life, Justine?"

"The period between birth and death."

Howard took out his notebook. In his preparation for the interview he had copied dictionary definitions of the word "life". "That's one definition. But there are others. Things like animate existence …union of soul and body…but the first definition in my Oxford Dictionary is this: 'the capacity for growth'. Surely an unborn child in the womb has the capacity for growth."

"It's not a child, it's a foetus."

"Well, a foetus then. If anything has the capacity for growth surely a foetus does."

Justine was getting annoyed. "Switch off the tape, please."

Howard complied.

"Off the record – agreed?"

"Agreed."

"I believe the pro-life lobby have put you up to this. Am I right?"

"No way. *The Announcer* doesn't take orders from any pressure group. We're strictly independent and impartial. But they do have a point, don't they?"

"No, they don't. If life just meant the capacity for growth it would mean older people aren't alive because they've stopped growing. Try telling that to pensioners."

Howard had anticipated this argument. "Growth doesn't just mean physical growth. Old people grow mentally, spiritually...in wisdom. *They grow older!*"

"Semantics, Howard. And I certainly don't accept the bit about union of body and soul. I'm an atheist. I don't believe in the concept of a human soul."

"Are we back on the record?"

"Provided we drop this line of questioning."

"Right." He switched the voice recorder back on and pushed his luck. "Many people see abortion as a tool of population control. How do you feel about that?"

"I asked you to drop abortion."

"OK, but on the broader issue of population control...what's your position? There seems to be a growing movement in favour of restricting population growth on genetic grounds..."

"You mean embryo research...to screen out embryos with severe genetic defects?"

"That's right. Disabled people say they have a right to be born like everyone else. Once you start screening out embryos with genetic defects, where does it end? Do you move on to the blind, then the deaf? They fear it's the thin end of the wedge."

"What nonsense. All we're saying is that, in the most severe cases, it would be better – more humane – to spare the embryo an intolerable quality of life."

"But isn't quality of life a subjective thing? Isn't it all relative? Your idea of the quality of life may not be mine, for example. The handicapped may not be able to lead a full life but surely half a life is better than none. You never hear disabled people say they're sorry they were born. They're just glad to be alive."

"I suspect that many of the most severely handicapped aren't – that's why they ask for assisted suicide."

She had led him to his next question. "Am I right in thinking you support voluntary euthanasia?"

"In principle, yes. Provided adequate safeguards are in place. There's a bill going through at the moment...Baroness Witherspoon's assisted dying Bill. It would make it legal to end the suffering of terminally ill people when they had requested it. Not by lethal injection, nothing like that. By withdrawing food and fluids."

"What do you say to those who claim that withdrawing food and fluids from a dying patient is inhumane?"

"It's more humane than keeping them alive, in pain, indefinitely."

"Critics say palliative care is now very sophisticated…that doctors know what they're doing. Why do you need to kill?"

"If the patient has requested it, you're not actively killing. You're helping them to die – when they're powerless to do it themselves."

"But what if they change their minds? People often do."

"You can't legislate for human unpredictability. All we're trying to do is help them end their suffering. I can't understand why you reactionaries have a problem with that."

Howard smiled. "I'm not a reactionary. I'm just playing devil's advocate. Even reactionaries accept that your motives are of the highest…"

"But…"

"But they fear the slippery slope. They say euthanasia has been tried before. Look what happened in Germany in the thirties. It was introduced by well-meaning idealists but then they made it compulsory and the thugs moved in."

"That won't happen here, I assure you. Economic conditions are quite different for a start. And the political situation…we live in a democracy."

For how long, Howard wondered. "Human nature hasn't changed though, has it?"

"Call me an idealist but I believe it has. We're more enlightened now than in the 1930s."

The time had come for Howard to slip in the key question. "Some say there's a population control agenda behind abortion and euthanasia…that a secret group of eugenicists wants to make them compulsory for people on state benefit. You know how rumours get around. Does that ring any bells?"

She gave him the withering stare. "It's certainly news to me, Howard."

It was the evasive answer he had expected, neither yes or no. She seemed to tense up but it could just be irritation.

"Do you know anyone called Tina?" he asked casually.

Her stare never wavered. "Can't say I do offhand. Why?"

"It's just a name that's cropped up in our investigation," he said vaguely. "Could be the agenda's mastermind – or rather mistressmind."

"Sounds like another wild conspiracy theory to me."

"That's what we think at *The Announcer*." Howard smiled brightly, adding under his breath, "Some of us." It was time for his last question, to end the interview on a lighter note. "I want to ask you about your views on love. Do you believe in it?"

Her reaction was startling, to say the least. "Love..." she declared with a dismissive gesture. "The world is obsessed with the wretched word. What does it mean...lust, sentiment, physical attraction, masochism? I think it's a phase you go through in life – like dyeing your hair pink or wearing a ring through your nose. It's something you grow out of. It's an old-fashioned illusion, a source of endless misery. Love causes more trouble in the world than religion. Do I believe in it? In a word, no."

Howard switched off the recorder and grinned at her. "Thanks, Justine. Sorry I asked."

After she had posed impatiently for Barry, the two journalists headed back to the office. In the cab, Howard asked his colleague: "What did you think of our famous feminist?"

The young snapper stopped fiddling with his equipment for a moment. "Not a lot. Why are they always so unfeminine?"

There was no answer to that.

*   *   *

Marcus C Quinn III was on his fourth Bourbon on the rocks of the evening when the phone rang. It was Justine.

"Is it a secure line?"

"As always."

"*The Announcer's* been round to see me. A reporter called Howard Mitchell. Magazine interview, he said, but I don't believe him. He asked too many awkward questions."

"Such as."

"Such as what did I know about a secret population control agenda and did I have any friends called Tina."

"Really."

"It's just as we thought, Marcus. William must have opened up to him before…"

"Before his unfortunate accident. Yes, but what exactly did the old guy tell him? That's what we need to know."

"Well, he obviously named names. You could be next in line for a visit."

"Thanks for the warning. I'll have to make myself 'unavailable for comment'."

"Will you inform the Director?"

"Of course. I keep him fully briefed. He's already taken quite a dislike to *The Announcer*. Was Mr Mitchell alone?"

"No, there was a young photographer with him."

"Did he record the interview?"

"Yes."

"What did you tell him?"

"Nothing of any importance."

"Are you sure?"

"Of course. I'm not stupid, Marcus."

"Better not talk to *The Announcer* again, all the same. I think we know whose side they're on."

"Not ours."

"Exactly. The matter is in hand. Our friends in Brussels are dealing with it."

"The intelligence unit?"

"That's the polite term for it."

"Do you think it will work? You know what the Press are like…they don't give up."

"Neither do I, my dear. Neither do I."

*　　　*　　　*

Following Howard's interview with Justine, features department ran an edited profile of the famous feminist next day, since they couldn't find anything else, and Fiona published the full interview in the magazine two weeks later. The text was arranged artistically around one of Barry's carefully airbrushed portraits of Justine looking soulfully into the middle distance and, for once, a magazine sub had come up with an inspired headline. It read:

Women or children first?

A woman's right to kill

It was Howard's turn to take Sally to Brownies. Once more the Rover was pressed into service as a neighbourhood taxi for his daughter and two of her friends, primly perched on the back seat in their freshly ironed uniforms with yellow neckties and shiny brown belts . . . the picture of innocence in contrast to the grimy, corrupt world which it was his misfortune to observe every working day.

Innocence, that was their precious possession, but for how long? How long before the sex education predators, circling impatiently on their commercial masters' business, robbed them of it...abuse disguised as protection? Then, when the 'protection' didn't work, which of these three little maids from school would end up another pregnant teenager or, worse, in the clutches of the abortionists? God forbid it would be Sally.

Dropping them off at the church hall, he adjourned to the Church Inn to wait for them. He was becoming quite a regular these days. The barman recognised him and they got chatting over Howard's pint of bitter. Would Crystal Palace do any better next season or would they have to sign new players? That was part of the trouble, it was felt. Too many new players. If you never had a settled team you didn't have much chance of building team spirit.

Howard wasn't sure how the conversation got round to abortion – it might have been because one of the Palace players' girlfriends was said to be expecting – but soon there was a lively debate in progress among the regulars at the bar. The pros and cons seemed to divide almost equally in line with public opinion generally. Supporters backed the popular view that it was a woman's right to choose while objectors maintained that they did not have a right to kill. Men didn't, so why should women?

It all seemed to hinge on the question of killing. How could you kill something that wasn't alive? Howard answered that in the same way he had with Justine. An embryo was, in a moral if not a legal sense, alive. But was it a *viable* person? Justine had made the point that it wasn't viable because it couldn't survive on its own. This stumbling block appeared to settle the argument in favour of the pros but it left Howard unsatisfied. There was only one thing for it: ask Barbara.

While Sally was taking a bath and Chris played his computer games, Howard turned to his Special Adviser on Medical and Social Issues and asked her: "What's the answer to those who say abortion's OK because the embryo is not a viable person?"

"Do I get a part credit for this?" Barbara asked mischievously.

"You get a part credit for everything. You just don't get a byline."

"You're the journalist. What does viable mean?"

"I always thought it meant workable, something achievable."

"Get the dictionary."

He went to the bookcase and took down the OED. "Feasible," he read. "Like I thought." But there was more. "Capable of living and surviving independently."

"Exactly. They say a foetus isn't viable because it's not capable of living and surviving independently. But then, how many newborn babies are capable of living and surviving independently? None. They depend on their mothers just as much out of the womb as they did inside it. It's years before they're capable of living and surviving independently. Does that make them unviable...is it OK to kill them?"

As rhetorical questions went, it was a classic. The oracle had done it again.

*   *   *

Edgar gazed miserably at the broken egg yolk in the frying pan. He just knew it signalled trouble ahead. And it wasn't long in coming. No sooner had he sat down to his regular full English, liberally laced with ketchup, than his better half stormed into the kitchen waving a copy of the *Brawton Bugle*.

"Have you seen this?" she demanded. Which was rather silly because the paper had only just come through the letterbox. She thrust it in front of him. "You're on the front page."

They'd certainly given the story the full treatment. Splashed across the top half of page one was a full-width picture of Edgar's brush with the law at the Town Hall the previous week. It was a perfect example of the Press photographer's art. It showed two burly officers manhandling the slight, balding figure of Edgar and actually captured the dramatic moment when his placard splintered in the struggle.

Below, in large type, the headline read:

Meadow rebel held in Town Hall demo

Edgar stopped eating and scratched his dome where it itched, as he read the report of the futile bid by residents to halt the proposed IPI factory. They'd described him as an 'office worker' rather than his full title of Head Messenger at *The Announcer* and had got his age wrong. He was fifty-eight, not fifty-nine. There was no mention of his eminent standing in the community and, unforgivably, no reporter had bothered to ask him for a quote, although they gave a full account of the chief planning officer's harangue in favour of the factory development.

When he reached the part where the Lodge traitor, his brother Mason, appealed to all right-thinking Brawton citizens to welcome the factory, Edgar had to stop reading. He had been well and truly stitched-up by IPI and their handsomely paid supporters. Even the local Press had got in on the act and were now putting the boot in. He pushed his plate away. He could eat no more.

If nothing succeeds like success, then nothing fails like abject failure. As if this total humiliation wasn't enough, he could hear words like 'laughing stock' and 'what will the neighbours think?' ringing round the kitchen. Janice was in full flow.

"I might have known you'd put us to shame. You'd been drinking hadn't you? You know you can't hold your drink. They could have arrested you, put you in a cell…"

"Yes, but they didn't, did they?"

"They should've done."

"Do leave off, Janice."

"It's all very well for you. You work nights, you never see the neighbours. I see them every day. And there's my Avon…what will the customers think when they see this? I'll never be able to live it down." She snatched the newspaper away scornfully. "You even broke the placard it took me hours to make," she trailed off, tears in her eyes.

"It took *us* hours," he corrected. "And anyway there'd be no point keeping it now would there…even if it wasn't broken?"

But there was no consoling her. "I've had enough. My angina won't stand it. What with all the hassle over the Meadow, the pressure on us to move house...and now this. You're supposed to have influence, but where is it now – when we need it? I'm fed up with you, Edgar. I really am. You're neither use nor ornament."

He sat with his head in his hands. Janice couldn't find her hankie so she tore off some kitchen roll and dabbed her eyes. The accusatory silence that followed, punctuated by muffled sobs, was even worse than the nagging. He couldn't stand it any longer. Beneath the gentle, impassive manner he was seething, not with Janice but with the wretched mess they were in and most of all the treachery of his brother Masons. Silently, he got up and went into the conservatory to check his tomatoes and plot his revenge.

"That's right," she shouted after him. "That's all you care about...your bloody tomatoes."

*　　　*　　　*

In common with every self-respecting journalist, Howard had read all about Messrs Woodward and Bernstein's celebrated Watergate achievement yet he was still surprised when he received a call in the newsroom from his own version of Deep Throat. The man sounded as if he was suffering from the Sars virus as he tried to disguise his voice.

The informant would only say that he was "a civil servant...a Whitehall insider" but, as leaks went, it was pretty useful. Did Howard know that the consultation committee which considered Baroness Witherspoon's Euthanasia (Assisted Suicide) Bill was heavily loaded with members of the Euthanasia Society? There were no opponents on it."

"Really, not even a token one or two?"

"Not one."

"Who took the decision to exclude them?"

"Who do you think?"

(Click).

Howard recalled what William had said about loaded committees. It was time to talk to the redoubtable Baroness.

When he telephoned her on her unlisted home number she was ready for him. Someone had obviously tipped her off. She was far too busy to see representatives of the reactionary (that word again) Press. She was due to go on holiday shortly to the Maldives and in the meantime the pressures of her Parliamentary duties left not a single window in her appointments diary.

Howard sympathised. He understood the pressures on high-profile politicians. If she could just spare him a few minutes now they'd made contact.

"Very well, but keep it brief and off the record. Do you agree?"

He had no option. "OK. About your Euthanasia Bill…do you expect it to become law in the next session?"

"I don't see why not. No doubt your vocal pro-life friends will do their best to sabotage it but we're used to that."

Howard let it pass. "I understand there are concerns over the short time allowed for opponents to lodge objections to the parliamentary committee."

"They've got until September 1st, that's over a month."

"But most parliamentarians and civil servants will be on holiday throughout the August recess. Isn't the September deadline effectively a guillotine device?"

"There's no question of any guillotine."

"You're perceived as rushing the Bill through, all the same. Critics claim that proposals for deliberate starvation, dehydration and neglect of disabled people are too controversial for the fast-track treatment."

"You're using typically emotive terminology, Howard. There's already been a full consultation process."

Then he played his ace. "As I understand it, Baroness, the consultation committee was heavily loaded with members of the Euthanasia Society. There were no opponents on it. Who took the decision to exclude them?"

There was a slight pause. "I don't know where you get your information from. At no time was a decision taken to exclude them. Pro-life groups were co-opted to the committee at a later stage."

"How much later?"

A longer pause. "About six months, I think."

"Why weren't they appointed in the first place?"

A much longer pause. "There were administrative problems. It was not possible in terms of time and resources for officials to contact them."

It sounded horribly lame and they both knew it. Howard pressed on about widespread concern among disabled people over lack of safeguards in the proposed legislation.

The Baroness sounded indignant. "My Bill contains numerous important safeguards; the disabled may be assured of that."

"Yet they're saying they're increasingly frightened to go into hospital because of the euthanasia campaign."

"If that's true then it's entirely down to the alarmist tactics of papers like yours. Anything else? I'm a very busy woman."

"Just one more question, Baroness. A reliable source claims a secret Right-wing think-tank is preparing a policy of eugenics in this country – through compulsory abortion and euthanasia for the poor. In other words, population control by the back door. It's code-named Tina. Do you know anything about that?"

"First I've heard of it. If I asked who your mysterious source was you wouldn't tell me would you?"

"You know I can't do that. Journalistic ethics."

"Then why should I tell you anything?"

"Because I'm asking in the public interest."

"I believe what I'm doing is also in the public interest. Now if you'll excuse me, I really must go. Thanks for your call."

"Thanks for your help, Baroness," Howard said.

But the line was already dead.

*   *   *

It had not been a good day for Marcus C Quinn III, the contraceptive pill mega-millionaire. He had spent most of it trying to extricate a large and painful thorn from his side in the shape of a greedy television producer. The guy had been on the IPI payroll ever since the firm's market researchers discovered a correlation between sales of their morning-after pills and explicit TV sex the night before.

Certain enterprising television executives had been quick to catch on, demanding the sort of sweetener they claimed some condom companies had handed out for years to ensure every drama contained its quota of 'adult scenes', however gratuitous. No-one, not even the most dedicated clean-up TV fanatic, had ever twigged the real reason why there was so much sex on television.

Anyway, to cut a long and rather grubby story short, this particular producer was giving him a hard time by demanding the sort of raise he must have known was impossible. Everyone knew the score and not to rock the boat, or rather derail the gravy train. The schmuck had gotten greedy and Quinn had told him so.

"No rise, no steamy sex scenes," the producer had threatened but Quinn refused to be railroaded. The guy was getting on. Younger executives were coming through who were so keen on the 'safe sex' myth they'd do the job for nothing. Once Tina took control, IPI would hit the jackpot anyway. They wouldn't need TV sex to stimulate sales any more.

So the IPI tycoon was not best pleased when Baroness Witherspoon phoned him to report Howard's call. "You didn't tell Mr Mitchell anything, of course?" he said when the Baroness paused for breath.

"Of course not, Marcus. He's just digging, hoping he'll find something. He suspects there's a secret think-tank plotting state population control by the back door, as he puts it, but that's as far as it goes."

"That's far enough. Did he mention Tina by name?"

"Yes, I was quite shocked. He quoted a reliable source."

"They always do, even when they don't have one."

"I just told him what's already common knowledge about my Bill. It was all off the record anyway."

"That doesn't always protect you, Your Ladyship. It might be wise not to talk to *The Announcer* again. Confine your interviews to our compliant friends in the media."

"If you say so, Marcus."

"When he finds he's getting nowhere, he'll put it down to another conspiracy theory."

The Powers that be

"Conspiracy theory. That's what they all say when they're up to something. Works like a charm." Bernard Baxter, the veteran news sub was sharing the late shift again with Howard. Although Howard was on special assignment, he couldn't escape the graveyard shift every four weeks.

"It's the parrot cry of every crook and political shyster in this mendacious world of ours." Like most Liverpudlians, Bernard could wax lyrical with the best, especially when 'relaxed' after a long supper break in the Dog and Partridge. "I'll bet Nixon and his cronies used the phrase a few times when Woodward and Bernstein were sorting them out. That and 'witch-hunt'. Whenever you're getting close to the truth you can be sure someone will cry 'conspiracy theory' and accuse you of pursuing a witch-hunt. That's when you really sit up and take notice."

The two journalists were alone in the vast newsroom, reclining in laid-back mode with their feet on the news desk and drinking coffee from the vending machine. It was 2.30 am and, after a late-breaking story about a jail rooftop demo in the edition area, which Howard wrote and Bernard subbed, the third edition had finally gone to press.

Howard completed his late check calls and closed his notebook. PA, Reuters and UPI had nothing on screen. All quiet. Bernard wanted to know how his colleague's investigation was progressing so Howard updated him on his conversation with Baroness Witherspoon.

"The ruling class," Bernard declared contemptuously. "Bribery and corruption are rife in this country and it's all due to the example handed down from the top. They get away with murder."

Tell me about it, Howard thought. They had taken out William with the greatest of ease. He didn't mention this to Bernard. There were limits to what he could reveal even to fellow hacks at this stage.

"What amazes me is the gullibility of the people," Bernard continued. "The ordinary man in the street never sees through them. You know why? Patriotism…the ludicrous Honours system…play your cards right and they might give you an OBE. The empire doesn't exist, for God's sake. They should rename it the ONEBE – the Order of the Non-Existent British Empire!"

Bernard was well into his stride. "I mean, it's a joke...yet the public never catches on. Any system that awards a knighthood to a rock musician, for example, has got to be a laughing stock."

"I take it you don't support the paper's line then?" Howard asked disingenuously.

"All that *Land of Hope and Gory* stuff, you mean? You've got to be kidding. After bleeding us dry with taxes all our lives...why should we feel loyal to them?"

"Good question."

"Who are *they* anyway? No-one seems to know any more. Who are they, Howard...'The Powers that be?' Who's running the country?"

Howard drained his plastic cup and threw it in a waste bin. "Search me. Obviously it's not the Queen."

"Obviously. 'There are powers at work in this country about which we have no knowledge'." Bernard, adopting a plummy accent, intoned the immortal words that had shaken the nation some months earlier.

"What about the Four Estates...the Lords Spiritual, the Lords Temporal, the Commons and the Press?"

"Right, let's take the Lords for a start. The Lords Spiritual have always been a joke. They represent a church founded by a serial killer, adulterer and divorcee...and now hopelessly split over priestesses and gay bishops." He took a swig of his coffee. "Which church has the highest number of practising members in this country?"

"I believe it's the Catholics."

"Correct. By a long way. Yet there isn't a single Catholic among the Lords Spiritual. Twenty-six Anglican bishops and archbishops but not one Catholic! That's why they're just a joke. Then there's the Lords Temporal. You'd think they'd have some influence in our strictly secular society but since the hereditaries – the real parasites – have been kicked out, they're on the verge of extinction. Those that are left are too terrified of further purges to upset any apple-carts. They know they're an endangered species – like the fox-hunting Hooray Henries, a species nobody will be sorry to lose.

"Then there's the Commons. No-one seriously believes that MPs have any power. Fifty years ago, maybe. But the world has moved on. Nowadays they're just clones of the party leaders...programmed by the chief whips. They're told what they're allowed to think and what they're not. If they step out of line, bang goes their nice little earner. Not that they actually *earn* their money. They don't even turn up half the time… why bother when you still get paid?"

"And their exes put ours in the shade!"

"Too right. Plus all the foreign freebies and diplomatic junketings. At the end of the day, the Commons is nothing more than a talking shop for political puppets, overgrown public schoolboys, free-loaders and faggots."

"They're not all gay, Bernard."

"Most of them are – either that or serial adulterers. That leaves us… the Press. Some of us – *The Guardian* for example – like to think we have an input but we're deluding ourselves. We're just hacks who write on the backs of advertisements…for aristocrats who regard us as naff riff-raff. They'd get rid of us tomorrow if it wasn't for the union."

Howard laughed. He knew all about the rumours of redundancies but someone would have to churn out the four editions a night. "Who'd do the work then?"

"Non-union hacks, of course. For half the wages. The nobility's nephews and nieces…your Tarquins and Sebastians, your Amandas and Jemimas…anyone who can operate a computer. You don't need journalists these days, all you need are glorified computer operators."

Howard looked at his watch and grinned. You had to hand it to Bernard once he was in full flow. "So much for the Four Estates. You've managed to write them off in less than four minutes. What about the Cabinet?"

The elderly sub laughed. "Stooges of the Prime Minister, as you're well aware. Ventriloquist's dummies. Take the Foreign Secretary, for example. He even *looks* like a dummy. At least the ventriloquist himself has some power but basically he's in the pocket of America and the CIA."

"So who *is* running the country – apart from America? Big Business?"

"Close."

"MI5?"

"Closer…but still no cigar."

"Who then?"

Bernard took his feet off the desk, bent down and slowly rolled up a trouser leg.

Howard watched him, fascinated. "Don't tell me you're one of *them!*"

"Course not. I'm a Catholic. We're not allowed to join. Not that we'd want to. We've got better things to do in our aprons – like washing up!"

He unrolled his trouser leg and resumed his laid-back position. "Have you read *Inside The Brotherhood*, Howard?"

"Of course. Required reading for every journalist."

"What did you think of it?"

"One of the most important books ever written."

"Opens your eyes, doesn't it. Everyone used to think they were a bunch of overgrown Boy Scouts. Must admit I did myself. Took them at face value. Forty years in journalism and I still didn't know my arse from my elbow."

"So you think these privileged plonkers are running the country?"

"Absolutely. Like it or not, they're effectively the secret police. And I'll tell you something else. They hate Catholics. We're their sworn enemies."

"I'm not surprised – if they're all like you!"

Bernard's well-filled frame shook with laughter. "*Touché, mon ami.*"

"Let's suppose," Howard went on, "for the sake of argument...that *another* secret organisation were to link up with the Brothers...use them for ulterior motives. What would be the chances of sussing them out?"

"Nil."

"As high as that?"

Bernard laughed again. "Sounds like the ultimate unholy partnership to me. The Boaz brigade are bad enough on their own."

Howard recalled William's words: "Tina is virtually impregnable. I know you will regard this mission as a challenge."

Some challenge!

Exaltation

The lone magpie strutted across Edgar's patch of lawn as he watched from the conservatory. He had been anxiously counting young tomatoes on the vines now arching across the confined, overheated space and had totalled two fewer than the previous day. This was worrying. Janice wouldn't have taken them. She didn't like tomatoes. And anyway they were barely ripe. He was about to repeat the process when the magpie appeared.

One for sorrow. Edgar waited patiently for its mate to arrive so he could get on with his counting. Nothing. The magpie stopped and began pecking viciously at the immaculate surface. He rapped on the glass and it flew off. Uneasily, he resumed his audit and this time counted three fewer than before. He gave it up. He must have miscounted and it was too hot to try again.

As he settled in the lounge with *The Announcer's* quick crossword (the cryptic one invariably baffled him), Janice popped her head round the door. Was there anything he wanted from the Co-op?

Could she get some more tomato fertiliser?

She snorted and was gone.

Even the quick crossword could be a swine. He cast it aside. It was obviously going to be another of those days. He was nodding off when the telephone next to his armchair rang and startled him. Still with a vague sense of foreboding, he picked it up.

"Hello."

"Is this Mr Ed Brierley?" asked an educated American voice.

Edgar had been taught to be cautious. "Who's calling?"

"My name's Quinn. Marcus Quinn. I'm Chief Executive Officer of International Pharmaceuticals UK. Is this Mr Ed Brierley?"

"Speaking." Edgar was wide awake now.

"I understand that you are unhappy with our proposals to develop The Meadow, Mr Brierley, and I wondered if it would be possible to meet with you."

That was putting it mildly. Edgar was totally brassed off with IPI and felt like saying so but discretion got the better of him. Perhaps they were going to call the whole thing off and build their factory elsewhere. It would do no harm to find out. "What is it about?" he asked suspiciously.

"It's too important to discuss on the phone. When would it be convenient to meet with you?"

"Well, anytime really...except mornings. I work nights."

"I know, Mr Brierley. You have a prestigious job. We wouldn't want to interfere with that."

That sounded slightly more promising, Edgar thought. The next day was his day off. "I could see you tomorrow afternoon if you like."

"That would be swell. Say about 2 pm?"

"OK. Where?"

"What about Brawton Temple...would that be within your compass?"

Edgar got the message.

"I'll be there."

*   *   *

When Edgar drove into the Lodge car park the first thing he noticed was a dark green Rolls-Royce Silver Cloud occupying almost two spaces next to the gate. You couldn't really miss it. Unashamed and oblivious to the incongruity, he parked his battered Proton alongside and peered inside at the leather and walnut opulence.

It was the sort of car you would buy only in your dreams, after winning the Lottery. For a moment, he pictured himself and Janice reclining in the back sipping champagne, Janice in a large chiffon hat, as a liveried chauffeur drove them to Ascot – before the vision faded and left him with a slight headache.

It could only be Marcus Quinn's car. Even as the realisation took hold, he refused to be intimidated. This was his Lodge. He was the Worshipful Master. He could have Quinn thrown out if he felt like it, brother Mason or not.

The American was waiting at the bar. He was a large, fleshy middle-aged man with close-cropped grey hair, heavy jowls, small mouth and eyes too close together. They exchanged a Masonic handshake. "I'm honoured to meet you, sir, especially during your term of high office."

They sat with their drinks at a table in a recess even darker than the rest of the gloomy mausoleum, Quinn wearing an immaculate, grey double-breasted suit, hand tailored white shirt and dark blue silk tie, Edgar in jeans and T-shirt. It was the Rolls and the Proton all over again.

After more pleasantries involving various arcane code words, the oddly matched pair got down to business. "We've heard about your unfortunate experience at the Town Hall and I want you to know that we do sympathise," Quinn began. "As Chief Executive at IPI, I'd like to try and make amends. I can tell you, strictly between ourselves, that we're prepared to offer you the full market value of your house in…" he consulted a small notebook…"Meadow Drive, whenever you and your good lady are ready to vacate the property."

The offer was what Edgar had been half-expecting all along but he knew it would cut no ice with his 'good lady'. She had made it abundantly clear she wasn't going anywhere. It was the factory that would have to move, not her. This was a scenario which Edgar now realised – not that he'd ever been in much doubt – was as remote as the prospect of him scoring a century break at snooker.

"It's not about money, Brother Quinn. I'd accept your offer but my wife…she's already had one heart attack. She's determined to stay put. If she was forced to move…well, it might kill her."

Quinn downed his Scotch on the rocks in one go and ordered another. "I appreciate your dilemma, Worshipful Master. We must take care of the ladies, God bless 'em. But the deal doesn't end there. I'm mindful of the stress and inconvenience all this has caused a distinguished brother and, by way of recompense, I'd like to put your name forward for exaltation to the Royal Arch."

Even in the aftermath of *Inside The Brotherhood*, many Freemasons still believed the Third Degree of Master Mason was the highest they could attain – blissfully unaware of 'chapters' that reached as high as the 33rd Degree. But Edgar knew all about the Royal Arch. It was impossible to work in a newspaper environment and not be aware of the elitist order that included titled aristocrats, used human skulls in its initiation rituals and addressed God by His secret name of 'Jahbulon'. Never in his wildest dreams did he imagine he could aspire to its ranks.

For a moment he was gobsmacked. His hand shook slightly as he reached for his half of lager. Edgar Brierley, Head Messenger at *The Announcer*, on equal terms with *real* VIPs, not small-time shopkeepers, coppers' narks and town hall nobodies…rubbing shoulders with peers of the realm, perhaps even with His Lordship, the paper's proprietor. That would shake Arnold Hicks and the rest of the Brothers who'd deserted him in his hour of need. The prospect was so dazzling it brought on his headache again. Then he came back down to earth. There had to be a catch.

He cleared his throat nervously. "I'm deeply honoured, Brother Quinn, but what do you want in return?"

The American raised the second Scotch to his lips, drained it, chips of ice and all, and signalled to the barman for another. Drink-drive laws were for lesser mortals who drove lesser automobiles. "As it happens, there is one small thing you could do for us," he said, drying the rat-trap mouth on a linen handkerchief from his breast pocket. "As part of your important work at *The Announcer*, we'd like you to keep an eye on one of its reporters, keep us posted on his performance…who he speaks to…that sort of thing."

Edgar had been right. Intrigue was involved. But then, he was no stranger to that. "Which reporter?" he asked, knowing already who it would be.

"Mr Howard Mitchell."

Right again. They wanted inside information on Howard's ongoing investigation into population control. Edgar had read most of the printouts and could provide them with a great deal of valuable material. But somehow the idea of spying on Howard seemed repugnant – after all the patient snooker tuition the journalist had given him.

"I'll have to think about it."

"Sure. But we can't keep the offer open for long. Talk to your good lady. Think about the fellowship of the Holy Royal Arch and its unique benefits. I'm privileged to enjoy Grand rank so there'd be absolutely no problem. One word from me and you're as good as exalted." He handed Edgar his business card. "That's my direct line. Call me. Soon."

＊　　　＊　　　＊

"Daddy, why do boy sparrows have black bibs?"

Howard was reclining on his sun lounger by the hotel pool, gazing at a solitary, picture-book white cloud in an azure sky when Sally ran up in her swimsuit and posed the question.

"Because they're messy eaters."

His daughter turned to Christopher who had followed her, wearing shorts and a Crystal Palace shirt with the name Mitchell emblazoned across the back. "See, I told you."

"Why are there so many sparrows in Mijas?" Christopher wanted to know. "Have they all come from England?"

"I expect so," Howard replied. "The food must be better here."

The pair ran off, laughing. They had obviously read about the disappearing English sparrows. "Missing sparrows traced to Costa del Sol," he murmured to Barbara, lying alongside. "How about that for a foreign page headline? It is August after all – the silly season."

"Don't you ever forget about newspapers?" she said, without looking up from her murder mystery.

Well, no he didn't. Not for long. Even relaxing on holiday at their four star hotel, bathed in constant sunshine and surrounded by bikini-clad distractions, not least the one turning a delicate shade of pink next to him, his thoughts kept straying to the strangest assignment he had ever undertaken.

At this distance from *The Announcer* office, with poolside laughter, shouts and splashing filling the warm air, the notion of sinister forces bent on imposing population control in Britain seemed totally bizarre. Perhaps Andrew was right and it was just a conspiracy theory put about by reactionaries and Catholics. Ninety-five per cent of conspiracy theories were unfounded. He accepted that. Every journalist did.

And yet...and yet. The nagging thought kept returning. *Five per cent weren't.*

He turned on his side, dozed off and dreamt about sparrows.

*   *   *

Whether it was his pool-side siesta or the effects of the sangria at dinner, sleep was the last thing on Howard's mind that evening. Nightfall on the Costa can be a magical experience. The brilliance of the stars, the balmy stillness of the air and the overwhelming fragrance of honeysuckle and bougainvillea wafting across their balcony lent their erotic suggestiveness to the evening. There was even a guitar strumming somewhere.

Less subtle was the impulse to explore the intriguing white triangular patches left by Barbara's bikini on her stunning body as she stepped out of the shower, still drying her blonde locks. She was in no hurry to put on her wrap, it seemed. Any doubt about her message was instantly dispelled when she looked across the bed at him and smiled her irresistible smile. There was no mistaking the signal in the lustrous green eyes. It was green for go.

For a time afterwards, as they lay side by side with the ceiling fan adding a further blissful dimension to the relaxed after-glow, the only word the wordsmith could think of was 'Wow'. This was as good as it gets. For some reason, he recalled *Make it Happy,* the book advocating a full range of sexual perversions short of animal coupling and labelled those who opposed them 'old-fashioned killjoys'. Well, old-fashioned normal sex had certainly made *him* happy. He couldn't be happier.

He and Barbara had something going between them which the sad sexual 'reformers' would never understand. What was this mysterious, metaphysical quality? Well, love actually. A coupling involving body and soul. And it was the soul that made the difference. If you didn't believe in the human soul you didn't know what you were missing when it came to sex. You were to be pitied. Like poor Justine Harvey-Ozgood, who had exclaimed to him: "Love...what does it mean?" Well, now he knew.

Or did he? He turned to his Special Adviser, now dozing naked and delightfully dishevelled alongside. "Have I improved?"

She stirred and looked at him through half-closed eyes. "You can't improve on perfection."

He kissed her gently. "What does love mean, Barbara?"

"Oh no, not more philosophy," she said sleepily.

"Does it mean sentiment, physical attraction, lust...is it a phase you go through?"

She opened her eyes, now a darker but still smouldering shade of green. "Well, if it's a phase, it's been a helluva long one in our case. You're not going off me are you?"

He laughed and gave her a squeeze. "What do you think? No, I'm just remembering what a certain feminist told me some time ago."

"Who was she?"

"Justine Harvey-Ozgood."

Barbara kissed him lightly on the cheek and sat up, the horizontal white line across her slender back contrasting with the pink, now turning to light brown, of her skin. "I know who you mean. She's probably like most feminists…"

"Embittered?"

"Yes, but there's usually a reason. Women love more emotionally than men. Sometimes, if they have been deeply hurt in their youth, say in a broken relationship, they can carry the scars for life. They never lose their sense of loss. They just carry on grieving. Their lives become unfulfilled and barren. They turn elsewhere for fulfilment, in her case to feminism."

"And abortion…she also runs abortion clinics."

"That says it all, really. There must be acute pain there, so bad that she feels the need to deprive other women of their babies…because she has none herself."

"Tragic, really."

"Desperately. You should feel sorry for her – for all feminists. They're embittered because nobody loves them."

"But what *is* love? We're back to that."

Barbara turned on an elbow and her look, he thought, was love itself. "What do you think it is?"

"I think love is caring for someone the same as you care for yourself."

"It goes deeper than that. It's caring for someone *more* than you care for yourself. I'll give you an example. In my hospital, we've got a patient who's been in a semi-coma for 40 years. He's called Thomas. Every day his wife still visits him. Her name's Bridget. She's seventy-one and he's seventy-four. He suffered severe brain damage when he was hit by a car.

"He was in a full coma for months but then came out of it. But he still can't walk or speak and some days he doesn't even recognise Bridget. But every day *for forty years* she's come to see her husband. She's devoted to him. That's what you call *real* love…in sickness and in health, for better or for worse…"

Howard was moved by the story of Bridget and Thomas. It was the perfect answer to Justine Harvey-Ozgood's petulant outburst. But she would never understand it.

"It's selflessness, really, isn't it?"

"That's right, darling. Putting someone else before yourself."

He thought some more. "Like we do for each other...and for Sally and Christopher?"

"Yes, and number three."

"Number three?" he said blankly, though his heart had skipped a beat. She kissed him again and this time her smile was sublime. "That's right. I'm pregnant."

A Rock and a hard man

Howard surveyed the main course artistically arranged before him: roasted pigeon and truffled eggs in a puree of capers and raisins with bread sauce, braised leeks, sautéed potatoes and a rich red wine jus…and suddenly felt an overpowering longing for a plate of egg and chips. After ten days of hotel cuisine, he almost wished he was back in *The Announcer* canteen sampling one of Mervyn's unpretentious specials. It was time for a day trip to Gibraltar.

"It's like going back home for a day," Howard explained to his family as he drove their hired Seat through Fuengirola and out along the coast road towards Marbella and the distant Rock. "Everything's British – the pubs, the banks, the shops, the telephone boxes, even the police – everything except the climate."

By the time they had sped through Estepona and downtown La Linea they'd drunk all their bottled water and the heat was stifling. Then, as they neared the towering lump of limestone they were forced to wait in a long line of traffic at the airport checkpoint while a plane landed (the runway at Gibraltar bisects the High Street). Howard was gasping for a pint of real bitter when they finally made it to a typically English pub. Even Barbara abandoned her usual red wine and soda for a glass of lager and lime as they sat in a shady corner, safe from the scorching sun.

Christopher and Sally wanted to take the cable car to the summit and see the Barbary apes, said to preside over British rule on the Rock. Howard had bought yesterday's issue of *The Announcer* and was happy to stay where he was so Barbara donned her wide brimmed sun hat and took charge of the expedition.

Her husband relaxed with his pint and studied the newspaper. Nothing much had changed in the world. Israeli tanks were still keeping busy. Bird flu fears grow. UK deports terror suspects. Global warming blamed as thousands die in French heat-wave. Policemen accused of child pornography. Gay bishop row splits Anglican church. Grouse season reopens in Britain. (His Lordship would be pleased).

Howard studied the paper from cover to cover. It was the first British newspaper he had seen for nearly two weeks. When he had finished with the features and sports sections, he turned idly to the cryptic crossword. William had assured him it was getting easier but it took almost ten minutes to solve the first clue:

Mirth from lady drinking vermouth (8)…Answer: Hilarity;

He followed up this success with:
Bill is cut short, strange to tell (8)   Answer: Acquaint;

Another, involving an anagram:
But lira was exchanged about noon in court (8).
Answer: Tribunal;

and:
Exclude copper with well-dressed person
(two words, 3 and 3)   Answer: Cut off.

By the time he completed half the puzzle and was beginning to fathom the tortuous mind of its compiler, he realised almost two hours had elapsed since the departure of Barbara and the children. He had made his pint last all that time. He strolled to the bar and ordered another. It would be evening before he drove back to Mijas.

The pub had a restaurant attached and he studied the menu. Sure enough there it was, halfway down: Egg and chips. Better still: Sausage, egg and chips. All meals served with tea and bread and butter. When Barbara came back with the children they'd sample this ambrosia.

He was about to return to his shady nook when the face of a tall, well built man standing at the bar struck him as familiar. Howard wasn't too good with names but, like his friend Bernard, he rarely forgot a face. He found himself staring at the man, feeling an eerie sense of *déjà vu*. The face was definitely familiar but there was something fundamentally different about him. Then everything clicked into place. The man was dressed in casual slacks, T-shirt and trainers. The last time they'd met he'd been wearing police uniform.

He went over and introduced himself. "Hi, sergeant. Howard Mitchell, from *The Announcer*. Small world eh?"

Peter Scott looked startled but recovered quickly. "Hello, Mr Mitchell. You've finally tracked me down then."

Although the meeting had been a pure fluke, Howard saw no reason to say so. "Long arm of the Press, sergeant. What are you drinking?"

"Newcastle brown. And it's Inspector now."

Howard ordered him another. "Congratulations on your promotion. So this is where they've hidden you. The Royal Gibraltar Police. Cute, I must admit. At least you've got all the comforts of home here. Brought the family with you?"

"Yep."

"Strict orders not to say anything, I suppose?"

"'Fraid so, Mr Mitchell."

"Especially about car tyres."

"What car tyres?"

"Ah yes, I forgot. They changed the one with the hole in it, didn't they?"

The inspector drained his glass and pulled the fresh one towards him. "What hole?"

Howard grinned. "I understand. Official Secrets Act and all that. Ever have any contact with Sir William's family? I know Dominic, his son, was keen to meet you."

"No. Never met any of them."

"That's easily remedied. I'll have to update Dominic on your whereabouts now, you know."

"Don't threaten me, Mr Mitchell. If Dominic, or any other member of his family, came out here, I'd tell them the same thing: exactly nothing. There's nothing to tell."

"Sir William was a brave man. You said that yourself...the way he steered clear of other vehicles when his tyre blew."

"Very true. Could have been a mass pile-up."

"Surely he deserves better than this...this cowardly cover-up?"

Scott took a swig of his brown ale and turned to face his interlocutor. There was controlled anger in his eyes and his face had turned slightly florid. "I'm no coward, mate. I've got three commendations for bravery plus the Queen's Police Medal. Sir William's dead. Nothing we can do will bring him back. I'm keeping quiet because I know what's good for me and my family. Strictly between ourselves, you should do the same."

"No way."

"You don't know what you're up against."

"I've a good idea."

"You're looking at very big people. They're on the square…untouchable. You'll never expose them. They'll hang you out to dry first."

Howard smiled. "Nobody hangs *The Announcer* out to dry. You underestimate the power of the Press."

The inspector wagged a finger in Howard's face. "You'll never win… never in a million years."

"That's fighting talk, sergeant."

"Inspector." He took a deep breath and pulled himself together. "Thanks for the drink, Mr Mitchell. But I really shouldn't be seen talking to you. Give my love to London and my 'friends' at the Met." He set off for the door.

"The bigger they are, the harder they fall, you know," Howard called after him.

The burly figure checked and turned. "Just make sure they don't fall on *you*." And he was gone.

Moments later Barbara and the children appeared. "Who was that man you were talking to?" his wife wanted to know.

"Just a contact."

Her eyebrows arched incredulously. "Out here, in Gibraltar?"

"You know me…contacts everywhere."

"So that's why you brought us here."

"Don't you believe it, darling. Take a look at this menu. We've come here for a proper lunch."

Losing contact

The newsroom thermometer read 20°C but Howard, now deeply suntanned, felt cold. It was still summer in England but the cold had hit him the moment they'd got off the plane at Heathrow. It had been late at night and a chill breeze had gone right through his lightweight holiday clothes. Still, it was always good to come home – even sitting at the news desk alongside Andrew.

The news editor was lounging in his usual languid style while scanning the final editions of that morning's newspapers. He was much amused by a silly season tabloid story about an obscure religious sect prophesying the end of the world. Dressed in white robes, they had assembled on the mid-wicket boundary at Trent Bridge, where an important Test match was in progress. They waved banners proclaiming 'The end is nigh' and 'Prepare for Armageddon'.

Andrew guffawed as he read about the efforts of the police in trying to restrain them from invading the pitch. "It's not cricket is it, old chap?" he asked Howard.

"Makes a change from streakers. What's the score?"

"England are 360 for four. We're in danger of winning."

"That *would* be the end of the world."

"Armageddon," cried the journalist nicknamed "the moron" as he turned to the page three girl. "Armageddon a hard-on!"

Howard grimaced. Now I know I'm back, he thought.

He needed to pick up the threads of the population control campaign and first off was a call to Dominic Greaves to tell him about his chance meeting with Inspector Scott in Gib. He unlocked his drawer and reached for his contacts book.

It wasn't there.

He opened the drawer wider and rummaged through the contents. Notebooks, printouts, pads of copy paper, *Announcer* stylebook, cuttings, photos from old stories, ballpoints, envelopes, rubber bands, glue, paper clips, string, scissors, ruler, his tea mug, headache tablets, a small cube of snooker chalk…they were all as he'd left them. Panicking, he leafed through his stored copies of the *Journalist* and was mightily relieved to find William's letter still concealed among them. But of his irreplaceable contacts book, the work of so many years' painstaking compilation, there was no trace. No longer cold but sweating slightly, he checked through it all again. Zilch.

"Andrew, have you seen my contacts book?"

His still chortling chief looked up. "What?"

"My contacts book. It's gone. You've not seen it, have you?"

Andrew cast aside the tabloid titillation and came over. "Course not. I don't have a key to your drawer. Are you sure it's not there?"

"Positive. See for yourself." He pulled the drawer out of its sockets and placed it on his desk.

Andrew stared at it and scratched his stubble. He inspected the drawer itself. "Not broken into. They obviously had a key. Are you sure you left the book in there?"

"Quite sure."

"And locked the drawer?"

"As always."

"Anything else taken?"

"No, I've checked."

"This is serious. Better tell the Editor."

"Whoever took it had a key – and knew what they were looking for," Howard said when he and Andrew conferred with Julian in his office later. "But they missed William's letter."

"Well that's something, I suppose," the Editor said. "Have you warned everyone?"

"Yes, I've e-mailed them all."

"There's going to be a lot of worried people around. They'll give you the cold shoulder for a while."

"They usually do anyway."

Julian grinned. The tension ratcheted down a notch. "Any duplicate keys to the drawer?"

"Only one. I keep it at home."

"Is it still there?"

"Yes, I phoned Barbara."

"You wonder about the security people," Andrew put in. "They have keys to everywhere."

"But not to reporters' drawers, Andrew. Have there been any other thefts from the office?"

"None that I know of."

Julian stood up abruptly, went to his wall safe and tapped in the combination known only to himself. He checked that everything was in order and closed the heavy door. "Right," he said decisively. "I'll have all the locks changed immediately on reporters' and sub-editors' drawers. Better let me have William's letter too, Howard. They've missed it this time, let's not give them another chance."

"Who do you think 'they' are, Julian," Andrew asked with only the slightest trace of scepticism.

"Spooks. Who else? Conspiracy theory starting to stand up would you say, Andrew?"

*   *   *

Next day's *Announcer* carried front page stories on the schism in the Anglican church over gay clergy and another householder charged with assaulting a burglar, but the real eye-opener was a report that the Department for Work and Pensions was proposing to crack down on incapacity benefit. Recent figures had shown a steep rise in people claiming the handout and fears had been voiced that they might not all be genuine.

The Department had commissioned a 'task force' to review eligibility to the benefit after preliminary investigations had suggested the system was open to widespread abuse. Howard felt a frisson of *déjà vu* as he read the report. Another of William's predictions had slotted neatly into place. Tina was beginning to emerge from the shadows.

On an inside page *The Announcer* carried a brief summary of a conference held in Oxford the previous day and attended by liberal establishment clones from Britain, the USA and Europe. The carefully trimmed beards and neat ponytails of the men and close-cropped heads of the assertive, self-important women were captured in a four-column picture alongside a smaller picture of shaven headed, tattooed gentlemen thought to be BNP members and described by the organisers as gate-crashers.

The theme had been one of universal happiness to be achieved through global population management. Stalls in the foyer featured blown-up photographs of happy people and even happier animals. Somehow, even the whales looked happy.

Justine Harvey-Ozgood was the main speaker. The world's food supplies were being threatened, the well-fed columnist and abortionist declared. Oilfields were drying up. Fish stocks were dwindling. Energy levels were failing to match increased demand. Transport systems were breaking down. Hospital waiting lists grew longer each year. The world was rapidly approaching a Doomsday scenario, she added happily.

In Britain, our housing and welfare systems could no longer cope with homeless families, single mothers and their spiralling benefit claims. Chaos and confusion were rife. Our beloved islands were bursting at the seams. There were simply too many people. We had to be realistic. The nation's population needed to be progressively reduced to 45 million by the middle of next century. Unpalatable measures would be necessary to achieve this Utopian objective. She did not elaborate. It would only have spoilt the party.

Another speaker, a popular TV wildlife broadcaster, welcomed her concerns for the environment. Her principled stance would "save the planet" and protect such endangered species as the North African salamander and the South American web-footed river turtle.

*　　　*　　　*

The theft of Howard's contacts book caused only a slight hiccup in *The Announcer's* crusade to unmask the mysterious Tina. When he was finally able to tell Dominic Greaves of his chance meeting with Inspector Scott in Gibraltar, the son of the former whistle-blower was momentarily lost for words.

"What a breakthrough, Howard," he was finally able to say. "Now I can take a trip to Gibraltar myself…sort the guy out. What do you think?"

"You could try. But I really don't advise it, Dominic. He's taken a vow of silence when it comes to all mention of car tyres. He's the personification of omerta. The Mafia would be proud of him."

"I'd be prepared to pay, you know…to persuade him."

"That could be a bit dodgy…offering a policeman money."

"But it wouldn't be bribery, would it? It would be for telling the truth, not covering it up."

"It's up to you, Dominic. Let me know what you decide."

"I'll discuss it with the family. It just seems like our only hope. We've heard nothing more about an inquest. Whenever we make inquiries all doors are closed in our face. No-one knows anything."

"Tell me about it. Coroners aren't the brightest people. It can take years to wake them up."

"If only we knew what really happened...and why. It would help us come to terms with Dad's death. Why should anyone want to kill him? He was just a Treasury adviser."

Howard felt a little enlightenment was called for. "He was doing very valuable work, Dominic. He was operating under cover and that's always dangerous."

"How do you mean, under cover?"

"Did your father ever say anything about population control?"

"Population control? No, nothing. Dad never discussed his work with us. We knew he was involved in top-secret government business. But we'd no idea it had anything to do with population control. What's going on, Howard? We have a right to know."

"I accept that, Dominic. All I can tell you at present is that moves are afoot to restrict the number of social security claimants in Britain..."

"Asylum seekers, you mean?"

"No, the poor in general. Some very powerful people want to stop them breeding – to halt the drain on the national economy."

"Sounds rather sinister."

"Believe me, it is. We particularly need to know the name of their director, their Mr Big...an internationally famous VIP. It seems your father knew – and he paid the price. I don't suppose he gave you any hints, did he?"

Dominic racked his brains but no name sprang to mind. "Dad moved in high circles, Howard. It could be anyone. He was always flying over to Brussels, if that's any help."

"That's a start. Did you notice anything unusual in the week before he died?"

There was a long silence. "Not really. We did have some strange guests over for tennis at the weekend. Americans. Mother didn't care for them."

"Can you recall any names?"

Dominic thought hard. "Well, there was one. I think it began with a Q... oh yes, Quinn. Mr Marcus Quinn."

An effective method
of birth control

Sweetest little fellow,
Everybody knows,
Don't know what to call him
But he must be one of those...

Andrew was treating the news desk to his own version of an old song *Mighty Like a Rose*. The lyrics had been altered in keeping with a PA story he had on screen about Paul D'Arcy, MP. It seemed Mr D'Arcy had taken issue with the organisers of a House of Commons football match between Labour and the Tories.

Not a single 'gay' had been selected for either side. It was nothing short of blatant discrimination on grounds of sexual orientation, he declared. The teams chosen were not representative of either political party. There were enough gay MPs to make up several football teams. (Probably enough to form their own league, although he didn't say so). He knew of many who would have been happy to turn out. He himself was prepared to play – in goal, of course, he added hastily.

What made it worse was he had written a strong letter to *The Times* about it which they had refused to publish. Even the Race Relations Board had declined to intervene, though why he felt they should was not clear. These responses were symptomatic of the homophobia blighting our society. The time had clearly come when MPs' football teams should include an appropriate quota of homosexual players. Indeed, he proposed that this measure should be extended to *all* football teams, starting with the Premier League to set an example. Minority groups were simply not being represented in sport...

There was a lot more of this drenge cluttering the screen.

"MP calls for gay goalkeepers," chortled Andrew, as Howard looked over his shoulder. "Which poor sod should I send to interview him?"

The MP's name rang the necessary bell for Howard. "I'll go if you like."

"You're on special assignment."

"I need to talk to someone like him. Part of the investigation. This story would give me a good excuse."

"What's he got to do with population control?"

"Well, everything if you think about it. You can't get more effective birth control than sodomy."

"I see what you mean. Go on then."

*   *   *

Like most gay activists, Paul D'Arcy was only too keen to talk to the media. Anyone with a camera, voice recorder or notebook was always welcome in his House of Commons office, whether they be from TV, radio, national newspapers, the *Isle of Man Observer* or *Needlework Weekly*. He wallowed in publicity like a pot-bellied pig in, well, potato peelings.

Of course *The Guardian* and *Independent* were his favourites but his image consultant had advised him that you couldn't afford to be choosy. Howard's telephoned offer of a feature in the up-market *Announcer* magazine had come as a surprise since he had not visualised that publication as a likely vehicle for his particular brand of evangelism. Still, it would be glossy paper and his photograph would reproduce that much better on it.

He had a large selection of expensively-produced studio portraits of himself in various poses, with expressions ranging from deeply studious and caring to arch, jovial and even raunchy, as far as that was possible at over sixteen stone. The consultant had emphatically advised against sitting for Press photographers as their work was often less than flattering.

So Howard was unaccompanied by a snapper on being admitted to the MP's panelled room at the House. D'Arcy extended a flabby hand and they sat on opposite sides of his Georgian, leather-topped desk. The MP was in his late forties or early fifties, it was hard to say. His round face was pale and boyish, with long tinted hair done up in a ponytail. He wore the politicians' uniform of dark lounge suit, stretched tightly over his corpulent figure and, as evidence of limited literary pretensions (he wrote pamphlets on pagan rituals, the infallibility of runes and New Age herbal remedies), a large purple bow tie.

He gave Howard a lubricious smile. "Well now, this is an unexpected pleasure." The voice was a fruity baritone with a patronising edge. "Where shall we start?"

Howard produced his digital recorder. "Do you mind?"

The MP waved a podgy hand. "Not at all, carry on."

"I didn't know you played soccer, Mr D'Arcy."

"Call me Paul. No, I don't of course. Not built for it really. I was just upset that our football teams are so, well…unbalanced if you like. I mean, as I told the Press Association, there are enough gay MPs in the House to make up several football teams, yet not one was selected for either side."

"Perhaps none of them like football. It's a rather rough game, after all."

"Not as rough as rugby. Used to play myself at Winchester, you know."

"You weren't a hooker, were you?"

D'Arcy smiled. "No, I was a prop forward. Pretty useful in the scrums, I can tell you."

Howard could believe it. The mind boggled. But he needed to guide the conversation towards population control. What were the MP's views on the subject, what was the strength of feeling in his party and, above all, what if anything did D'Arcy know about Tina? It had to be done by a process of gentle osmosis. He checked his notebook. "Then you went up to Oxford and gained a second class degree in theology?"

"That's right…wanted to be a priest but I soon grew out of that. Lifestyle too disciplined. I was more of a free spirit."

"Do you believe in God?"

"Not any more. I used to before I became a pagan. Now I regard all mainstream religion as a form of pseudo-science…on a par with UFOs… all that rubbish. How can you believe in God in a world like ours? The wars, the cruelty, the hatred, the wickedness, the suffering? No, I'm what you might call a devout atheist nowadays."

As the professional talker paused for breath, Howard managed to slip another question in edgeways. "So you became a waiter, then an insurance salesman, then a broadcaster, then a writer…"

"That's me. Jack of all trades and master of none, to use a well-worn cliché. Shouldn't use them, I know but I do. My literary agent is always nagging me about it."

The last thing Howard wanted to discuss was D'Arcy's naff literary output. Sensing more waffle, he put in hastily: "What made you become an MP?" He had a good idea what the reply would be...taking on a new challenge in life, desire to serve the public, duty to represent the hopes and aspirations of his constituents. There would be no mention of self-advancement; lavish salaries whether you worked or not; regular opportunities to vote yourself inflation-busting pay rises; fat pensions; tax-free fringe benefits including world travel freebies; sexually compliant secretaries (of either gender), expense accounts to make a tabloid hack blush and holidays beyond the wildest dreams of even the teaching profession.

D'Arcy settled for another cliché. "I suppose you could say it was a desire to put back into society some of the benefits I had taken from it."

Howard studied the 'running order' for the interview, the notes he had hastily scribbled earlier. "You do come from a privileged background, of course. Comfortable middle class home, never had to struggle to make ends meet?"

The MP smirked and offered one of his favourite witticisms. "Nonsense – I've worked my way up from the top to the bottom!"

Returning swiftly to the script, Howard ploughed on: "Yet coming from such stable family roots it seems strange that you have an antipathy towards the family unit yourself. Why is that do you think?"

"If it's strange it's because I'm a queer. I have an unconventional take on the world. I read the papers – even yours sometimes – and I see that most murders are committed within the family circle. So maybe the family unit isn't all it's cracked up to be. It's high time the bias in favour of the heterosexual home was corrected – and that's what I'm trying to do."

The self-professed devout atheist and alternative lifestyle guru rambled on: "In this day and age, when discrimination on the grounds of sexual orientation is supposed to be outlawed at all levels of society, homosexuals should receive equal treatment when it comes to bringing up children. We'd make a damn sight better job of it than you lot, I can assure you."

Somehow, Howard doubted it. But as the vehement tirade had temporarily abated, he jumped in quickly with: "Isn't homosexuality the direct opposite of procreation and fertility? Where would the children come from?"

"We'd adopt them of course…if they'd allow us to."

Somehow, with the best will in the world, Howard couldn't picture D'Arcy as a father figure. "So you're calling for acceptance of homosexual families?"

"Absolutely. My own Private Member's Bill is listed for next month."

"But don't children need a stable home environment? Would such family units be in their best interests? There are so few stable homosexual relationships, after all."

"I know of many."

Howard had mugged up on his statistics. "Fewer than one per cent of all cohabiting couples, I'm afraid. Homosexuality is essentially a promiscuous lifestyle."

"Plenty of children are brought up by single parents these days, why not by a single gay parent?"

"You're right, of course. But there's an unfortunate correlation between children of one-parent families and rising crime. One-parent families are bad news *per se*…nothing to do with sexual orientation."

"Don't kid yourself, Howard. It's all about entrenched prejudice…it's etched in the national psyche. Gays are regarded as pariahs. Well, my Bill will change all that."

There was a pause of about half a second so Howard seized his chance to slip in the key question. "Could I ask you about the perceived connection between homosexuality and population control?"

"Well, the country's bursting at the seams. Something's got to be done. I suppose you could say homosexuality was an infallible method of achieving it. As such, I heartily recommend it," he laughed.

"I don't know whether you've heard but word is going round about an unofficial project to promote enforced population control. Does the name Tina mean anything to you?"

D'Arcy suddenly became preoccupied with the view of Westminster through the dusty leaded windows. The sky had become overcast and a light shower had started. "Tina? No, I don't have girlfriends as such." He was doing his best to be nonchalant, but you could tell he wanted to change the subject. "If what you say is true and they really want effective population control, they should make *buggery* compulsory!"

Howard had to smile. They'd all heard the joke about the Geordie who decided to emigrate to Australia. When asked why, he replied that two-hundred years ago homosexuality was punishable by death. One hundred years ago you were sent to prison for it. Now the government had made it legal. He was leaving before they made it compulsory.

Typical homophobic joke, D'Arcy declared when Howard reminded him of it. The law may have changed but attitudes hadn't. We were supposed to be living in enlightened times yet homosexuals still faced a culture of abuse which, if directed at racial minority groups, would result in criminal prosecutions. "I'm frequently referred to as a poof and a shirt-lifter, for example, which I find grossly offensive."

"Why...isn't that what you do?" Howard asked innocently.

There was, of course, no answer to that. D'Arcy stared balefully at this man who had stormed the citadel of his inflated ego. "Switch it off."

Howard pressed the 'stop' button on the voice recorder.

The MP hauled his gross form out of his chair, crossed to the door and opened it. "Interview concluded," he snapped. The voice had lost its fruity mellifluence.

"I should've known better. Strictly off the record, you're just another hack slavishly plying your newspaper's noxious agenda. Well, you'll never discredit homosexuality. It goes back thousands of years. It's like trying to discredit..." he looked angrily around for inspiration and noticed the light spattering of rain on the windows..."rain".

Howard could take a hint. He pocketed his recorder, pen and notebook. Pausing on his way out, he said: "That's an interesting analogy, Paul. But doesn't rain make the world more fertile – not less?"

The door slammed shut behind him. For all his bulk and bombast, D'Arcy was really a delicate flower at heart. Pity he hadn't given him a photograph.

The backlash

Driving home through the traffic later that night, Howard could not get rid of an uneasy feeling. Something was not right and he couldn't work out what it was. He'd routinely checked the Rover's tyres and petrol filler cap when he'd unlocked the car in the basement car park and placed his laptop in the boot. Nothing had been amiss.

The two-and-a-half litre engine hummed as sweetly as ever as he headed along the A3 towards Wimbledon. When traffic allowed, he checked the brakes. No problems there. The power steering remained finger-tip positive. Gearbox smooth as velvet. Heater and air conditioning all normal. No strange noises. No stowaways lurking in the back. What was he worrying about?

He switched on the radio for the news bulletin. It had been a slow news day and there were no updates on any stories. The Classical channel was dispensing mournful Schubert lieder. He turned it off. He wasn't in the mood for Schubert. There were some jazz CDs somewhere but he couldn't find them.

His thoughts turned to the profile on D'Arcy that he'd just filed for the magazine. The MP's evasive reaction when he'd hinted at the Tina Project had been significant but you couldn't read too much into it. Then there was Dominic Greaves's revelation about his father's unusual tennis guests a few days before he died. William had said Quinn was the only member of Tina who knew its director's identity. Could he have let slip the supremo's name over the Pimms and orange squash? Hence the enigmatic hints in Williams letter?

All Howard's efforts to interview the IPI chief executive had run into the proverbial brick wall. There was still a lot of work to do before he could expect a breakthrough in his quest for Tina's elusive Mr Big. The pointers suggested he was on the track of a mega-scoop but for some reason he couldn't focus his mind on his next moves.

Traffic grew lighter as he drove through Kennington and for a time he concentrated on his offside door mirror as a procession of deranged bikers swooped past, shattering the speed limit. Try as he did to relax, the feeling that something was wrong would not go away. It was a pure gut feeling. *Something* was not as it should be. Only when he had to brake sharply at traffic lights, glancing up at his interior driving mirror to check on following vehicles, was the mystery solved.

Nothing was reflected in it. That was because it had been turned the wrong way. Hastily, he turned it back and instinctively slowed down. At the first opportunity, he pulled in and did a careful, all-round inspection of the car, checking under the bonnet with a torch and paying particular attention to the wheelnuts. Short of a full MoT test, he was satisfied nothing else had been tampered with.

You had to hand it to them for subtlety, whoever they were, Howard admitted as he resumed his homeward journey. What they were telling him was that they could have messed him about a lot more if they'd felt like it. Perhaps not as drastically as they did William but the outcome would have been more than a little unpleasant just the same. The car park at *The Announcer* was kept padlocked at all times. Since the first of the suicide bombs, security had been intensified with CCTV monitored round the clock by private guards. No outsiders were ever admitted, whoever they were, VIPs or otherwise.

So the message being delivered was loud and clear: not only did 'they' have a key to his desk drawer, they also had one to the company car park, one to his car and had somehow eluded the security cameras. He'd been on the receiving end of intimidation before, of course, especially in Northern Ireland but there the methods had been comparatively crude. The people he was dealing with now were not bombers, sectarian fanatics or drug gangs, they were more sophisticated. That was becoming clear. Who were they? Spooks, obviously, as Julian had observed. But not as we knew them. These were the Euro-spooks in Brussels. They spoke a different language.

He thought about phoning *The Announcer's* chief security officer but instinctively decided against. Senior management needed to be alerted but none would be in their offices at this time of night. In any case, the managing editor was a wally of the first water, a shooting crony of His Lordship and probably holed up legless in some remote Highland hideaway plucking birds, perhaps not all of the feathered variety. Even if Howard had known his mobile number, the old boy would not have taken kindly to some unknown hack ringing him up in the middle of the night to tell him his driving mirror had been turned the wrong way round.

The Queen hadn't died nor had there been a terrorist atrocity, but he would have to call Julian at his home, he decided as he turned into his own driveway. As soon as he had unloaded his laptop and pecked Barbara on the cheek, he called the Editor's private residential number. A Spanish maid answered and put him through when he impressed on her that it was urgent.

"Sorry to bother you at home, Julian but a rather cute stroke's been pulled that I think you ought to know about." He explained in detail, stressing the fact that the company's car park security had been breached.

"You're quite sure there's no innocent explanation for the mirror?"

"Positive. If there was any doubt in my mind, I wouldn't dream of calling you. It's par for the course, Julian. After the stolen contacts book...this. These people have got keys to everything..."

"They're taking us on, aren't they," Julian said calmly. "You'd think they'd know better. OK Howard, leave it with me. This is a matter for the Met. I'll phone the Commissioner immediately."

Howard grinned. That was the style. Straight to the top. No messing about with Press officers, chief superintendents or assistant commissioners. He put the phone down and embraced his wife properly. He knew she had overheard.

"Tell me about it," she said wearily.

They went into the lounge and he fixed the drinks. She looked as if she needed one. She was pale and drawn due to an early bout of morning sickness. But she remained cool and composed as he updated her on his latest investigation.

"This one could be the toughest so far," he said when he'd explained the full picture.

The eyebrows arched and she managed a wry smile. "That's what you said last time. All those Belfast drug-runners...surely it can't be worse than that."

"They all got sent down," he reminded her.

"Yes, but they were criminals. The people you've just told me about... they're different. Superficially, they're all respectable. *They* won't get sent down will they?"

"Maybe not, but they've got to be stopped just the same."

"I knew you were up to something when you asked about abortion and euthanasia."

"You're not worried are you…being pregnant and everything?"

"Of course I'm worried. Not for me but for you…and the children."

"*The Announcer* will look after us, like they did last time. And the police have to, as you know, under the human rights law. They even protect gangsters from each other these days"

"But *will* they protect us? We can't rely on the human rights law, can we?"

She was right. They couldn't. For a moment, he wanted to hug her and tell her it would be all right, he'd back out of the investigation, hand it over to someone else. But the challenge was too formidable. It was his duty to tackle it – for William's sake and ultimately for society's sake. "No, but you can rely on me," he said at length. "We have to go through with this, Barbara. What we're looking at is a potential totalitarian state…a police state. Two children will be one too many."

She patted her stomach, shook her head slightly and gave a thumbs-down gesture.

"Exactly. Three will get people arrested. It won't stop at the underclass. It'll spread to everyone. You've told me yourself about euthanasia…the hidden agenda. They start with the terminally ill then, when nobody objects too strongly, they move on to the paralysed. Then the semi-paralysed. Then the severely handicapped. Where does it end…with the epileptics, the mentally ill? Then the disabled, the blind and the deaf?

"This quest for purity and perfection…everyone seems to forget that it's been tried before. You start with deluded scientists and you end up with a deranged dictator. It'll be the 1930s all over again. You don't want them to get away with *that* do you?"

"Of course not. It's just…oh, never mind."

"What?"

"Well, the backlash seems to have started already."

"What backlash?"

"We've had a few 'silent' telephone calls."

"I see. When?"

"Today…and yesterday. I was bit upset because Sally answered the last one."

"They didn't say anything to her?"

"No, she just kept saying hello but no-one answered. She thought it was one of her friends who couldn't get through."

"What did you tell her?"

"I told her it was probably Mr Nobody playing a joke."

"I'll get on to BT."

"No point in changing the number, I don't suppose?"

"Not really. They'd sniff out the new one in no time. Computer speaketh unto computer. I've got contacts at BT. They can trace a lot more calls now. In the meantime, we'll go on interception. That'll give us some peace."

"I could use some of that right now," Barbara said, finishing her Scotch and heading for the door. "I need an early night."

"We'll have to beef up security for a while. I'll talk to Julian. He'll fix it, don't worry."

"Easier said than done. How long do you expect it to go on for this time?"

"Not long. Just remember the family motto."

The hall of the Mitchell home boasted a spoof coat of arms presented to Howard by a previous *Announcer* cartoonist in recognition of his award-winning journalism in Northern Ireland. Its motto read: *Necesse accipere arduum cum onere intolerabili,* which, roughly translated, meant: You have to take the rough with the intolerable.

His wife grimaced. "I'll try."

"Soon be over, darling, you'll see."

She smiled thinly. "I believe you."

*   *   *

Events moved swiftly following Julian's call to the Commissioner. Strings were pulled with a pizzicato precision. Within two days, *The Announcer's* car park guards were replaced, razor wire was fitted at the top of the compound's perimeter fence and the old iron gate replaced with one topped by twisted metal points that resembled a portcullis upside down. The padlock made way for a coded keypad and all users advised of the code, which was to change periodically.

Even Wimbledon police, not noted for their response times,

immediately set about installing CCTV around the Mitchells' home, together with a monitor in their dining room. The gateposts were fitted with an infra-red beam which activated an electronic buzzer in the lounge and main bedroom should any unsuspecting night prowler pass between them. The high beech hedge surrounding the house was considered a fairly effective barrier, although there were some small gaps in it.

Before they left, the officers told Howard and Barbara they'd think about a direct alarm link to a local police station if there were any problems although, due to budgetary cuts, many in the area were now closed at night.

"The place is like Fort Knox without the gold," Barbara observed after the last panda car had departed.

Oscar, who had been taking a keen interest in developments, bounded up for some attention. Howard bent to rub the tousled head. "And, as our last line of defence, there's always, Oscar."

"Don't kid yourself. All he barks at are cats."

*   *   *

The art of taking the rough with the intolerable was not confined to the Mitchell family. Andrew Moran had spent a convivial evening at the Press Club where he tried his hand on the club's snooker table, his highest break being three – one red and one yellow. The game remained an impenetrable mystery to him. He could not understand what Howard saw in it.

After a consoling double Scotch he left the club and made his way along a badly lit alley to an adjoining taxi rank. He never made it. Being mildly intoxicated, he didn't really feel the blows but he did feel his arm snap sickeningly as he hit the pavement. He was vaguely aware of two thugs running away as a car's headlights briefly lit up the scene. Then he woke up in hospital.

On arriving at the office the following afternoon, Howard found his boss in his usual recumbent position but noticed he was flicking through the day's newslist with only one hand. The other was in a sling. His stubbled face was also extensively bruised and one eye was almost closed.

"I told you to take more water with it, Andrew," Howard said, switching on his terminal. "What happened?"

"Mugged, old boy. Outside the Press Club last night. Two large gentlemen jumped me. One black, one white. They may be criminals but they got the racial mix right."

"You're a tough nut, Andrew, but you shouldn't have come in today. There's no way you can work in your state."

"Watch me. I can still walk and I can still type with one hand."

"Is the arm broken?"

"Yep, in two places. I'll be like this for weeks. Lucky it's not my drinking arm."

"You obviously put up a struggle."

"You bet. Kicked them both where it hurts. They ran off – but not very fast."

"Did they take anything?"

"That's just it. I had over £200 and all my credit cards plus my mobile phone but they didn't touch a thing. It seemed they just wanted to beat me up."

"Did you report it to the police?"

"Don't make me laugh, old boy. It hurts when I laugh."

Alarm bells were ringing in Howard's suspicious mind. This was obviously no ordinary street mugging. Tina was developing an unladylike streak to her character. "How's the conspiracy theory sounding now, Andrew?"

"I'd say it still sounded a bit paranoid if it wasn't for one thing."

"What's that?"

"I think they were French – or possibly Flemish. They spoke a couple of words to each other. They weren't English, that's for sure."

The incident's significance was certainly not lost on Julian when the wounded hack updated him later that afternoon. Firstly, the Editor gave him a pep talk about the dangers of walking around alone at night, especially after 'relaxing' at the Press Club. Then he insisted his news editor should get the police to install security cameras at his Holland Park flat, similar to those round Howard's home. If both journalists had become targets, then both their homes needed protection. The safety of Andrew's partner, Britt, was also a concern, although she was out of the country on a flight to Australia at present.

Julian realised there was a positive side to the latest development.

It finally removed any lingering doubt about conspiracy theories. You knew you were on the right track when people started attacking your staff. Bristling with indignation, he decided on his own brand of counter-punch. The spooks needed to know that the Press were still on the case. If they wanted a fight they could have one. He fired off another editorial broadside headed:

We will not be silenced

There have been serious developments in *The Announcer's* investigation into plans to impose state population control on the British people by stealth. Members of our reporting staff have been subjected to violence and threats, which confirm suspicions that we are dealing with a powerful lobby of dangerous fanatics.

Our inquiries lead us to believe that they are motivated by delusions of eugenics long thought to be obsolete and discredited by history. A secret European intelligence unit (exposed recently by this newspaper but still in existence) is clearly active in the United Kingdom. Those who stand in its way – including journalists going about their legitimate business – now face determined efforts to silence them.

The Announcer regards it as its duty to stand in its way.

And we will not be silenced.

*   *   *

Abortion-related stories dominated Andrew's news schedules over the following week. Figures released by the Department of Health showed a five per cent increase in terminations during the previous month but, in the case of teenage girls, the total had risen by seven per cent. Some of these had been performed on girls as young as fourteen without their parents' knowledge, a development backed by progressive elements but described by the Pro-Life Alliance as "profoundly disturbing".

It was a symptom of a society which had completely lost its conscience, an Alliance spokeswoman told Howard. "For every baby born alive to these young mothers, another is torn from the womb and put to death."

No sooner had he completed the story for the front page than Andrew handed him another. The growing popularity of *The Announcer's* crusade had led to cracks appearing in enemy ranks, as often happens when a newspaper captures the high moral ground, and a mole had surfaced with a juicy revelation about Planned Families.

In an anonymous letter to Julian, a disaffected PF member tipped him off about a split that had developed between the group and the NHS. It seemed the 'family planners' were deeply miffed about an NHS decision not to make abortion a priority – a decision revoking an earlier agreement.

The mole enclosed a photo-copy of a confidential PF report that showed they wanted the law changed to allow abortions without the signatures of two doctors, and for the procedures to be performed by nurses in doctors' surgeries. The tip finally reached Howard's desk with a request for a short piece to tie on to the abortion statistics.

Planned Families' only concern when he phoned them seemed to be the source of the leak and the terrible fate awaiting him. But the Pro-Life Alliance were more forthcoming. They were encouraged by what they saw as a split in the enemy camp. "Perhaps the NHS are finally seeing the light," a spokesman said. "Abortion is the deadliest form of terrorism. It targets human life at its most vulnerable. We want less of it, not more. A truly civilised society would want none."

*   *   *

The white ball sped straight at the blue, potted it in the middle pocket, then spun sharply backwards and rolled into the opposite pocket. It's a shot all beginners are taught if they are to master the art of deep screw. You place the object ball on the blue spot in the centre of the table and position the white cue-ball between it and the middle pocket. Then you lower your bridge and strike the cue-ball below centre.

Howard again demonstrated the shot as Edgar, his mature student, watched. It wasn't difficult once you knew how it was done but Edgar simply could not acquire the knack and it was starting to irritate him. He usually managed to pot the blue ball but the white then rolled after it into the same pocket. Sometimes the white would leap over the blue, which was disconcerting. The nearest he came to executing the stroke correctly was when he potted the blue and the white stopped dead.

"That's because you're just stunning the ball," Howard explained. "To screw it back you need to strike a little lower and follow through a bit further." He played the shot once more. "There are four things you need to remember: keep the cue level with the table; hold the cue *lightly*; check before you follow through, and *keep your head down*.

Edgar was listening. He was determined to get it right. He chalked his cue and crouched into his ungainly stance, the overhead light reflected on his hairless dome, shiny as the pink ball on the snooker table. Slowly this time, he drew the cue back, checked momentarily, then followed through like a pro. The blue shot into the pocket and the cue-ball zipped smartly into reverse, rolling to the lip of the near pocket, where it hung for a second before dropping.

"Ye-esss!" the head messenger cried, straightening up and holding his cue aloft, Dennis Taylor-style. You'd have thought he'd just scored a maximum.

"Well played, Edgar," Howard said. "Keep practising the shot…you'll soon be able to play it every time."

"I don't think I'll ever reach that standard."

"Don't sell yourself short. We'll make a fifty-break player out of you yet."

Edgar laughed. "I've never made twenty, let alone fifty"

"It'll come, you'll see." Howard said, hanging up his cue in its case.

"Thanks for the coaching, Howard. I really appreciate it."

And he did. The more Edgar thought about all the patient tuition the reporter had given him, the guiltier he felt about taking his contacts book.

The Decision

It all happened so quickly. One minute Janice was pushing her trolley towards the customer service desk in the Co-op to complain about the shocking state of their cauliflowers; the next, she felt a crushing pain in her chest and the supermarket started going round. Seconds later she became aware that her head was resting on the tiled floor and an elderly man was bending over her asking if she was all right.

She remembered thinking what a daft question it was. Did she *look* all right, lying there staring at the wheels of her trolley? Other faces gathered above and a checkout girl placed her seat cushion under her head as a pillow. Then a shelf-stacker held her hand and told her they'd rung for an ambulance.

Though she could hardly breathe, Janice managed to draw the assistant's attention to the trinitrate spray in her handbag and after a frantic search the poor girl found it. A supervisor with some first aid knowledge joined her and successfully applied the spray under Janice's tongue. The pain eased slightly and they brought a chair but she was still gasping for breath and couldn't get up.

Janice had gone off God since He let her beautiful little daughter die at birth all those years ago. But now, as she lay helpless while shoppers shuffled past and stared, she found herself praying. "Please God, don't let me die here in the Co-op...not in front of all these people. Some of them might be my Avon customers. What will they think? Please let me get home and die there."

It seemed an age before the ambulance arrived but at last two cheery paramedics appeared with a stretcher. They took her pulse and blood pressure and placed an oxygen mask over her nose and mouth. Lifting her lumpy figure effortlessly on to the stretcher, they wheeled her out, past more curious faces, to the ambulance. Then it was 'lights and music' all the way to Brawton Infirmary, which fortunately wasn't far.

The accident and emergency department was crowded when they brought her in but she was rushed through for emergency assessment by a junior doctor who looked as if he might be doing work experience on day release from school. He gave her a nervous, cursory examination and, under instruction from a staff nurse, an injection to ease the pain.

She was wheeled into a curtained cubicle where two more nurses fitted a new oxygen mask and cuffed her arm to the automatic blood pressure machine. They briskly undressed her and draped her in the standard hospital gown with draw ties round the back. She'd be kept in overnight at least, they told her. It was a suspected heart attack but they couldn't be sure until tests had been carried out. She was breathing more easily now and was able to tell them her name, address and next of kin. She asked them to phone Edgar before he left home for work. There would be things he needed to bring. Her medication, for a start.

They'd take care of that, the nurses said. They were friendly and professional but you could tell they were stressed out. The department was very busy today, she was told, so there would be a wait before they could do the ECG and blood test. They gave her an alarm buzzer to press if the pain got worse. "Try to relax," one said. And with a swish of the curtain, both were gone.

To say Edgar was gobsmacked when they phoned him was putting it mildly. He had only just woken up. They had called earlier, they said, but there'd been no reply. The staff nurse explained what had happened and asked if his wife had any history of heart trouble. He told her about the heart attack over seven years ago and her ongoing angina. They'd have all the details in their records.

The nurse asked if Janice had done any heavy lifting recently. He didn't think so. No more than usual. There were her Avon packages, of course, but they weren't very heavy.

Did she take her angina medication regularly?

Regular as clockwork. Never missed a dose as far as he knew.

Were any anxieties or serious emotional problems bothering her?

That one pulled him up. The memory of Janice in tears when she'd seen his picture on the front page of *The Bugle* still hadn't faded. Although they had now been offered the full market value for their bungalow, he knew his wife would never come to terms with moving. Not after thirty-five years. It was too much to ask of any woman.

After a moment's hesitation, he answered: "No more than usual." Edgar didn't believe in telling lies but he knew how to be economical with the truth.

The nurse told him what to bring – all Janice's drugs, toiletries, toothbrush, dressing gown, nightie, slippers, underwear, change for the phone, reading material...

*　　　*　　　*

She'd been moved into a room in the cardiac care unit when Edgar arrived at the hospital, carrying a grip containing his wife's belongings and her medication in a bulging plastic bag. He'd seen it all before, of course, but the sight of Janice lying there wired up to all that electronic gadgetry shook him just the same. You had to put on a brave face, try to be cheerful. He managed his characteristic grin.

"I've heard all about it," he said, drawing up a bedside chair. "You'll have to keep out of that Co-op." He tenderly kissed her unusually pale cheek and stroked her untidy grey hair. "How do you feel now?"

"Weak," she answered weakly. "They don't know if it's a heart attack... got to do more tests." She tried to smile but the oxygen tubes in her nostrils made it difficult. "Told me to relax! How can you relax in a place like this?"

"You can now I'm here, Janice. I've phoned them at *The Announcer* – taken the night off. They'll have to get the paper out without me."

"Will they let you stay here?"

"Let them try to stop me." He rummaged in the plastic bag and began unloading the bottles, jars and boxes of his wife's pharmacopoeia. "I've brought your things. They told me to bring reading material but I didn't think you'd feel much like reading...so I brought you this." He handed her the latest Avon catalogue and she seemed pleased. "Should keep you quiet for a bit."

She reached for his hand. "I do love you, you know."

Tears welled up in his eyes. It had been a long time since he'd heard her say that.

He bent to kiss her again. "I love you too, Janice."

"You do mean it, don't you?"

He held her hand tightly. "Course I mean it...you know I do."

"If anything should happen..."

"Nothing's going to happen. It'll be angina, just a false alarm ... you'll see."

177

"But if it should…you won't ever move out of our home will you?"

Edgar felt the tears rising again. "No way," he managed to say. He really meant it.

"I wouldn't rest if I thought…"

"Believe me, Janice, there's no way I'd leave."

"It's been thirty-five years, Edgar."

He squeezed her hand. "Nearly thirty-six."

"Stanley grew up there…and our little girl…she would've done."

He turned away to hide his tears from her. They both missed their son since he'd married and emigrated to Australia. But they never spoke of the daughter, stillborn at their little bungalow. The memory was too painful. But now it all came back to him…the icy day in January, the snow-covered Meadow…even the doctor's attempt to comfort them after his efforts to resuscitate the tiny waxen figure had failed.

"Into every life a little rain must fall," he'd said. He hadn't mentioned the deluge of distress that afflicted the Brierleys for years afterwards. It changed them all, even young Stanley. He'd grown away from them emotionally long before he left them physically.

The grief was like a splinter of ice piercing your heart. And it never melted. They called their little angel Charlotte. The hospital had offered to 'dispose of' the body, as if their beloved daughter was some kind of waste material, but they'd made sure she had a Christian burial. There were only three people at the funeral – Edgar, Janice and the Methodist minister. They'd tried to sing *All things bright and beautiful, All creatures great and small* but Janice broke down in tears, so the minister read out the words. Then the tiny white coffin was lowered into the iron hard ground and Edgar had to hold his wife tightly to stop her from fainting. Charlotte would have been thirty now, if she'd lived, Edgar thought. It was alarming that Janice was suddenly talking about her.

A nurse bustled in to check the wall-mounted heart monitor. Edgar tried to suppress a panicky feeling. He didn't like the way his wife was talking. Not one little bit. "Is she going to be all right, nurse?"

"She's stable now, Mr Brierley. But she needs to sleep. It might be an idea to get some rest yourself. We'll call you at home if there's any change."

"I'd rather stay if you don't mind."

For several hours he sat staring at the TV in the visitors' lounge, seeing nothing. Slowly though his mind worked, the significance of his wife's illness was taking shape. There was a lesson to be learnt from it. If Janice survived (and even if she didn't, though he blocked out that particular thought) it was his duty to resist the planning blight on their bungalow, not run away. Their home was their castle, albeit a small one, and it was worth fighting for. IPI were bullies and bullies had to be stood up to. If all else failed he would stand in front of the bulldozers himself.

True, after he'd accepted Quinn's offer, his new spymaster had been as good as his word and nominated Edgar for undreamed-of status as a Holy Royal Arch Companion. But seeing his poor wife reduced to her present state, after all the hardships of their married life, crystalised his conflict of loyalties. She'd stood by him through all their misfortunes – Charlotte's death, his accident, his operations, his periods out of work when they were struggling to raise Stanley.

It was time he realised where his first duty lay and stood by her. Some 'noble causes' were nobler than others. He needed to get his priorities right. From now on his own personal noble cause had to be Janice. As for the factory, it had not been built yet. There was many a slip twixt cup and lip. OK, he'd lost the early rounds but he was still on his feet. If he was smart, options were still open...

When the night shift came on they offered him a folding bed in his wife's room but he told them he was a night worker like them. He kept a lonely bedside vigil and was encouraged when his wife started snoring. That was more like his Janice, he thought. She must be getting better. He did nod off for an hour as dawn broke. But not before he had reached his Decision.

*   *   *

Edgar had been right after all. It wasn't a heart attack but an acute oesophageal spasm aggravated by her angina. All the tests proved it. The ECGs, the echocardiogram, the X-rays and several blood tests. Say what you like about the NHS, they'd been very thorough. When the consultant came round he increased Janice's medication for her blood pressure and cholesterol. He'd write to her GP, who would 'keep an eye on her'. She had to rest, take things easy for a while and *avoid all kinds of stress.*

The ward sister repeated the words with heavy emphasis as the couple prepared to leave three days later but Edgar had already got the message. False alarm or not, it had concentrated his mind wonderfully.

The buggers

The Rolls-Royce Silver Cloud caused quite a stir when it glided majestically into Meadow Drive. Quinn hadn't come himself but had sent a chauffeur to collect Edgar for his initiation as a Royal Arch Companion. Net curtains twitched in more than one window as the chauffeur led the dark-suited Edgar to the limousine, opening a rear door for him and respectfully touching his peaked cap.

Janice, now fully recovered from the heart scare, also watched with pride from the lounge of their bungalow as her husband set off for what she regarded as his long-overdue promotion. True, they hadn't always seen eye to eye about things and recently his old head injury seemed to have been bothering him. She just hoped he didn't drink too much. At least they'd bring him home in style if he did.

Edgar was deeply impressed as the sumptuous Rolls rolled across London to the Royal Arch temple in St James's. Despite his nervousness when they produced a human skull, a central element in their arcane ritual, the initiation ceremony passed off without a hitch. It had been quite a bombshell for Edgar to learn that Masonry's Supreme Degree regarded lesser degrees as counterfeit. All those oaths he'd solemnly taken involving throat cutting and the tearing out of tongues for betraying secrets were bogus, the Companions assured him. Darkness was for those without. Only Companions of the Royal Arch were allowed to share the 'Grand Omnific Royal Arch Word of Jahbulon', pronounced Yahbulon.

To enact this solemn rite, the top of their Royal Arch 'altar' was adorned with a brass plate inscribed with a circle on which was written Je-ho-vah, divided into three syllables. Within the circle was a triangle and on each side of the triangle was written Jah-bul-on, also split into three. During Edgar's thirty years as a third degree Craft Mason, no-one had ever told him the secret name of the Great Architect of the Universe.

Despite his exalted new status, he'd felt hopelessly out of his depth at first. His new Companions were all toffs: company directors, professional men, an Anglican bishop and a sprinkling of nobility as he'd expected. No fish and chip shop owners here. But when Quinn introduced him as 'editorial manager' at *The Announcer*, he soon grew in confidence. It sounded more impressive than head messenger, he thought. It was surprising how much better you felt about yourself when people believed you were important – even if you weren't.

At the festive board, they dined on sautéed *foie gras*, roast venison, baby asparagus, Swiss chard and glazed chestnuts washed down with a Hermitage La Chapelle 1990, the like of which he had never tasted in his entire life. This was, without doubt, how the other half lived.

Later, Marcus guided him into a luxuriously appointed private room and opened a box of Romeo y Juliettas. Although Edgar didn't smoke cigarettes, he enjoyed an occasional cigar, particularly when they had been specially imported from Havana. The two Companions settled in their massive, hand-tooled leather armchairs and a steward brought them their whiskies with a small crystal jug of iced water. The American ordered that they were not to be disturbed and, when the steward withdrew, came straight to the point.

"Ed, I want you to know how much we appreciate the swell job you did in, ah, acquiring the contacts book."

His guest grinned self-consciously. He was beginning to feel uncomfortable again.

"However," Quinn continued, exhaling a large cloud of blue smoke towards the ceiling, "the book, though helpful – don't get me wrong – fell rather short of expectations. Nearly all Mr Mitchell's contacts seem to be government public relations people, MPs, peers and peeresses, professional bodies, various pressure groups…unfortunately not a lot to take us forward at this time."

The tip of the cigar glowed red as the millionaire took another long drag. "We were wondering if you could possibly, ah, acquire more intimate material. It's important we find out who he's talking to privately. Could you get hold of his personal diary, for example…"

Edgar tried to appear nonchalant but he kept thinking of his last snooker session with Howard when he finally began to acquire the knack of deep screw. His journalist friend had gone out of his way to help him master a beautiful game and this was how he repaid him. He'd got himself in deep with Quinn. The deeper it got, the more uneasy he felt. "They've tightened up security since I took the contacts book," was all he could say.

"So we understand. But you're our man on the inside."

"It'd be too risky. I don't even know where he keeps his diary."

"In his jacket, I guess."

"I can't pick his pocket, can I?"

"Of course not, Ed. Not while he's wearing it. But doesn't he take his jacket off?"

"Yes, he hangs it on the back of his chair."

"Suppose he were to get up for a minute and leave it there?"

The bald head shook vigorously. "I can't watch him all the time. I have my own work to do. In any case, someone would be sure to see me. I'd be sacked. I'd lose my pension."

Quinn knocked the ash off his cigar into an ornate pedestal ashtray.

"If that were to happen we'd look after you, of course. Mutual help and support, you know."

Oddly, Edgar still preferred the security of his pension. "I'm sorry. You've been very kind and I'm grateful for my promotion but it's just not on."

The Royal Arch Grand Commander thought for a time. Then he reached into his jacket pocket and took out a small package. "In that case," he said, "I suggest we try this."

He very carefully unwrapped what looked like a jeweller's ring box and took out a tiny metal capsule. It was slightly larger than a 20p piece. "State of the art microchip technology," he smirked, holding it aloft between a podgy finger and thumb.

A bemused Edgar cleared his throat. "What is it?"

"This, sir, is one of the most sensitive listening devices money can buy," Quinn said proudly.

"A bug, you mean?"

"Precisely."

*   *   *

"The buggers!" Andrew exclaimed, his arm still in a sling but his fondness for a facetious pun undimmed.

"How's the conspiracy theory looking now?" Julian asked him.

"Sorry I doubted you, Julian."

Andrew, Howard, Julian, Edgar and a fifth man were huddled round

183

the Editor's desk, with Edgar's prize exhibit lying on his blotting pad.

Julian's bushy eyebrows positively bristled as he examined the tiny listening device. Then he looked up at Andrew. "You were right to doubt, Andrew. It's our job to be sceptical. But once you begin to see the truth – once the dots are there – it's for us to join them up."

He turned to his chief messenger. "Who gave you this, Edgar?"

"Mr Quinn…Marcus Quinn. He told me to fix it under Howard's desk."

"It's not transmitting now by any chance is it?" Andrew asked.

The fifth man, a middle-aged bespectacled electronics expert called Steve Prentice, shook his head. "No, it's shut down." He indicated a minute aperture. "You press there with a pen or anything pointed to activate it."

"How powerful is it?" Julian asked.

"Very powerful. It's the latest microelectronic superbug, works within a mile range."

"Incredible. It's so small."

"Microchips keep on getting smaller. The big breakthrough is a computer the size of a postage stamp. My firm's working on a prototype voice recorder that'll fit inside a small matchbox. Could be useful to journalists."

"And you're sure there are no more of these gadgets in the office?" Julian asked.

"Quite sure, Mr Geldard. We've swept all your offices. They're all clean."

Julian turned to his head messenger. "How long have you known Marcus Quinn, Edgar?"

"Only a few months."

"Through your Masonic connections?"

"That's right."

"I realise you can't go into those. I do appreciate your courage in coming to us with this. You've performed a very great service. It must have been quite a conflict of loyalties – your fraternal oaths and all that."

Edgar wasn't going to tell them about the contacts book. That would only complicate matters. But his change of heart had lifted a huge weight from his shoulders. All too clearly now, he saw his primary loyalties were to Janice and his employers. The blood-curdling oaths he'd taken as a third degree Craft Mason held no terrors since his Royal Arch Companions had assured him they were meaningless. He no longer felt any conflict of loyalties. He had finally got his priorities right.

"I've been a Freemason for over thirty years, Mr Geldard, and I would never betray their secrets. This is something else..." He indicated the microchip device. "It's not the Brotherhood who're doing this, its IPI. So you can count me in. First things first."

"You've done the right thing, Edgar, and we're proud of you," Julian said. "Just when it seemed we were up against a brick wall you've given us the vital breakthrough. We're going to need your services again if you're agreeable."

Edgar flushed at the fulsome praise from such an exalted quarter. "I'll help all I can."

"Good man. But remember...not a word to anyone outside this office."

Edgar grinned. "I can still keep a secret. Would you like your tea now, sir?"

"Tea!" the Editor exclaimed. "He talks about tea at a time like this. It calls for a toast."

He opened a desk drawer and took out a bottle of 14-year-old Scotch and glasses he kept for visits by His Lordship and other VIPs. Edgar had just qualified for that category. Julian poured out generous measures and handed them round.

"Edgar," they chorused, raising the amber nectar to their lips.

"Our new undercover agent," Julian added.

When the embarrassed head messenger had returned to his newsroom duties and Steve had also departed, Julian turned to Howard and Andrew. "Well, gentlemen, where do we go from here?"

*   *   *

There was no version of *The Announcer* on Sundays. Management had considered launching a Sunday paper but had thought better of it. The market was already saturated with heavyweight weekend supplements and magazines. It was doubtful if there was room for one more. And with circulation shrinking inexorably, it seemed like just another way of losing money. *The Announcer* was already doing that very well thank you.

Some *Announcer* hacks worked Saturday night casual shifts for Sunday papers. They were nearly all sub-editors desperately trying to make ends meet. But for the reporting staff, Saturdays were a time to rejoin the human race and reintroduce themselves to families who rarely saw them during the week. In Howard's case, this meant 'bonding' with Chris and Sally, and catching up on TV viewing with Barbara.

The couple were comfortably curled up in their lounge watching the late horror film when a strange thing happened. The night had turned chilly and the gas fire cast a mellow glow across the darkened lounge. Outside a breeze stirred the shrubbery and a climbing rose tapped lightly against the french windows. It was 2.40am when the film ended. Howard was about to switch off the set when Barbara, who had been lying on the settee, sat up suddenly and grabbed his arm.

"Sshhh…" She was staring at the window.

"What is it?" he whispered.

"There was a noise."

"It's only the rose bush."

"No, listen. There's someone outside."

Perhaps the horror film they'd just watched had set the mood but, for a full two minutes, they remained frozen, staring at the french windows. Then slowly, very slowly, one of the brass handles began to turn.

Shock does weird things to the central nervous system. Even as he dashed to the window, Howard felt a frisson of static chase through his head and shoulders…and an odd sense of detachment, as if he were observing events but was not part of them.

He became aware of a loud noise from the kitchen. It was Oscar's barking. He leapt for the light switch on the wall, realising too late that the light would only alert the intruder. A tall dark shape slipped round the side of the house. They ran into the hall and opened the front door. The shape dissolved into the darkness. They heard a car start up. Howard ran to the gateway and saw it speed away, tyres squealing.

There had been something quite remarkable about the car, Howard thought as he slowly retraced his steps. On its roof was an illuminated sign. It didn't say TAXI. It said POLICE.

Oscar's barking had woken Sally. She was standing anxiously at the top of the stairs clutching her teddy and Barbara went up to put her back in bed. "It's those cats again," she said. "They come out to play at night and Oscar doesn't like them in his garden."

When she came back downstairs, Howard was studying the CCTV monitor in the dining room. There was no sign of the intruder on the tape. No-one had passed between the gateposts. He must have found a gap in the hedge. Howard resolved to seal the gaps next day. He'd get some wire mesh from the garden centre.

"Have you called the police?" his wife asked.

That was a bit rich, he thought. But he said: "Not much point. Whoever it was will be miles away by now. I'll stay up for a while. You go to bed."

She kissed him good-night. "It's started hasn't it?"

"You never know. It could've been a burglar."

"You can't fool a seasoned campaigner like me."

She kissed him again. Longer this time and tenderly. It was a kiss that said she had every confidence in him. There was nothing to fear. "Who'd be married to an investigative journalist?"

Her trust in him was ineffable. The anxiety he'd felt earlier slipped away and he relaxed. After all, they'd both been here before.

All the same, Howard didn't go to bed that night. For a time he sat gazing out of the dining room window. Barbara's Renault was parked on the drive. The Rover was safe in the double garage, which was so crammed with junk that there was no room for the Renault. He would have to clear it out – and soon. Cars were usually the first target when it came to dirty tricks.

He scanned the stretch of lawn towards the gateposts with their invisible infra red circuit connected to the bedroom alarm. That had now been switched off so that Barbara could sleep undisturbed. She needed her sleep, especially now. He didn't. Morning newspaper journalists soon learnt to go without sleep for long periods.

When the dawn sky began to lighten, he clipped the dog lead to Oscar's well-worn collar, collected his camera in case of more excitement, and set off to patrol his garden. It wasn't large – about a quarter of an acre – but it had plenty of character. Enclosed within the beech hedge were a rose garden, flower beds, a vegetable patch, tool shed, a child's swing, apple trees and a lawn big enough to play a sedate form of cricket, using a tennis ball and miniature stumps.

Howard always enjoyed the beauty of dawn unfolding...the imperceptible lightening of the sky, the cool freshness before the heat of a summer's day, the sharp sweetness of the honeysuckle around the back door, the way the dahlias and hydrangeas seemed to change colour as the soft light intensified. It was a magical time, experienced only by night workers. For an hour the dawn chorus echoed round the deserted gardens and the animal kingdom ruled unchallenged. You saw hedgehogs, rabbits, squirrels, even foxes at play in the middle of the road, as if cars had never existed. But then the first milk float of the morning would trundle round the corner and the spell would be broken.

This time something else broke the spell. As man and beast reached the smaller front lawn, with its shrubbery and conifers, Oscar strained at the leash and led his master to a small, grey object lying near the dining room window. Howard smiled grimly. It was not the first dead rat he had found outside his home. It probably won't be the last, he thought as he fetched a shovel and consigned the corpse to the dustbin.

It must have been left there by the driver of the police car. The message was obvious. Sometimes it was boxes of live matches, burnt round the edges, or newspapers with banner headlines about murders. Parked cars were also a favourite target. He checked the Renault carefully but there was no sign of scratched paintwork or slashed tyres.

What amazed him was that the low life who resorted to this intimidation always made the same crucial mistake. They always operated by night. Whoever they were, and in whatever country, they assumed nocturnal harassment would work as effectively against him as it did against people leading normal lives. Such victims, who did daytime jobs and slept at night, were easily terrorised by their tactics. But the spooks failed to see the obvious: that journalists on a newspaper which came out in the early morning would be awake throughout the night. So whatever strokes they pulled, he would always be ready for them.

*   *   *

Towards the end of September, as a golden summer turned gently to bronze, a strange thing happened to *The Announcer's* circulation figure. It stopped going down. In fact, it started going up. The paper's campaign against state population control had clearly struck a sympathetic chord with the reading public. While the litter press, the *Sun* and the *Star,* continued to ply their readers with a daily diet of fantasy by way of news, sex by way of entertainment and football by way of escapism, a more serious mood could be detected among thinking people.

Julian Geldard was too old a hand at the game to predict a sea change in public opinion just yet. It was too early to make an informed judgment. But the signs were promising. The ABC figure, released that day, showed circulation had increased by over 25,000 copies in the past month and had returned to just over a million, an important psychological figure. It was the first monthly increase for four years.

In addition, advertising revenue was rising and there was an unprecedented flow of letters from readers worried about euthanasia. Many were elderly and fearful of going into hospital. Who could blame them?

Even more encouraging was the steady drip of intelligence from sympathisers (paid and unpaid) among the enemy. The latest took the form of leaked internal memos produced by the Centre for Reproductive Rights which revealed secret long-term plans for legalising abortion on demand worldwide.

The source at the CRR was one of the paper's most reliable and diligent informants. The incriminating memos contained all the details needed for another front page story and the last one summed it up neatly. It read: "There is a stealth quality to our work. We are achieving incremental recognition of values without a huge amount of scrutiny from the opposition."

We'll see about that, Julian thought as he flagged the leak for Howard's attention. Times were changing and *The Announcer* was instrumental in changing them. The shrewd old scribe had taken a massive gamble. He had stuck his neck out and transformed editorial policy on the strength of a hunch. And the hunch had come good sooner than expected. Official demographers were already hinting at the need to reduce the UK population to 45 million by the middle of the next century. Justine Harvey-Ozgood had said as much recently. Granted, it had been at a lunatic fringe junket. The public had not taken her seriously. They didn't realise they were being softened up for something unthinkable. They didn't know about Tina.

He decided to run special features using Howard's copy on the unsavoury pioneers of the culture of death. The truth about Malthus & Co should open a few eyes, especially those of younger readers. If the response merited it, he would make more space available for readers' letters, maybe another half page.

The staid, straitlaced *Announcer* had never been regarded as a crusading newspaper. It was on the verge of a startling metamorphosis. There would be no more talk of folding, or speculation about redundancies. No more buy-ups of weirdoes in a desperate attempt to shore up circulation. There was only one way for the paper to go now – that was up.

The day's events called for a modest celebration, Julian felt. He reached into his desk drawer for The Macallan. A trip to the Palace may still be some way off but he was beginning to feel quietly confident.

*   *   *

Most hacks are frustrated novelists. Many have had books rejected by publishers. Some have even had them published but they've never become bestsellers. So it's been back to the bread and butter of daily death, disaster and destruction served up in the newsrooms. But there is nothing journalists like better in rare moments of relaxation than to indulge their suppressed creativity by way of punditry and original wordplay – strictly between themselves, of course, not for publication.

So when it was decided to activate Edgar's bug, fix it under Howard's desk and pretend they didn't suspect a thing, they were like children with a new toy. Andrew, in particular, still typing one-handed, was in his element. During a lull in the flow of copy, he winked at Howard and casually asked: "How are you getting on with the population thing?"

Howard caught on quickly. "Slowly but unsurely."

"Any luck with Tina?"

"She's proving a feisty lass. She's fighting back. We're getting harassment at home."

"What sort of harassment?"

"Silent phone calls, car tampered with, dead rats on the garden..."

"Par for the course, old boy. Unbalanced people. We've all had it."

190

"I know, but the pressure's starting to get to Barbara. We need a breakthrough on their Mr Big but there's no sign of one."

"Hey, look at that on PA," Andrew interjected. "The neo-Nazis calling for compulsory abortion for pregnant asylum seekers…they're muscling in on the population control lobby!"

Howard checked his screen. There was no such story on PA. He scribbled a note and threw it across the desk to Andrew. It read: "Let's not go OTT!"

After that the conversation became desultory, with Andrew remarking on the paucity of the day's news list, how the editorial staff still faced mass redundancies and his progress in 'cultivating' the Editor's secretary as a source of information in that area. For good measure, he also threw in a few bawdy comments about Diane's outstanding potential as a bed partner.

The object of this imaginative charade was to convince Marcus C Quinn III, when he listened to the taped conversation, that Edgar had done his job well and his electronic eavesdropping device was living up to its state-of-the-art specification.

He would also be gratified to know that Tina's foreign spooks were earning their euros with comparatively restrained methods of intimidation at the Mitchell family home. It seemed Howard's wife was already cracking and they hadn't seen anything yet.

Slaves of the lamp

Have you ever wondered as you descend the packed Tube station escalator at 5.30 pm, who that lone figure on the up escalator might be? There he is, quite smartly dressed and carrying a laptop, gliding upwards in splendid solitude while you and about 950 other home-going commuters stand jammed together on the plunging, rattling stairs, barely able to take a deep breath.

For you, the day's toil may well be over but for the night worker going the other way it's just beginning. Maybe he's a plain clothes police officer, a nightclub owner, postal supervisor or ambulance controller. Then again, he might be a morning paper journalist, a "slave of the lamp and servant of light", in the immortal words of Sir Edwin Arnold – or, as Howard might have put it, a hack heading for another date with insatiable printing presses, even now being oiled and reeled-up ready for their nightly thunder.

One of your inalienable human rights is the right to true information – and to read it at your breakfast table without giving it a second thought. For Howard and his colleagues, it was their privilege to provide that service, often despite threats, smears and other attempts to stop them which most people would regard as bizarre, not to mention completely outrageous.

Howard had come to work by Tube that evening because of one such occurrence: Barbara's Renault had been sabotaged. And, because her life-saving job was even more important than his, she had been obliged to drive to hospital in the Rover.

On waking that morning, she had found both front tyres on the Clio were flat. As far as she could see, they had not been slashed. They were just flat.

Howard was asleep and Yvette, the *au pair*, had taken Chris and Sally to the school bus. Barbara tried inflating the tyres with a foot pump but it was clear they had not just been let down but punctured. One wheel she could have dealt with because she knew how to fit the spare, but two rendered the task impossible.   As she had to be in theatre in less than an hour, there was no alternative but to unlock the garage and take the Rover. She left Howard a hurried note, telling him what had happened.

When he inspected the damage at lunchtime he cursed himself for not clearing out all the clutter from the garage. He phoned the police and reported the damage – strictly for the record, though he recognised it was a pointless exercise. Then he phoned his local car mechanic and ordered two new tyres for the Renault. Immediate delivery and fitting. It would cost an arm and a leg, he knew, but it would go on expenses.

Then he called a skip hire firm. Once again, money talked. They'd deliver a skip within the hour and they'd remove it that evening. Tradesmen would usually drop everything if you offered them double the rate for the job. Cash up front, of course. It was a deal. He kept an emergency stash in the bedroom safe.

In the few hours remaining before he had to resort to public transport, he manhandled on to the drive the discarded bunk beds the children had slept in years earlier, rolls of mildewed carpet he'd forgotten all about, a broken electric fire he knew he'd never be able to fix, half-used tins of paint and brushes with bristles hard as concrete, stacks of yellowing newspapers, boxes of ceramic tiles left over from their bathroom makeover, a rusting tricycle and pedal car that brought back memories of Christopher as a toddler, and one very old dilapidated armchair. Over the years, they'd produced more rubbish than Channel 4. Why did people accumulate junk in their garages? Garages were for motor cars.

He knew Barbara would be sad about the armchair. When the children were tiny they called it the Getting Better Chair because whenever you fell and grazed your knee or you got stung by a wasp or you were sick after eating too many sweets, Mother would apply expert first aid, then sit you on the Getting Better Chair and you'd feel fine again in no time. It worked like magic. He had to admit he felt a pang himself as he lifted the poor old chair on to the pile of rubbish. But two of its legs were broken beyond repair. It had clearly lost all its healing powers.

The District Line route to work was a good deal quicker than by car. And less stressful. The train was almost empty, in contrast to those heading the other way. There was time to tackle *The Announcer* crossword (with only limited success), and read about England's encouraging progress in the Test match. The only drawback was the absence of regular news bulletins on the radio. He felt strangely bereft without them.

On reaching the office he was surprised to find a party going on in the

Editor's room. "Haven't you heard?" a sub said. "The Euthanasia Bill's been defeated. But that's not all — our circulation's gone back over a million."

"Nice to hear some good news for a change," he told Julian as he joined the party. They were watching Baroness Witherspoon being interviewed on BBC Television. She seemed surprised by the loss of her Bill but characteristically unbowed.

The measure had been defeated by only nine votes, she pointed out. The setback was just a blip in her campaign to create a more liberal-minded and compassionate society. She blamed it on misguided propaganda by a certain reactionary newspaper. A cheer went round the office when she said that.

Her campaign would go on. A new and more comprehensive bill would be drafted. Plans were afoot even as she spoke. Countries throughout Europe were adopting enlightened legislation for 'living wills' and assisted suicide. Britain would fall into line. It was 'historically inevitable'. And it would happen sooner than many expected.

When the programme turned to the entry into Britain of an extremist Muslim cleric, hacks drifted back to their desks and the task of producing a 36-page first edition in three hours. Howard updated his chief on the previous night's dramas and presented him with a hefty expenses claim.

More than usually mellowed by several tots of The Macallan, Julian signed it without a second glance. He was full of the paper's reviving fortunes and future strategies. *The Announcer* was about to regain its original status as Britain's pre-eminent paper of record. Edgar entered several times bearing proofs of early City and Features pages. Then with a Sports page trumpeting England's sensational Test match triumph.

Julian waved the page aloft. "If England can do it, Howard...so can we."

A change of tune

September for the junior choir at St Peter's meant rehearsals for the Harvest Festival the following month. As it was Howard's night off, he took Christopher, protesting as usual, to the church and listened while the choir practised their first hymn, *We plough the fields and scatter*. It was one of his boyhood favourites. As he drove home (another parent was on the pick-up run) he hummed the next lines: "…the good seed on the land; but it is fed and watered, by God's almighty hand…"

Back home, he was comfortably ensconced in his favourite armchair with *The Announcer* crossword, grappling with the clue: Sheer chaos in Surrey (5), when the phone rang. Esher, he thought, before picking up the handset.

"Is that Mr Mitchell?" a cultured male voice inquired.

"Yes."

"The guarantee on your Singer has expired."

"I beg your pardon."

"The guarantee on your Singer has expired." The cryptic message was followed by a click, then the dialling tone.

With a sigh, he checked 1471 but, of course, it was 'number withheld'. This was a new one. If it was Mr Nobody again, he had found a way of bypassing interception. But could it be something to do with Barbara's sewing machine. A bit late to be calling about it, and surely the caller would have elaborated.

He seemed to remember that the sewing machine wasn't a Singer but a Pfaff. It was years ago when she bought it but the advertising slogan had stuck in his mind: The Pfabulous Pfaff. He strode into the dining room and lifted the machine's cover. Yes, it was still the same old Pfabulous Pfaff. Perhaps Barbara was going to exchange it for a Singer. She hadn't said anything. But if that were the case the guarantee would hardly have expired before she'd bought it.

Another mystery. Eat your heart out Alfred Hitchcock. He returned to the crossword but could no longer get his head round the clues. His mind kept returning to the phone call. Could it be some kind of code? Had a hidden meaning escaped him? Suppose it were a crossword clue…

195

The guarantee on your Singer has expired.

Your Singer.

Your singer.

There was a subtle difference. "The good seed on the land"…the youthful voices echoed in his ears.

He dropped the newspaper and rushed out to the Rover. Wildly, he drove across town to St Peter's, overtaking, undertaking, ignoring red lights. Losing his cool? You bet he was. If anything had happened to Chris he'd tear Tina apart with his bare hands. On reaching the church, he leapt out of the car and vaulted up the steps, breathless. The children were singing *Come ye thankful people, come.*

A young woman approached him, smiling. "Can I help you?"

"I'm looking for Chris…Christopher Mitchell. Is he here?"

"Yes, but they've not finished yet."

A wave of relief swept over him as he spotted his son, singing with the others in a corner next to the organ. "That's OK. I'll wait."

"You're his dad, aren't you?"

"Yes."

He sank into a rear pew. His hands were shaking.

"Are you all right, Mr Mitchell?"

"I'm fine…just thought I was late."

The woman laughed. "You're early. They won't be finished for another twenty minutes."

"I'll wait…listen to the hymns." He managed a weak grin.

His son came running towards him when they'd finished the rehearsal. "Hi Dad…I didn't know you'd be meeting me. I thought…"

"It's all right, I'll tell the other mother I'm collecting you."

"Why Dad?"

"Thought I'd listen to the singing for a bit. You're all very good."

"Not the girls…they can't sing for toffee."

"Then I thought you might like to go to McDonalds."

"Brilliant. Thanks, Dad."

*　　　*　　　*

When the children were safely tucked up and Howard told Barbara what had happened, they marvelled at humanity's capacity for malice. If you could call them human. Low-life was too flattering a description for them. They were subterranean.

But they were clever, you had to admit. Theirs was a sophisticated form of terrorism, without the bombs. They knew all about the human rights law – that they would have the National Crime Squad on their backs if Howard or his family came to any physical harm. The same applied to Andrew and Britt now that they also enjoyed police protection.

But the spooks had done the crash course in psychology and knew the *threat* of violence could be as effective as violence itself. Each stroke left you wondering if there just might be an innocent explanation. But when you added it up, you knew there wasn't. It could all be bluff, of course, but you couldn't be sure. You daren't risk calling it. There was no way you would rely on the human rights law when your children were involved. 'Accidents' could still happen. 'Relentless pursuit of truth regardless of personal cost' was one thing. When the cost became personal to your family, that was quite another. Again, he asked himself if it was time he bottled out? Julian would surely understand. But what about William? Would he?

Barbara read his mind. "You mustn't give up now. Remember the family motto."

"Yes, I know. But there are limits, even to intolerability."

"It'll be half-term soon. I'll take them to Brighton – stay with my parents."

The dark moment passed. Howard pondered the idea. It might work. His mother could go with them. It would be a break for her, and the kids loved their Gran. At least, it would take the heat off for a time. He'd have to be careful they weren't followed, of course. He could lay a false trail for the benefit of the news desk bug. Yes, it might work. And if Edgar's briefings lived up to expectations, the whole grimy affair could soon be over.

Then he'd ask for a transfer to sub-editing.

197

A new market for IPI UK

Red, black, red, black, red, green…Edgar was on a roll. For the first time in his life he'd made a twenty break. Six balls potted consecutively. And one shot involving deep screw, as Howard had taught him. That was the icing on the cake. Howard had watched every stroke and applauded at the end of the break.

It was late afternoon, before their shifts started, and they had the snooker room to themselves. They weren't playing a full frame, just practising. Flushed with success, Edgar decided to quit while he was ahead. He hung up his cue in its case, pocketed his chalk and sat down next to his tutor. There was something he needed to tell him.

"They want me to nick your diary."

"Do they now? I'd better hang on to it then."

"They're after personal information – who you talk to privately outside the office."

"Well, I'm talking to you, Edgar."

They both laughed.

"I told him – Mr Quinn – there was no way I could do it. I couldn't watch you all the time till you took your jacket off, I had my own work to do."

"Someone would see you, anyway."

"That's what I said. Told him I couldn't risk my job."

"When are you meeting him again?"

"He's coming to our lodge next week."

Howard pondered on how best to lay a false trail for Quinn and his spooks. Then he had an idea. "Tell him I'm into bee-keeping. Tell him you think I'm a member of East Cheam Bee-keeping Society and that I could be contacting someone there."

Edgar grinned. "They might get stung."

"It has been known."

"I like your style, Howard."

"And suss him out on their next move. That's what we desperately need to know."

"I'll see what I can do."

"Thanks, Edgar. You're definitely improving, you know."

"What, as a spy?"

"No, as a snooker player."

*　　　*　　　*

CATHOLIC SCHOOLGIRLS TAUGHT TO USE CONDOMS
Parents 'outraged' by three-in-a-bed sex lessons

Marcus C Quinn III felt an uplifting sense of encouragement as he read Howard Mitchell's latest exclusive. He had long regarded the six million-strong Catholic community as a rich potential market for IPI products. It had been a closed sector for far too long due to the Church's repressive policy on artificial contraception. But it seemed they had now adopted a more enlightened approach to sex education.

The breakthrough had apparently been made when a rival condom company infiltrated a Catholic school in the Midlands. The school had agreed to teach girls of fourteen how to unroll the company's products on an enlarged model penis. Courses for boys included homosexuality and anal sex. He could only marvel at the power of the liberal propaganda machine in not only persuading Catholic teachers to instruct Catholic pupils in sodomy but to use condoms in the process. It was doubly priceless. He chuckled so much that he had to stop reading for a moment while he wiped his eyes.

It appeared that when parents first learned of the classes they feared an element of child abuse, mental if not actually physical, because the children, who had previously been happy at school, told them they did not want to attend on certain days. Parents again, Quinn thought contemptuously. Their children should be compelled to attend. Parents should be prosecuted if they kept them away.

The story got better. Pupils at the school received handouts, written by a 'specialist sexual health adviser', which offered advice on homosexuality, three-in-a-bed sessions, masturbation, oral sex, kinky outfits, bondage and sex toys.

Although *The Announcer* article adopted a negative tone and was heavily biased in favour of the old-fashioned parents involved, Quinn knew there was no such thing as bad publicity. Here was a golden opportunity to expand his company's activities in a previously closed sector. If his rivals could manage it with their dodgy condoms, IPI could surely go one better with its far superior pills and new range of contraceptive jabs.

The RC community was opening up and he had to make sure IPI had its foot in the door of this massive potential market. The fact that one Catholic school had already been converted to progressive thinking on sex education meant that others would surely follow. All that was needed was a gentle push from his marketing division: introductory offers of free morning-after pills for a month, that sort of thing.

The real beauty of it was that teachers were willing to do his salesmen's work for them – without a penny being paid in commission. Howard Mitchell and *The Announcer* may be giving him a hard time but the liberal establishment dominating education was certainly offering him an easy one.

*   *   *

The yellow and brown colours with pink spotted cap swooped round the final bend into the home straight at Goodwood well ahead of the rest of the field. His Lordship's horse, Face the Music, was a stayer and that was why his jockey had been instructed to send him into an early lead.

There were some speedier animals in the field but the front-running tactics were designed to test their stamina. They would use up their speed trying to catch the leader. That was the script, anyway, and it seemed to be working as Face the Music passed the two-furlong pole some five lengths clear of the chasing pack and showing no signs of flagging.

Shouts of "Go on boy" filled His Lordship's private box as the gap between his horse and the others started to shrink. With a furlong to go, Face the Music's lead had been cut to less than two lengths and the jockey had got his whip out. His Lordship, binoculars pressed to his eyes, seemed to be keeping his cool but Her Ladyship, a skinny woman much younger than her husband, started waving her race card and calling: "Keep going, my beauty."

The whips were flailing now and excitement rose in the box as another horse joined Face the Music in the lead with fifty yards to go. Among the invited guests, Julian and his wife, Claire, also trained their binoculars on the runners. They had felt obliged to back Face the Music, albeit with a modest £100 each way. At the post, there was only a short head in it but when the photo finish camera had done its work, the short head was not that of Face the Music.

"The lazy swine," Her Ladyship declared, tearing up her bookie's ticket which had just cost her a grand. "Couldn't hold out for one more yard."

Julian made a sympathetic face but felt the verdict rather harsh coming from someone who had just been calling the horse her beauty. The wretched beast had given its all. It had set the pace, out in front alone, for the best part of one-and-a-half miles then, lashed mercilessly in the closing stages, had courageously dug deep to find something extra, only to be pipped on the line by a younger and faster animal. It had still hung on to finish second. Her Ladyship should have backed it each way.

His Lordship, his ruddy aristocratic features animated by the excitement, took a more philosophical view. "We had a run for our money, my dear. The going didn't suit him, I'm afraid."

Other members of the party, well-heeled relatives, friends and *Announcer* executives, the men in their best suits and the ladies in their designer dresses and frilly hats, commiserated with their host. Reservations were expressed about the trainer's tactics. Front runners seldom seemed to win. Few jockeys could master the art, it seemed. Perhaps he had been 'sent on' too early. The ground wasn't right. A longer distance might suit him better...

Still, there was always the next race. As they returned to their champers and nibbles, and studied their race cards, His Lordship drew Julian to one side. "I'm glad I've had this opportunity for a quiet word, dear boy." He always called Julian "dear boy" even though he was only a few years older. "I've been thinking about the campaign on population control."

So he'd finally noticed, Julian thought. His Lordship exercised his right of editorial input only sparingly but, when he did, you listened. And you took note. If you upset His Lordship, hardship would surely follow. Julian would have felt a lot less apprehensive if Face the Music had won its race rather than finished second.

"I've been talking to a lot of people – advertisers, business advisers – and I'm wondering if we're doing the right thing. We've been running it quite a time now. What's your view?"

"Circulation's up by 25,000, My Lord."

"Do call me Jack. Everyone does."

"Well, Jack, we're back above a million. First increase in four years."

"I know, and it's terrific, but I'm not sure if what we're doing is within our compass." He paused for effect but there was no reaction from Julian. "We seem to be upsetting a few people it would be wiser not to upset, if you follow me..." Still no reaction.

His Lordship sighed. "I know we're in the business of selling newspapers and the board will be pleased with our progress...but we do need to strike a balance, dear boy. Our advertisers, you know..."

"Advertising revenue's up as well, Jack," the Editor reminded him. "Display and classified – both up by ten per cent. Only the Magazine's not pulling its weight in that area." It was a well-aimed arrow and it found its mark. The Magazine's editor was Fiona Templeton, His Lordship's niece and noted both for her professional limitations and lesbian liaisons, which His Lordship often went to great lengths to hush up.

He was quick to defend his niece. "Fiona has a lot of problems. The advertising will pick up, I'm sure."

"I'm sure you're right, Jack." Julian launched another pre-emptive strike. "By the way, is there any truth in the rumour about Fiona and that TV woman, Justine something or other?" The question was asked in a casual, throwaway manner but its sensitive and mind-concentrating implications were quite unmistakable.

Julian, champagne in hand, looked innocently at his employer. His Lordship, a morsel of smoked salmon half way to his mouth, looked balefully at his employee. Both men fully understood each other.

"None at all," His Lordship snapped. "Fiona's private life is her own affair. I wouldn't dream of interfering."

"Of course not, Jack. What was it you were saying – about our population control campaign?"

Jack had suddenly spotted a shooting crony he needed to talk to at the rear of the box. "Oh, er...nothing. Just tone it down a bit, that's all."

Julian drained his glass and breathed a sigh of relief. He'd headed off a very nasty moment. He was sure the plug had been about to be pulled on his campaign. Astute diplomacy had saved the day.

*   *   *

It was time to harvest the tomatoes. At least the fairly plump crimson ones – that vivid shade of red Edgar remembered so well from Stanley's childhood picture books, even from his own before them. The ripened fruit were fewer this year. All told, it was a strangely disappointing crop. He had watered, fed, pruned and nurtured them with the same dedication as always but, for some reason, they had not thrived with their usual vigour.

Brawton and District Horticultural Society had sent their customary invitation to exhibit his produce at their annual show but he realised the modest specimens he was gently separating from their vines were far from prize-winners. They wouldn't even rate a 'highly commended'. He decided not to enter them. He had had enough humiliation for one year...

After placing the ripe fruit in the fridge, he set off for his daily walk round The Meadow. It was cooler now in the afternoons. The milder days of September had come as a welcome relief after the long hot summer. The wild flowers were mostly fading and one or two of the lofty elms were ever so slightly tinged with yellow. You couldn't avoid a feeling of sadness with the approach of autumn. It would be another seven months before the rustle of spring restored the heady hawthorn blossom and the enticing powder blue carpet you dare not walk on.

Except, of course, it wasn't going to happen. The trees which had escaped the deadly Dutch elm disease rampant elsewhere now faced the ignominy of a chainsaw massacre. Sure, IPI promised to save a few but you couldn't believe them. The bluebells and wild primroses would flower no more. Within months his little private paradise would be torn apart and flattened with concrete. The speed with which breeze block buildings were erected, the chemicals factory would probably be up and running by next spring.

Even as the depressing thought crossed his mind, he saw through the undergrowth a group of men with long poles, measuring tapes and theodolites. The surveyors had arrived already. The Meadow's days were numbered.

An occupational hazard

Howard had first noticed the slight tremor in his hands towards the end of a closely contested frame in the snooker room a week or two earlier. Only the pink and black balls remained to be potted and the scores were level. The cue ball was in a difficult position next to the pink and he had to raise his bridge hand to address it. As he did so, his hand trembled and he miscued. It was a foul stroke and it cost him the frame.

He thought nothing of it at the time but the tremor gradually grew worse, to the point where he was unable to carry a cup of tea across a room without spilling half of it. Barbara knew all about the journalistic creed – the relentless pursuit of truth regardless of personal cost – and she suspected that her husband's latest assignment was beginning to exact its personal cost in the form of stress.

She noticed that he had also lost weight and that he became breathless on climbing their flight of stairs. In bed he was feverishly hot and could not stop scratching to relieve constant itching. All these symptoms made them both irritable and impatient with the children. To cap it all, their sex life, erratic at the best of times, became non-existent.

Barbara knew a sick man when she saw one. "If you don't go and see the doctor, I'll get him to call here and see you," she threatened her husband after he'd reduced Christopher to tears over some petty misdemeanour.

Howard didn't like doctors. He'd coped with plenty of stress in the past. It was an occupational hazard. You just didn't let it get to you. But then his snooker deteriorated further and he couldn't pot a ball. This had never happened before. This was serious. Reluctantly, he agreed to tests.

It was just as well that he did. When the results came back, the GP informed him he was suffering from an over-active thyroid gland and told him to take two weeks off work. "Have you had any worries or emotional upsets recently?" the doctor inquired.

Howard had to laugh. "You could say that, doctor." He realised that the medic probably wouldn't believe him if he elaborated so he didn't bother trying. Fortunately, his condition, though serious, could be treated by medication. He took his prescription and walked out of the surgery smiling to himself and slightly envious of the comfortable, hassle-free lifestyle enjoyed by members of the medical profession.

No-one bugging their phones, tampering with their cars or threatening their families. And that, he realised, was probably just for starters.

For Howard Mitchell, 'the nightmare' was well into its stride.

*   *   *

In fact, it did feel like a bad dream when, at 11 pm a few nights later, the electronic alarm from the gateposts buzzed in the lounge. Howard, still on sick leave from the office, had been drinking coffee in the kitchen with Barbara when they heard the buzzer. He reached for his camera and went to open the front door, fastened on its chain, just as the doorbell rang.

The porch light illuminated two heavily built men wearing anoraks and dark trousers. "Howard Mitchell?" one asked.

"Yes."

"We're police officers." An ID card was flashed. "May we come in?"

"Yes, of course." Howard placed his camera on the hall table, removed the chain from the door and opened it. He wondered if they had traced the person who had punctured his wife's tyres. It seemed unlikely but you never knew. He showed the CID officers into his lounge. "Do sit down. It's rather late to be calling if it's about our security."

They sat massively in the two armchairs and regarded him with the ponderous alertness of expression that is the hallmark of detectives the world over. One was about forty, with a round face, neat moustache and an amiable manner. The other was younger, taller and ominously truculent.

"It's not about your security," the younger officer said distastefully. "It's about your computers."

Howard leaned forward on the settee, mystified. "My computers?"

"That's right. How many have you got, Mr Mitchell?"

Howard knew he didn't have to tell them anything but the question seemed innocuous enough. He was about to say "two" when he recalled that Julian had taken over his laptop when he began his sick leave.

"I've only got one: my PC."

The policemen exchanged meaning glances and, at that moment, Barbara came in carrying the cup of coffee Howard had left in the kitchen. As he took it from her, his hand trembled, spilling coffee on his trousers.

"You'd better go to bed, darling," he said, wiping his trousers with a handkerchief. "This is just par for the course."

Barbara had no intention of going to bed. She sat on the settee next to him. "Not yet. I want to know what's going on."

"So do I," her husband said, raising the cup to his lips but again spilling coffee in the saucer.

"The detectives watched him silently. You could see their minds working. Here was an obviously guilty man who was hiding something.

"Where is it – your computer?" the truculent officer demanded.

"It's in my bedroom."

The officer got up abruptly. "Show me."

Howard rose to his feet, politeness now forgotten. "I sincerely hope you've got a warrant."

The amiable officer also stood up. "That's right, Mr Mitchell. We do have a warrant." He produced a piece of paper from his pocket and handed it to Howard. "You'll see it also authorises us to remove your computer for examination."

Howard scrutinised the document. It looked authentic. "Examine it…what on earth for?"

"Child pornography," the younger policeman almost snarled. "We have reason to believe you have downloaded images of child pornography."

Howard and Barbara looked at each other. This was a lot more than par for the course. As dirty tricks went, this must rank with the murkiest. If there was one sure way of discrediting anyone it was to allege they had downloaded child porn on their computer. Careers had been wrecked by the tactic. Some well-known people had been permanently damaged by it. Even when found to be completely innocent of the charge in subsequent inquiries, they never recovered. Throw enough mud and some of it is bound to stick.

All these thoughts flashed through Howard's mind as the police officers headed for the stairs. He thought of standing in their way but if he did they could charge him with obstructing an officer in the course of his duty. The children were asleep and Yvette would be watching TV in her room. There was no point in creating a disturbance. Best to let the law take its course as quietly as possible.

Few nocturnal happenings escaped Sally's attention, however, and as Oscar started barking in the kitchen and two burly strangers appeared on the landing carrying Howard's personal computer and trailing cables, she stood watching at her bedroom door, as always clutching her teddy.

"Why are those men taking your computer, Daddy?" she demanded.

"It needs to be repaired, darling" he assured her. "It's got a virus. Go back to bed now, that's a good girl. There's nothing to worry about."

Satisfied, she returned sleepily to bed.

Bed, however, remained some way off for Howard. When the two heavies had finished stowing all his computer equipment in the boot of their police car, while communicating progress into their crackling personal radios, the nice half of the nice-nasty partnership said: "I'm sorry, sir, but I must ask you to accompany us to the police station."

"What on earth for?" Howard asked irritably, realising it was the second time he'd asked the question and how feeble it sounded.

"To answer a few questions."

"I can answer your questions here."

Mr Nasty stepped in. "Either you come voluntarily or we'll arrest you," he declared aggressively.

"I see. Am I allowed to change into my shoes first?" He was wearing his slippers.

The older officer nodded but, as Howard was half way up the stairs, the other shouted: "I'll go with him."

There was a commotion in the hall as Barbara tried to intervene. The shock of all the bizarre intrusion shattering the peaceful domesticity was too much for her. "Leave him," she cried. "He's not done anything. This is our home."

Howard turned on the stairs. Ridiculous though it seemed, they suspected he might be trying to escape. The situation was getting out of hand. Barbara was losing her cool, Oscar was still barking and there was a risk of disturbing Sally again. Enough was enough. Better to phone the NUJ's lawyers and go with the officers. So after telling Barbara to phone his union's on-call solicitors and assuring her he'd be home within the hour, he was escorted to the police car.

But not before Barbara let it be known they hadn't heard the last of the matter. "You realise this is blatant police harassment, don't you? There's no child pornography on my husband's computer and you damn well know it. We'll sue you for wrongful arrest." But her parting shot was a real classic: "I'm a nurse and I treat a lot of policemen at my hospital. I won't harass you if they bring you in – but I'll make sure you feel the injections."

It might have been the dim light from the street lamp but the two heavyweight plods suddenly looked pale. And the tall one winced visibly. Howard had never seen Barbara in such a temper. When they reached the car, he turned and waved to the defiant figure standing in the porch. He was proud of her…although even he baulked at the thought of this irate nurse brandishing a hypodermic needle with intent.

It was midnight and raining heavily when they arrived at Brawton police station, and Howard's slippers were soon saturated. The building was ablaze with lights but there was little activity. He was taken before the duty sergeant, who glanced up briefly from his desk and ordered Howard to turn out his pockets. It was no use protesting. They were only doing their job. He extracted his wallet, mobile phone, pen, diary, keys, handkerchief, thyroid medication, nail file, comb, some small change and a well-worn block of snooker chalk, placing each item carefully on the desk.

"Now your watch and cuff-links," the duty sergeant said curtly.

Howard felt like a criminal. "I wish to place on record that you are abusing your powers, sergeant," he said, controlling his mounting sense of outrage with difficulty.

The officer picked up Howard's personal diary. "You can make a statement later. Watch and cuff-links."

Howard removed his onyx cuff links and gold wristwatch. "How long do you propose to hold me? You should know that the NUJ's lawyers have been informed."

The sergeant was reading Howard's diary. "Interesting life you lead, Mr Mitchell." Howard said nothing. The diary contained no details of his investigation.

"What makes a journalist like you interested in kiddie porn?"

"What makes a police officer like you make such a slanderous statement?"

The sergeant looked up. "Slander is it?"

"That and wrongful arrest, malicious prosecution, causing fear and alarm to law-abiding citizens, violating human rights and attempting to suppress free speech."

"I'm sure you know how to make an official complaint, Mr Mitchell."

Howard wasn't going to be led into that blind alley. "I'm not talking about the discredited PCA. I'm talking about a High Court action against you and your officers."

"Now I'm really worried," the sergeant scoffed. "You're being held for questioning as part of our continuing investigations into the activities of a paedophile ring in the United States and this country. We're acting in good faith on information received."

"From whom? Who's put you up to this?"

The officer grinned. "Reliable sources, I think the phrase is." He beckoned to a uniformed constable and Howard was led down a corridor into a small interview room containing only a table and two chairs. He sat wearily on one and the constable stood between him and the door.

"I'm not going to escape," he said in an attempt at humour.

The young constable stood smirking at him as if enjoying his moment of power. This was probably a ploy to unnerve suspects, Howard thought, so he kept his trembling hands in his pockets. They had caused him enough trouble already.

It was 2.15 am when the young, abrasive CID officer entered the room. There would be no questioning tonight. The NUJ's lawyers had obviously acted fast. They'd had plenty of experience in springing falsely arrested journalists from police custody. He was told his computer would be checked by experts. Everything he had written and looked at would be recorded. If any images of child pornography were found, he would face criminal charges. In the meantime he was being released on police bail.

With a shaking hand, Howard signed the receipt for his belongings, which were then tipped unceremoniously out of a plastic bag on to the duty sergeant's desk. Could he telephone for a taxi, as there was no credit left on his mobile? Not from the police station. Against regulations. But there was a public call box about a hundred yards away.

The rain was still pouring and by the time he'd reached the phone box his feet were again saturated. He had to wait half an hour for a taxi. Worries or emotional problems, doc? You name them.

The deal

Marcus C Quinn III was feeling rather pleased with himself. The morning had gone well. He had approved a direct mail campaign targeting Catholic schools with an offer of free morning-after pills and had finally negotiated a deal with the intransigent television producer. A compromise had been reached over his sweetener, with the necessary adjustments made to the company's PR budget.

It was a strictly short-term agreement until Tina took effect. The guy had to be kept onside for two reasons: he could guarantee ongoing, sexually stimulating programme content and veto any storyline about promiscuity causing sexually transmitted diseases.

Once Tina's measures for compulsory population control were introduced there would be no more need for televised brainwashing. The schmuck could go take a running jump. IPI would be printing its own money, with new factories like the one prudently earmarked for Brawton taking care of the projected surge in production.

But what really made Brother Marcus's day was the coded e-mail he'd received from a police source detailing Howard's uncomfortable experience the previous night. It seemed that the journalist's curiosity about Tina might finally be on the wane. The latest intelligence revealed he was suffering the shakes and was taking medication for a serious glandular condition. His private diary had also been perused and certain sensitive data noted.

At last, Quinn had some good news for his tetchy Supremo when he next phoned. He'd been asking awkward questions about tactics recently as *The Announcer's* campaign gained in strength and popularity. Now, it seemed, they'd got Mr Mitchell on the run. It was all highly gratifying.

Success always stimulated Quinn's libido and he decided on a quickie before lunch. When the butler brought in his elevenses – coffee made from beans specially imported from Brazil and a large cognac on a silver tray – he inquired about the whereabouts of Sandra, his favourite maid.

"She's in the pool, sir."

"Send her in, Robert."

"Very good, sir."

Robert, along with everyone else on Quinn's extensive domestic staff, knew all about the quickies in the study but, like the other servants, had soon learned to pretend he didn't.

*   *   *

After lunch, Quinn planned to motor over to Brawton to meet 'that guy, Ed' and check on the progress of his company's £30 million investment. The architects and surveyors were still mapping out The Meadow site for the new factory and he wanted to discuss the building's precise location. He was particularly concerned about the positioning of its foundation stone, which was to form the centrepiece of an elaborate, American-style inauguration ceremony. All senior IPI executives would be present, as well as local VIPs and civic dignitaries, plus, of course, the media for a big publicity splurge.

The occasion would provide the perfect prelude to Tina's long-awaited summit conference, when plans would be finalised for groundbreaking reforms determining the future shape of Britain's population. This top-secret seminar, like all the other meetings, required the same conditions of maximum security offered only by a Masonic temple. There could be no more ideal venue than Brawton Lodge 15392, less than a mile-and-a-half away.

The set-up was perfect, he said, outlining his plans to Edgar in the bar of Brawton Masonic Hall later that day. 'Ed' who, as well as being a Royal Arch Companion, was still, of course, Master of his Lodge, agreed. He was getting the hang of his role as double agent and managed to appear enthusiastic about the grandiose plans for the IPI factory's 'inauguration'.

He told Marcus the Brothers would be honoured to host the secret seminar. Would it be a Royal Arch function? He would need to know how many delegates would be attending and, as far as possible, who they were. This was a slightly tricky one for Quinn. How much, if anything, Edgar knew about Tina was uncertain. But as his proficient spy in targeting Howard Mitchell, he must have worked out what the intrigue was about. How far could he be trusted? Not as far as inviting him to the seminar, maybe, but as Lodge Master, his hospitality would have to be recognised.

Tina's members had been consulted beforehand on this delicate question and, after careful consideration, it had been decided to offer him the prestigious appointment of Grand Tiler for the meeting. In company with hand-picked security officers, he would be responsible for guarding the outside door of the conference chamber. Masonic tradition also required a Grand Inner Guard on the inside.

The Royal Arch Grand Commander had been chauffeured over to Brawton in the Rolls, in anticipation of a day's uninhibited drinking and even his capacity for indulgence had reached saturation point when he finally put this proposition to Edgar, as if bestowing on him the supreme accolade. Edgar, who had consumed only his customary half of lager, was disappointed. He felt his eminent Companion could do a lot better.

As well as having been taught to be cautious, he knew never to accept first offers. He was quite firm about it. He told Quinn there was no way he could sanction a meeting in his Lodge without knowing exactly what was going on…who the participants were and what was being discussed. In return for providing all necessary facilities and hospitality, he expected to be fully informed as a matter of courtesy.

"You're quite right, Ed." Quinn's speech was slightly slurred as he downed his fifth double Scotch on the rocks. "You're a swell guy and we owe you. We wouldn't want you to feel unhappy with the arrangements. What do you have in mind?"

Edgar was mindful of Howard's instructions: *The Announcer* needed to know about Tina's next move. Here was a golden opportunity to find out. "Well, a list of invited guests, for a start."

"Sorry, Ed. Top secret. Just wait till you see them. Then you'll know why. You've heard about VIPs…these people are VVIPs."

"At least what they'll be discussing. I have a right to know that as Master."

"Relax, Ed. Would I sell you a bum steer? They're top people. They won't be plotting a revolution." If only he knew, Quinn thought.

"I'm not asking for their agenda in detail…just some brotherly assistance." He drew his hand twice across his right eyebrow, the signal of a Mason in Distress.

Quinn realised Edgar's dilemma as Lodge Master. As a brother Mason, he was sworn on oath to respond. "OK, let's put it like this…it's a summit meeting of highly respected intellectuals who share a vision for improving the health of the nation. We call it the Tina Project…and that's absolutely all I can tell you."

Edgar made a mental note. He'd write it all down as soon as possible because his memory was so poor. In the meantime, it was clear he was calling the shots. "In that case, Brother Quinn, I'll be happy to authorise your seminar on condition that I'm appointed Grand Inner Guard. That is the least I can expect."

Quinn thought about it. You always had to compromise with the English. "OK, Ed," he said finally. "You got yourself a deal."

The apology

The miniature alarm clock at Howard's bedside showed 3.25 am when the phone rang. He'd just gone to bed after his first night at work following sick leave and he was shattered. So shattered that he'd forgotten to disconnect the bedroom phone extension. This could only be another silent call, he thought as he reached over and picked up the receiver. "Hello."

"Is that you, Howard?" It was his mother and she sounded distraught.

"Mother...are you all right?"

"I'm sorry to wake you, Howard, but I've had such a shock. I know it's late but can you come round? I'm in a terrible state."

He was wide awake now. "Of course. What's happened?"

"It was awful, Howard. I thought I was going to have a heart attack. The police have been here...at three in the morning. I didn't hear them banging on the door because I'd taken my hearing aid out. They woke the warden and she let them in."

The bedroom was warm but he suddenly felt cold. It was an effort keeping his voice calm. "At this time of night? What did they want?"

"Something about a missing woman...I couldn't hear most of it. I told them there was no woman here, except for me."

"They didn't hurt you, did they?"

"No, they didn't touch me...but they gave me a real fright. I thought something had happened to you...an accident or something. When *they* call, it's usually bad news...'specially in the middle of the night."

Two weeks on medication had steadied Howard's hands but they started shaking again. And they felt clammy. "Are you on your own or is the warden still there?"

"No, she's gone back to bed. I wish *I* could...I've still got palpitations."

"Have you phoned the doctor?"

"Pardon."

"I think you should call the doctor," he shouted, and turned to look at Barbara. She was still asleep.

"Doctor? You know what I think about doctors."

"OK, Mother. Make yourself a cup of tea. And keep warm. I'll be round in about half an hour."

"I'm ever so sorry to trouble you, Howard…I'm just all shook up…"

"It's no trouble. I wasn't asleep anyway. See you in half an hour."

The anger welled up inside him as he sped along the deserted roads towards Cheam. His innate self-discipline, honed by twenty years as a reporter, was starting to crack. However iron-clad your self-control, you were still human…you couldn't halt the flow of adrenalin. The strokes had been subtle at first but now they were getting seriously nasty – continental style. *Intolerabili*, indeed.

He realised how they'd got his mother's address, of course. Edgar had warned him they were after his diary. The duty sergeant had taken a great interest in it when they'd illegally held him at the police station. It contained several addresses, including his mother's.

In common with all journalists, Howard knew bribery and corruption were rife in the Force. Senior officers had admitted it. But for a policeman, a public servant, to cause alarm and distress to an innocent old woman disgusted him. What about the oath the man had solemnly sworn when he became a constable…to serve all Her Majesty's subjects *without favour or affection, malice or ill will*? Had he kept his fingers crossed behind his back while he was swearing it? His treachery would not have come cheap. It would have cost a lot of euros.

His mother was no longer hysterical when he arrived at her flat. But her face was drawn, her eyes anxious and her hair dishevelled. She looked even frailer than usual in her dressing gown and slippers. He gave her a long hug and squeezed her cold, arthritic hands. She was full of remorse for having dragged him out of bed in the middle of the night. "It's good of you to come, Howard. I feel so much better now. I shouldn't have phoned you."

"It's all right, Mother. I'm appalled at the way you've been treated. They've not heard the last of it, believe me."

She had brewed a pot of tea and they sat with their mugs (no china cups at times like this) in front of the flickering logs. "Tell me about it from the beginning," he said.

"Well, the first thing I knew was the light switched on and the warden standing by my bed shouting something at me. It was a shock to be woken up like that. I put my hearing aid in and she told me the police wanted to come in. I couldn't understand her at first. It was very frightening…I was afraid something had happened to you, or Barbara or the children."

"Did the policemen come into your bedroom?"

"Not then. They were standing at the door…two of them, both in uniform. They hadn't even taken their helmets off."

Insult added to injury, he thought. "Then what happened?"

"The warden made me get out of bed because the policemen wanted to look under it. I couldn't believe it. What did they think I was hiding – heroin or something? Anyway, I got up and they made me sit on the chair in the hall in my nightdress while they searched the whole flat. I didn't know *what* was going on. My palpitations started and I thought I was going to pass out, it was just so terrible…"

He felt the anger welling up again. "It must have been, Mother," he said sympathetically. "How long were they here for?"

"Not long. Less than ten minutes. Course, there's not much to see is there?"

"Did they say anything to you?"

"Nothing at all. No apology or anything. When they left the warden said they were looking for a woman who'd gone missing from home. They'd been told she was here. Who would tell them a thing like that?"

Who indeed. His poor mother didn't know the half of it. If he'd tried to explain, she would have thought he'd gone round the bend. "Search me," he said, trying to reassure her. "These things can happen, with the best will in the world." And the worst, he added under his breath.

"Anyway, I'm all right now – thanks to you. You're a good boy, Howard."

He forced a smile. She'd suffered a severe shock but she was a tough nut at heart. You didn't survive six years of war, the Blitz and the hardships of rationing without developing a stubborn streak. Hitler hadn't beaten her. It was unlikely that a few bent coppers would.

All the same, precautions were necessary. Now they knew her address, the next thing to expect were the silent telephone calls. He'd have to get her put on interception straight away. And he'd need to talk to the warden about security. The accommodation was supposed to be sheltered, after all. It would need to merit the description. Oddly enough, the one factor in his mother's favour was her deafness. If suspicious callers knocked on her door, she wouldn't hear them.

He got up to leave. "You sure you're OK now?"

"I'll be fine. Thanks ever so much for coming round. I don't know what I'd do without you."

"I'll sort them out tomorrow, Mother, don't worry. If there's any more problems, you must phone me again – day or night – promise?"

"There'll be no more problems, I'm sure."

"Promise…OK?"

"All right, if you say so."

Her hugged her again and kissed her dear, delicate old face. "That's my girl."

She smiled bravely. "You're a good boy, Howard."

*   *   *

There was some comfort in the thought that the Euro-spooks must be getting desperate when they targeted innocent and defenceless old women in sheltered accommodation. But as it was his poor old mother who was the victim, it didn't last long on his way home through the dawn mist. The malevolent bastards weren't going to get away with this. He'd make sure he got the Met Commissioner on the case if it was the last thing he did.

Tears sprang into his eyes as he recalled his earliest memories of his mother. He could still remember his feeling of utter desolation when she left him on his first day at primary school, aged five. Later, when she enrolled him at Sunday school, he recalled her peeping through a curtained window at him as he sat with other pupils on their tiny chairs in the Beginners' classroom. She hadn't thought he'd seen her but he'd been unusually observant even then.

He could vividly recall her beautiful young face close to his when she taught him how to tie his first necktie, knotted his shoelaces and combed his hair…how he had held her hand on department store escalators, jumping off excitedly when they reached the top. His mother was old now and ill but he loved her as much as he did then. He wanted to protect her in her vulnerability just as she had done for him in his.

Here was a truly good lady, who had never done anyone any harm in her entire life. Her only pleasures were her two grandchildren, going to church on a Sunday and watching the birds and squirrels from the window of her tiny flat. It was nothing short of a scandal that she should now be viciously victimised through no fault of her own, simply because her son was making things difficult for a gang of neo-fascist, culture-of-death fanatics.

His mother phoned the following afternoon just before he left for work. It had all been a mistake, like he'd said. An inspector and a policewoman had just been round to apologise. They were both ever so nice and had taken their hats off when they entered her flat. They had explained that they'd been looking for a woman called Maxwell who had run away from home and somehow the name had got mixed up with Mitchell. They said they were sorry for 'any inconvenience' caused.

It sounded horribly implausible to Howard. "Do you know anyone called Maxwell?" he asked her.

"That's just it. I've asked the warden and there's no-one by that name round here."

After he'd told her he would have a word with the warden and she had sent her love to Barbara and the children she rang off. She seemed none the worse for her experience. But Howard was still seething. 'Any inconvenience...' The words themselves were an insult after his mother's ordeal. As if a disingenuous explanation and half-baked verbal apology could undo the distress and trauma they'd caused. The shock alone could have killed her.

No doubt, in their cynically oblique way, that was what they were trying to do, while making sure they were not directly involved...a sort of murder by remote control, like William's had been. He'd see them in hell first. Once Julian was informed, it would go straight to the Commissioner. No messing about with the Police Complaints Authority or even CIB3, the anti-corruption unit. Heads would need to roll, starting with the duty sergeant's.

The double act

"Are you sure Julian's getting cold feet on the population thing?"

Andrew winked at Howard. The double act was 'on microphone' again. It was part of the feedback they were providing for Quinn via the bug below the news desk. Steve, the electronics genius, had assured them it was still working. The least they could do was use it to impart a diet of misinformation.

"Looks that way, Andrew," Howard replied. "He's talking about taking me off the investigation. I can't believe it…after all the work I've put in."

"Has he told you why?"

"Not in so many words. He thinks it's affecting my health but I've told him I'm OK. I've just got to keep taking the tablets."

"There must be another reason…I mean the campaign's putting on circulation. We're back over a million."

"Between you and me, I think that's all it is…a circulation stunt."

"Seriously?"

"Yep. They'll keep it going…go through the motions…as long as we sell more papers. But I've a feeling any day now he'll tell me to lay off Tina."

"That's show business. Can't say I'll be sorry. We've been stretched to the limit without you."

The conversation moved on to whether the proposed redundancies had been shelved, how Diane might perform in bed, the high-profile case of the burglar suing the householder who assaulted him…

Quinn's backroom boffin had heard enough. He pressed the edit button, rewound the record and when Robert came in with the coffee (instant for all the staff) handed the recorder to him for the boss. The boss was busy in his study with arrangements for Tina's summit when the butler brought him the instrument.

When he got round to playing it, he lit up a Romeo y Julietta by way of a small celebration. Everything was turning out just swell. One more creative push from his Euro-spooks would be all it needed. He thought of sending for Sandra but a woman was only a woman. A good cigar was a smoke.

*   *   *

The fringe-shaded light shone over the green baize in the snooker room and the brightly-coloured balls were all in position for the start of a frame but neither Howard nor Edgar was in a hurry to break off. By arrangement, they had come in early, before the start of their evening shift, when they knew the room would be empty. They were seated in a corner in a conspiratorial huddle.

"The summit's next month…November 4th, Mr Quinn told me," Edgar said, studying notes he'd made on a scrap of paper.

"Where…do you know?"

"I should do. It's at my Lodge…Brawton Masonic Hall."

"Why there?" Howard asked.

"They're laying the factory foundation stone on The Meadow that day. They call it an inauguration. Very big deal. The Press will be invited. Then they're holding the meeting afterwards. Maximum security. Press *not* invited."

"Can you get us in?"

Edgar laughed quietly. "No chance. It's strictly off limits. VVIPs only. Mr Big himself is coming."

Howard was listening. "You don't say. Who is he, do you know?"

"Don't ask me. But they've told me I'll know him when I see him. They've put me on the door. I'll be the Inner Guard."

Howard looked at Edgar with a mixture of admiration and incredulity. "You…on the door?"

"That's right. I'm Master of the Lodge…it's the least they can do."

"Then you could record the proceedings…"

Edgar laughed again. "Absolutely no way. Everyone'll be frisked for things like voice recorders. We've hired a whole firm of security guards… metal detectors, the lot. No minutes. No notes. No record. Officially they don't exist, you see."

Howard thought hard. "What about a bug? Could you plant a bug beforehand?"

"They've thought of that. The whole building's going to be swept for bugs before they start."

"An outside scanner?"

"The chamber's soundproofed. We made sure of that for our Lodge meetings. Graphite walls, acoustic baffles…the lot. We spent a fortune on it.

And there'll be security patrols outside as well."

"That's tough, Edgar. Looks like we'll have to rely on your memory."

"Not a good idea, Howard. I can never remember what day it is, thanks to this." He tapped the side of his gingery tonsure. You could still see the scar from the old injury. "I only remembered all this because I wrote it down straight away."

William had said Tina was 'virtually impregnable', which he knew Howard would regard as a challenge. 'Virtually' was the key word, the wordsmith decided. He'd cracked some tough challenges in his time. Tina would be no different.

Meanwhile, unstinting praise was called for. This unlikeliest of double agents had supplied him with priceless information – and at considerable risk to himself. "You've come up trumps again, Edgar. We won't forget it. There could be mega bucks in this for you."

"Some things money can't buy, Howard. Don't get me wrong, I'd be glad of a – what do you call it – a part credit. But at the end of the day, all Janice wants is the same view of The Meadow we've always had. Do you think that's too much to ask?"

"You never know, Edgar. You never know."

*　　　*　　　*

"They've brought your computer back." It was Barbara ringing him on his mobile as he drove home.

"That's big of them. When was this?"

"This afternoon. I was at work. Yvette was here with the kids. They all think it's come back from the repairers."

"Plain clothes officers then?"

"Yes. From what Yvette says, it seems they were the same two bruisers."

"Any note with it?"

"There's an envelope addressed to you."

"Open it, will you."

"Hold on." She opened the envelope and read the single sheet of CID-headed notepaper. "It just says they've completed their examination in accordance with powers vested in them under the Obscene Publications Act...section blah, blah, brackets sub-section blah, blah, blah. Your property is returned herewith. No further action will be taken."

"NFA eh? What a surprise. No apology or anything?"

"No, nothing else. No signature even."

"Well, it may be NFA for them but it's not NFA for me." They weren't getting away with it as easily as that. They'd put him through the wringer. First his car, then his contacts book, then Barbara's car, then his computer, then his mother and even his 'singer'. If he'd read it in a novel, he'd have said such pressure was well OTT. There'd be problems with that ultimate literary test 'the willing suspension of disbelief'. Yet it had all actually happened. Truth was indeed stranger than fiction – but soon it would be payback time.

Before then, however, lay other important matters. "What's for dinner, darling?"

"Beef stew and dumplings."

"With chips?"

"With chips."

"Who loves you, baby?"

* * *

The aphrodisiac qualities of beef stew and dumplings were amply vindicated later that night. Unusually for her, Barbara could not sleep afterwards. She turned to Howard, who never slept before 3 am, and said: "What are you going to do about it?"

He was writing some notes by the light of the bedside lamp. "Do about what?"

"You know…about the computer and the 'child porn' rubbish. You said it won't be 'no further action'."

"No, there'll be plenty of action…legal action. The union's looking into it. They're confident we've a good case for unlawful arrest, false imprisonment, human rights violation…you name it. We'll throw the book at them."

"Cast iron case, I'd say. But if it goes to court won't people think 'no smoke without fire'? You know what they're like."

"It won't go to court. They'll settle. They'd have to prove they had reasonable grounds to suspect a crime – and they didn't. It was malicious. Yes, they'll exploit the 'no smoke without fire' angle to exercise our minds but in the end they'll settle. They know they can't win."

"How much, do you think?"

"At least fifty thousand. Doesn't matter to them, it's taxpayers' money."

"Really?"

"Yes, maybe more."

"Whoopee!" She threw her arms round him and kissed him passionately.

He grinned at her. "You're too demanding, darling. I've got a headache."

They could still laugh.

"Then there's your mother's case," Barbara said. "She could do with fifty grand."

"That's a lot more serious. I still go cold when I think of it. At her age and in her condition, the shock might've killed her. But there's big problems…Mother's seventy and profoundly deaf. The ordeal of giving evidence in court would be too much. They'll exploit that, of course."

"It's all absolutely horrible. What's happening to the police? They never used to be like this. I remember when I was a child, going to school…my mum always used to tell me: cross the road with the policeman. You were brought up to trust them in those days. You can't now. It's a police state."

"That's right. They tried to clean up their act a few years back. Do you remember I told you about it? There was a secret meeting of ACPO…"

"What's that?"

"Association of Chief Police Officers…1998 I think it was. The minutes of the meeting were leaked to me. I do remember the key bit. They said police corruption in the UK was 'pervasive…at Third World levels',"

"That's appalling. And it's not got any better."

"There's still plenty of straight coppers, though. It's a mistake to think they're all bent. The trouble is the secret units in their ranks, like the Masons. They're poisoning the police and they can't seem to root them out."

Barbara was starting to feel drowsy. "Tell me a snooker story, darling."

Whenever Barbara couldn't sleep, Howard found that describing a recent frame of snooker to her worked like magic. "OK. The last time

I played Edgar – I give him five blacks start, you know – well, I got the thirty-five points back in one break. So that made us level. Then, you won't believe it, but he actually made a break of twenty – thanks to all the lessons I've given him.

"Anyway, it came to a blue ball game and I snookered him behind the pink. Well, he not only hit the blue off three cushions but potted it…what a fluke, you should have seen it. I had to tighten up the safety play after that but then he went in-off, leaving me just the pink and black to win. Pink was a straightforward half-ball pot into the middle but black was on the top cushion so I had to play a cannon with check side to develop it. Fortunately, the black rolled over the corner and that was it. Game over."

He glanced sideways at his wife. She was snoring gently.

*   *   *

They had rehearsed the script until they thought it sounded natural. With a wink, Andrew set the ball rolling. "So they've finally taken you off the case, Howard."

"'Fraid so. Julian told me last night. I'm gutted."

"Something about personal problems."

"You could say that…the bastards have started targeting my family. First my mother, now my son…"

"No way you can deal with that, old boy. No job's that important."

"All the same, I'm a bad loser as you know."

"Can't win 'em all…not even you."

"I'm just hoping the spooks'll give us a break now."

"I wouldn't bet on it."

"Exactly. So I'm packing the family off to the seaside for a while. Julian's putting it on exes."

"Where're they going?"

"Classified, old boy. Can't even tell you…strict orders from the boss."

"Give us a clue…off the record."

"Safe house on the Fylde Coast…that's all I can tell you."

*   *   *

Before setting off on the journey to Brighton, Howard got Steve Prentice to check the Rover for bugs and tracking devices. Nothing could surprise him any more, but the electronics expert gave him the all-clear. Just to make certain they weren't followed, Steve was enlisted to drive about a quarter of a mile behind them for part of the way.

When all the luggage had been packed in the boot, Gran and the kids stowed in the back with Oscar, and Barbara settled in front, Howard headed south along the A23. Traffic was surprisingly light for a Saturday afternoon. On reaching the M25, Steve turned off for his home in Caterham, after telling Howard on his mobile: "The only way anyone could track you now would be by spy satellite."

Even that wouldn't have surprised Howard, so omniscient seemed the Euro-spooks. But apart from Gran's hearing aid battery failing, they arrived on Brighton seafront just over an hour later without mishap. Fortunately, she'd brought replacements.

"This hearing aid's such a nuisance," she said apologetically," as Sally and Chris helped her out of the car. "It's such a fiddly thing. You're right Howard, I'll have to get a digital one, the sort that fit inside your ear."

A stiff breeze blowing off the English Channel snatched her words away. "Pardon," he said, cupping his hand to his ear. Everyone laughed. It was good to be able to relax at last. He only wished he could stay with them and forget all about Tina. But the 'impregnable' summit meeting was fast approaching and he was still racking his brains for a way of cracking it.

After tea in the small private hotel, kept immaculately by Barbara's middle-aged and energetic parents, Fred and Lilian, he said his good-byes. The kids were in their element, at the seaside with two Grans and a Grandpa to keep them happy, not to mention Oscar and his fascination for rock pools. It was reassuring to think that if the spooks were still interested in his family, they'd be looking for them at the other end of the country. All the same, Barbara had to stay vigilant.

"Don't worry, I won't let them out of my sight…not even your mum."

He hugged Sally and Christopher. Then his frail old mother. "Make sure you buy that digital…I'll pay for it," he shouted.

"No you won't. I won't let you."

But he could tell she was weakening. She'd heard so many good reports of the new hearing aids. They fitted ever so snugly, right inside the ear; no-one could tell they were there.

As Howard drove back up the A23 he put on a jazz CD and whistled along to the music. But he didn't go straight home. Steve Prentice had said something about a microchip the size of a postage stamp and a voice recorder you could fit into a small matchbox. When he reached Crawley, he called Steve on his mobile and headed towards the boffin's home in Caterham.

His mother had given him an idea.

*   *   *

"This is the external acoustic meatus," the elderly, sprightly Irishman said, pointing to a large diagram of the human ear pinned to the wall of Julian's office. Using a pencil, he tracked along the outer ear passage. "In Mr Brierley's case it's much wider than normal, due to the surgery after his accident." On reaching the inner ear, he continued: "I've examined Mr Brierley's inner ear under the microscope and his mastoid cavity is considerably enlarged. Most of the mastoid bone has been removed. I've never seen a cavity like it. It's like a cathedral in there!"

The Irishman, Prof Peter O'Brien, was the ear, nose and throat consultant at a leading teaching hospital. Julian had hired him, at prohibitive expense, because he was generally acknowledged to be the best ENT specialist in London. In addition to the Editor, the professor's attentive audience consisted of Andrew, Howard, Edgar, Steve and the senior sub-editor Bernard Baxter, the latter at Howard's special request.

The professor's blue eyes twinkled as he explained the functions of the incredibly delicate inner ear mechanisms…the incus, the cochlea, the tympanic antrum and the amazing semi-circular canals that hydraulically control our balance. Fortunately, these had not been damaged in the accident. The mastoid bone had simply been crushed.

But when he came to Edgar's titanium implant, he was full of praise for the doctors who had performed the reconstructive surgery all those years ago. "They didn't have the sophisticated equipment we have today," he explained. "But they've done a first class job in replacing the mastoid bone with a titanium implant. It still looks good as new. His only problem now is going through airport metal detectors!"

Julian held up a slim, shiny metal object about two inches long. It was Steve Prentice's prototype of a miniaturised voice recorder that he had adapted to open like a telescopic umbrella when in position. "You say

Mr Brierley's mastoid cavity is enlarged, professor and, as I understand it, would be big enough to accommodate this."

Prof O'Brien took the object, opened it up as directed by Steve, and examined it closely. "Without a doubt," he said. He knew what it was. Julian had told him after he'd expressed ethical reservations about Howard's inspired idea.

The Editor had explained that the Press sometimes needed to use subterfuge in their search for truth and that *The Announcer* would never do anything illegal or against the public interest. Once he understood the importance of the paper's investigation and had been assured of strict confidentiality, he agreed to participate.

"You are willing to insert it in Mr Brierley's ear?"

"Yes, as we agreed."

"Is there any risk to Mr Brierley?"

"None at all. It's a perfectly straightforward procedure."

"Would it be visible…if someone were to look down his ear, say?"

"Positioned in this particular mastoid cavity, no. Nothing would be visible."

"Would any anaesthetic be necessary?"

"None. I could insert it and secure it in five minutes…completely painless."

"And take it out later?"

"Certainly. No problem."

"Thank you, professor. You've been most helpful. We'll be in touch."

*   *   *

When the professor had left, it was Steve's turn to lecture the others. His prototype micro-recorder was longer and slimmer than the news desk bug, which had now ceased operating. But it took the art of miniaturisation several steps further. Though still in its experimental stage, it represented a breakthrough in microelectronics – a field dominated for years by the Japanese.

Once installed in Edgar's mastoid cavity, the device could be activated to open out by remote control. It could be deactivated and closed in the same way.

"What about possible detection?" Julian asked.

"Metal detectors would give a positive reading," Steve admitted. "But in Edgar's case, that would be consistent with his titanium implant…"

"Which everyone knows about," Edgar put in brightly. "They won't have a clue there's anything behind it."

"It's an ingenious idea, Howard," Julian said. "I congratulate you."

"Thanks, but Steve deserves the credit – and Edgar, of course," Howard said. Like everyone else in *The Announcer* snooker room, he'd known all about Edgar's mastoid cavity and titanium plate for years. It was only when his mother mentioned hearing aids concealed inside the ear that he remembered what Steve had said about his invention. On the way back from Brighton, he and the electronics wizard had worked on the adapted model now poised for its definitive test.

The Editor turned to his chief messenger. "It's all down to you now, Edgar. Are you happy to go through with this?" The two had spoken at length earlier, when Julian explained the importance of the project and its far-reaching implications for society. He'd also made it clear that, if it worked out as desired, Edgar and Janice would never have any more financial worries. Even if it failed, his courage and resourcefulness would be rewarded with a four-figure bonus.

Edgar thought about the money. He thought about the duplicity of his Brother Masons. He thought about Janice. And he thought about the wild primroses on The Meadow.

He cleared his throat nervously. "You can rely on me, Mr Geldard."

*   *   *

The flag fluttered proudly atop its temporary flagpole at the site of the IPI factory on Brawton Meadow. It was the long-awaited day of its inauguration, a historic day for the company and a deeply emotional occasion for its chief executive officer.

For Marcus C. Quinn III, the flag symbolised the invincibility of his people when challenged. He'd seen off all the local opposition to his factory – and he had seen off the national Press in the shape of Howard Mitchell. This persistent thorn in his side had finally been 'immobilised' and his family sent fleeing to the Fylde Coast, wherever that might be.

Ahead lay Tina's momentous summit meeting when he would be welcoming the Director himself along with some of the world's most eminent eugenicists. But right now he was celebrating another summit, the summit of his own personal commercial success.

Several of the elms which IPI had pledged to protect had been cut down to form a clearing, at the centre of which was the large foundation stone, draped by another IPI flag. Quinn stood at the head of a small group of civic dignitaries, senior company executives and curious local residents, flanked by a team of mini-skirted cheerleaders led by Sandra, his versatile maidservant. On the sidelines, marshalled by police, newspaper and TV journalists focused their cameras on the scene. Unknown to Quinn, Howard watched as the representative of *The Announcer*.

At a given signal, the Brawton Prize Silver Band, resplendent in new uniforms paid for by IPI, struck up with *The Star Spangled Banner*. It was a spirited rendition despite a certain lack of intonation in the trombones. If it sounded more like the *Star Mangled Spanner*, Quinn did not seem to notice. Dressed in an immaculate Armani black leather coat, as it was a chilly morning, he stood stiffly to attention, right hand clasped on heart, until the anthem came to a faltering halt.

Then His Worship the Mayor of Brawton, Brother Arnold Hicks, a magnificent figure in crimson and black robes and gleaming double chain of office, stepped up to the microphone to pronounce a civic greeting. Reading from notes, he declared it was a pleasure and a privilege to welcome such a distinguished entrepreneur as Mr Quinn and his IPI colleagues into their community on this auspicious occasion. He stood second to none in his admiration for IPI's culture and enterprise. Relations could only be strengthened by this exciting and imaginative project.

He would like to take this opportunity to say that Brawton was proud of their new friends and stood four-square behind them. He knew he spoke for all right-thinking citizens when he said the factory would "give birth to a new era of prosperity" within their community.

Polite applause greeted this slightly unfortunate analogy and it was the turn of a Baptist pastor to call down God's blessing on "this righteous enterprise", followed by impassioned prayers for the company's directors and "all those destined to attain personal fulfilment in their employment".

Quinn then reverently unveiled the foundation stone by removing the second flag to reveal a brass plaque engraved with an eagle and declaring:

"This foundation stone was laid by Mr Marcus Cornelius Quinn III, Chief Executive Officer of International Pharmaceuticals Incorporated UK" with the date elaborately carved in large Roman numerals.

As a chill breeze sent autumn leaves scattering across the clearing, he solemnly took a silver trowel and 'dressed' the stone at its four corners. Then he stepped back and saluted smartly. The cheerleaders swung into their choreographed routine and the band played *America the Beautiful.*

Not a dry eye anywhere, Howard thought. You'd think they'd just commissioned a squadron of B52 bombers rather than a Pill factory.

*   *   *

Contrary to popular belief, the Powers that be are not proud. When it comes to carrying out their dirty work, they are perfectly prepared to use anyone, however naff, to promote their interests – usually disowning them with a pained aloofness when they outlive their usefulness.

And so it was that, as *The Announcer's* campaign began to gain the high moral ground in the battle between society's entrenched pro and anti-life battalions, the elitist forces behind the Tina Project started to panic. What they needed was a subtle pre-emptive strike to discredit the newspaper and prevent the climate of opinion turning against them before the all-important launch date.

Since the project was still top secret, a conventional PR exercise was out of the question. So they decided to enlist the support, employing their usual methods of persuasion, of a cross-party coterie of amoral MPs whose vanity outweighed their flexible consciences. It was not a difficult task.

As a result, many Questions were asked in the House about reactionary elements of the Press abusing their powers with alarmist population scare stories that were little more than publicity stunts. Members whose previous eloquence on the vital necessity for free speech in a democracy had successfully delayed the passage of the Privacy Bill, now demanded that the worthy measure be brought forward as a matter of urgency.

It was noticeable that many of the Questions were tabled by a certain pony-tailed pagan, a man with a unique gift for being wrong about practically everything. Fixing his stern gaze on the Press Gallery, the Hon Member asked if *The Announcer* would be prosecuted under the Public Order Act for spreading false rumours and inciting fear and unrest among the citizenry.

In the time-honoured tradition of Parliamentary Questions, however, nobody bothered to answer them.

The sting

Bearing in mind the urgency of the timescale, the stakeout was organised with remarkable precision. First, they had to find a surveillance site overlooking Brawton Masonic Hall's rear entrance since, according to Edgar's feedback, that would be the door used by the VVIPs. It made sense. From long experience, the journalists knew that the more high-profile the public figures, the less inclined they were to use front doors. But just as a precaution, they posted two staff photographers in parked cars within range of the main entrance.

After Howard, Steve and Aubrey Vernon, the pictures editor, had scoured the immediate area, they settled on The Swan with Two Necks, a pub two streets away but with a first floor functions room from which the all-important rear entrance lay comfortably within telescopic range. The landlord was told the room was required for an important business meeting and they did not want to be disturbed. Mine host agreed with alacrity when offered twice the going rate, cash up-front.

Next, Julian picked his observation team. The fewer the better, he realised. Less chance of leaks. In addition to himself, the elite squad comprised Howard, Andrew, his left arm still in a light sling, Steve, Bernard, Irene and Aubrey, with a trusted senior photographer, Ken Lomas. Aubrey would be using the Samsung digital camcorder and Ken a state-of-the-art Nikon stills cameras.

They'd cut it fine, but by lunchtime on November 4 everything was ready. Prof O'Brien implanted the micro-recorder in Edgar's mastoid cavity without a hitch. On the journey from the professor's London rooms to Brawton by *Announcer* staff car, Steve anxiously tested his baby's remote control. No problems.

Upstairs in The Swan with Two Necks, Aubrey and Ken fussed over their light meters and viewfinders as windswept clouds occasionally dimmed the late autumn sun. Final checks were made on the battery of laptops and electronic equipment ready for relaying the scoop of the year back to head office.

Then, fortified by a half of lager and after all the surveillance team had wished him good luck, Edgar set off briskly for Brawton Lodge 15392, of which he was still Master, wired for sound.

Everything was going to plan. It couldn't last.

It didn't. As the time for the summit approached and tension grew in the observation gallery, Steve picked up a strange squeak on his bug detector headphones. "We're being scanned," he said calmly. "It's quite high-powered."

Almost at the same time, Bernard called out: "That's Jim Gledhill down there in that car... *Brawton Bugle* editor. I used to work with him on the *Gaydian*...he's their local stringer."

Julian uttered a four-letter word and it wasn't "drat". "I can't believe there's been a leak from one of us."

"Could be the landlord," Andrew said. "He may have seen us moving our gear in. Maybe he got suspicious and tipped off the local rag."

"After what we paid him. There's gratitude for you," Howard said.

"Not seen any other familiar faces, have you Bernard?" Julian asked.

Bernard scoured the surrounding streets through his binoculars. He'd been picked for the team because of his ability to recognise faces even when they were disguised or wearing dark glasses. He was earning his money already.

"Nope, but Jim's still sitting there. I never forget a face, although in his case I'd be happy to make an exception."

Irene laughed. "You can't beat Scouse humour."

"The great Groucho Marx actually," Bernard said modestly.

The electronic squeaks continued in the background.

"Can you get rid of it, Steve?" Julian called.

"I'm doing my best." He tweaked switches here and there and the squeaking stopped.

"Can they still hear us?"

"Don't know...probably."

While the journalists had been concentrating on the immediate vicinity, activity had built up in the Masonic Hall's car park, with police and security men gathering round its rear entrance.

"Right, listen up everybody," Julian said. "We need to cut the verbals from now on, just in case we're overheard. When the delegates start arriving, note their names in your notebooks. Don't speak them out loud. We don't know who might be listening. Let's keep quiet for now...OK?"

Everyone stopped chattering. Even Bernard. The only sound was the low electronic hum of Steve's equipment. Then the first limo rolled into the car park.

Cameras, lights, action…and silence. The sting was up and running. The occupants of the 'Press box' watched intently as two large gentlemen, one in a designer leather coat and the other in a dark suit climbed out of the car. One was Marcus Quinn, smoking a cigar. The other was the county's chief constable. Bernard wrote down two names and showed them to Julian, who nodded.

Two more cars, a Bentley and a top-of-the-range Saab, arrived in quick succession. Security staff directed them to reserved parking spaces and deferentially escorted their occupants to the entrance. There was no mistaking the swept back grey bun of Baroness Witherspoon or the gross, swaggering figure of Paul D'Arcy. Names were written in notebooks. The camcorder whirred. The Nikon's shutters clicked.

After a lull, the designer-suited Justine Harvey-Ozgood and the self-styled intellectual Martin Pratt arrived followed by a West African princess in exotic robes. Bernard scratched his head over her, then scribbled a suggested name.

As the flow increased so did the degree of incredulity. There were stifled exclamations of "I don't believe it" and "It can't be" as well-known TV celebrities including a game show host, a Tory comedian and a leading sports presenter were admitted. Several MPs and peers from all parties joined the procession, keeping Bernard and his fellow scribes busy.

Even Julian couldn't suppress a gasp of astonishment when a middle-aged, weird-looking woman was helped out of a Land Rover. "Surely not…she's a Catholic," he exclaimed.

"Sort of," Bernard corrected. "Left wing, pro-choice supporter."

The scientists were more predictable, especially the geneticists. As was an atheist university lecturer and self-publicist. Then came a known gay Anglican bishop. No surprise there. Some of the delegates wore shades but Bernard recognised most of them. Those who threw him were mainly the foreign dignitaries, especially a three-man Chinese delegation, ambassadors of their country's coercive abortion policy. He was more successful in identifying a European Union commissioner and a top United Nations official, both surrounded by bodyguards.

A millionaire entrepreneur turned up with a Left-wing trade union leader, incongruously sharing the same limo. When a high profile cabinet minister arrived equally incongruously by taxi, you began to wonder just how high this was going to go. "Not him...of all people," Julian gave a stifled cry.

The Press box cameras whirred and clicked and the pens scribbled furiously in notebooks. With admirable self-control, not a single name was spoken. Yet everyone present was aware they were witnessing the most sensational event of their careers. As experienced professional journalists, they had fondly imagined they knew what was what in the world. Yet here, parading in front of them, was living proof of their ignorance.

All these people, many of them household names, were population control freaks, yet no-one had suspected a thing in their dealings with them. The hacks all thought their knowledge of human nature was complete, that nothing could surprise them, and here they were reeling in amazement. It was a shock to the system, a humbling blow to their collective ego.

And still they had not seen Mr Big. Edgar had told them he'd be the last to arrive. The procession had dried up now and the car park activity subsided. The security guards lounged idly round the doorway. One or two lit cigarettes. The Press box waited patiently in silence.

It was broken by a knock on the door. Andrew opened it slightly. It was the landlord. Would they be requiring anything by way of refreshments, he wanted to know, peering through the crack.

"Nothing, thank you," Andrew said, and closed the door.

"Lock it," Julian instructed.

"Gledhill will have sent him," Bernard said. "He's still down there in the car."

"Remember, everyone. No names till we're out of here," Julian reminded them.

"Actually, I could have done with a cup of tea," Irene observed. "My mouth's gone all dry."

"All our mouths have gone dry, Irene," Julian said. "Don't worry, you'll get plenty to drink later."

Fifteen minutes passed. The guards were growing restless. But the Press gallery did not lower their lenses. They remained focused, fascinated...the scene already translating into vivid intros.

Suddenly there was activity around the doorway. Police and security guards sprang to life. Cigarettes were hastily extinguished as a gleaming black Daimler swept into the car park. No sooner had it stopped than four men, obviously detectives, jumped out. A rear door was opened and a tall, slim gentleman dressed in an immaculate dark blue suit and wearing sunglasses stepped out.

Even with the shades, there was no mistaking a face that regularly appeared on millions of TV screens.

The Director had arrived.

The security cordon parted before him as, with a shy grin and an airy wave, he strode into the building. It was over in seconds.

There are times when clichés can be justified. Two blocks away, in the journalists' eyrie, jaws dropped, literally, and there was a collective sharp intake of breath. They turned to each other, startled, eyes wide and uncomprehending. It was, as they say, a defining moment.

"Now I've seen everything," Julian breathed. "Life as we know it is about to change."

*　　　*　　　*

The chamber had been swept twice for bugs and, on arrival, each delegate passed through the arched metal detector. If it buzzed, the Tiler and his security officers respectfully relieved them of any possessions capable of concealing miniaturised recording or filming equipment, such as mobile phones, wristwatches and even pens. These were stored outside in safety deposit boxes.

When the guests had all assembled and it was Edgar's turn to take up his position as Inner Guard, the Tiler knew what to expect. As a member of Brawton Lodge 15392, he was well aware of its Master's titanium implant, so when the detector buzzed, he smiled. He did a routine search of Edgar's pockets and asked him to remove his wristwatch.

Of course, the detector buzzed again when Edgar passed through a second time but everyone laughed. Edgar, Tiler and security team all enjoyed the joke before he was waved through.

There was silence now in the chamber. The delegates sat in varying degrees of nervousness and expectation as they waited for the Director and the opening of the epoch-making seminar. Then there was movement outside the door and the Tiler knocked three times. Edgar, the Inner Guard, opened it with a flourish and in strode the great leader. All the delegates stood up. Some men, D'Arcy among them, even bowed.

When they were seated, the Director took out his notes and addressed the delegates in a quiet, slightly hesitant voice, using a hand microphone.

"Ladies and gentlemen, I welcome you all to this historic gathering. As you know, our little group does not exist," he said, to smirks and suppressed laughter. "No minutes, notes or records of any kind will be taken. You must keep everything in your head."

Edgar, who had been more than usually gobsmacked by the Director, had to grin when he heard that.

"There is only one item on the agenda – population," the great leader continued. "No-one would dispute that we live in an overcrowded island…" (I would, Julian thought. Only the cities are overcrowded. Has he never taken a walk in the Highlands or on the Yorkshire Moors?)

"…It has been estimated that, for society to function efficiently, healthily and decently, the present population should gradually be reduced. We are therefore aiming for an optimum figure of 45 million in this country by next century. This will require remedies which some of you, I know, will regard as distasteful but I assure you they are essential *in the national interest*…"

Turning to the Chinese delegation, the Director continued: "Sadly, voluntary methods of controlling population growth have failed in Britain and we must now consider a bolder approach. Our friends in China have pointed the way.

"There is a wider dimension to our principled stance on population than merely solving the nation's financial crisis. If carried to its logical conclusion, our vision of a society freed of its long-suffering underclass can be fulfilled. The dream of reformers down the centuries will be realised. *The poor we shall no longer have with us. We can make poverty history!*" (Howard smiled. He had seen the political spin-off coming weeks earlier. Even now the party politicians would be oiling their propaganda machinery.)

"To turn this dream into a reality, ladies and gentlemen, we must act…fearlessly and decisively. And we must act *now*."

The Director took his seat on Edgar's ornate Lodge Master's throne to sustained applause. You certainly had to hand it to the guy's speechwriter. Even some in the Press gallery had been swayed by his eloquence. Well, almost.

Then it was the turn of Justine Harvey-Ozgood to take the microphone. Dressed in a severe business suit with a pearl grey shirt, open at the neck, the TV chat show intellectual had been chosen to unveil Tina's 'distasteful remedies'. Her words brought everyone down to earth. The proposed strategy was a glorious euphemism for coercive population control, not to mention a breathtakingly arrogant assault on human rights.

Once ratified, it would eventually become law with the aid of a compliant Parliament and an already softened-up media. Remarkably few areas of potential resistance had been identified, she said. They would be overcome, as in the past, by judicious and generous methods of persuasion.

Bristling with reformer's zeal, Justine launched her vision of an orderly, caring but strictly loveless world. It was clear to everyone in national and local government that Britain's social services and welfare benefits system had reached breaking point. The problem was one of ever-increasing numbers: the sheer volume of non-productive welfare claimants had placed an intolerable burden on our economy.

This was no time to shrink from their duty as responsible citizens. The national interest demanded a logical, radical solution – a selective programme of birth control, sex education, abortion, sterilisation and euthanasia based on state direction. Compulsory sex education would be introduced in schools, beginning at age five. The right of parents to withdraw their children from the lessons would be abolished. Those who broke the law would be severely penalised.

Existing laws on voluntary euthanasia would be tightened under her Health of the Nation Bill. In cases where two doctors decided there was no hope of recovery, painless life termination would be applied by the withdrawal of life support, food and fluids. This policy was in line with procedures in enlightened European countries. It was clearly in the interests of incurable patients, many of whom were refused assisted suicide at present due to ambiguous ethical and outdated religious factors.

Their most urgent priority would be to restrict the number of children in disadvantaged families that lacked the means of supporting them. The irresponsible breeding habits of this anti-social group had long been a major cause for concern. Corrective measures were as much for their own good as the nation's. It was no use relying on voluntary methods and national guidelines. They had been tried and had failed.

Her proposed Bill would restrict benefit claimants in socio-economic groups D and E to one child in future. Four pilot areas had been selected for the project. They were Gateshead, Nottingham, Camberwell and Portsmouth. Mothers of one child would be subjected to compulsory contraception, by pills, injections or implants, at the direction of their GPs. If they became pregnant with a second child, they would be offered a grant to have it 'terminated', plus a further cash sum to be sterilised.

If they refused, the government would have to take a firmer line. Their social security benefit would be withdrawn and they would face a heavy fine. If they could not pay, they would be sent to a detention centre and their children taken into care until they agreed to be sterilised.

Mothers of more than one child who refused sterilisation would also have their benefit withheld and their children taken into care until they agreed.

(The unexpected harshness of Tina's agenda caused a stir among the delegates and cries of disbelief from the listening journalists.)

Opponents of social progress would condemn these measures as totalitarian and even a violation of human rights, as they had in China, but the policy had now been totally vindicated in that country. "It is time for Britain to follow their example. The national interest demands it. *There is no alternative.*"

She reminded her audience that government legislation had proved highly effective in correcting anti-social human behaviour in the past. It had been painful at the time but it had been for the people's own good.

"We stopped them drinking and driving. We stopped them speeding. We stopped them smoking. We stopped them eating junk food. What we need to do now is stop them breeding," she declared, to loud applause.

*   *   *

"Stop them breathing?" Irene asked in disbelief when the recording was played back in Julian's office two hours later.

"No, stop them *breeding* – but that as well!" Howard answered.

The reporting team had watched as Prof O'Brien, wearing his micro-lens 'loops' headset, had carefully retrieved the tiny recording device from Edgar's mastoid cavity, using a pair of surgical tweezers. Then, as the champagne enjoyed liberal circulation, everybody sat around in varying stages of wonder and astonishment as Steve played it back connected to an electronic amplifier.

The instruction to "keep everything in your head" was greeted with raucous mirth before Justine Harvey-Ozgood's recipe for state terror reverberated round the office and they were all too stunned to say anything. Julian, Howard, Andrew and Irene busily scribbled their shorthand notes, more from habit than necessity. Edgar, the lion-hearted hero of the hour, sat with the slightly dazed expression of a man not yet able to come to terms with the scale of his heroism.

Bernard was already working on his headlines. Prof O'Brien sipped his champagne and shook his head in disbelief at what he was hearing. Only Steve remained impassive, focusing his attention on his mini-miracle.

At last the strident diatribe came to an end and the seminar's delegates unanimously adopted the Tina Project in the form of a draft private member's bill, to be sponsored by Paul D'Arcy MP, and fast-tracked under the government's existing emergency powers.

William's dire prediction – "the supreme irony" – had come to pass. Howard's faith in him and Julian's inspired hunch had finally been vindicated. But that was only half the battle. Having established the truth, you had to make sure it prevailed. The enemy was no longer Tina. It was time. Five hours to the first edition deadline.

Julian was already calling Cyril Sharp, the tetchy night editor, on his internal phone. "There'll be some fireworks tomorrow," he said when the underling answered. "I want you to clear the first nine pages."

"Are you sure, Julian?"

"Nine pages, Cyril. Let's do it."

Then a call to the circulation manager. "Get those presses oiled, Harold. I'm ordering a double print run tonight. That's right…two million copies!"

*   *   *

Word soon got round in the newsroom as the tempo ratcheted up towards the first edition deadline. To keep the story under wraps until the last minute, Howard used Julian's terminal to write the splash, plus background material for the inside pages, much of it already prepared from his early research on Malthus, Galton, Stopes and the other control freaks.

Andrew and Irene were doing a joint colour piece on the day's extraordinary events in Brawton as seen from The Swan with Two Necks. Aubrey was organising two full pages of pictures of the visiting eugenicists. Bernard, splash sub for the night, also weighed in with a detailed report on the revolutionary hi-tech electronics used in the sting, with Steve as technical adviser, and Julian…

Julian was dealing with the bad news.

Half way through the evening, only two hours before the deadline, the managing editor had phoned. There was a slight problem. Lawyers acting for the Tina network had just served him with a High Court injunction prohibiting the naming of its director and members, pending a full court hearing next day. An application to prohibit publication of the remaining report had been refused.

How they'd got wind of *The Announcer* story after all the newspaper's precautions was a mystery, though the collective machinations of Jim Gledhill and the pub landlord were suspected.

Julian was only slightly miffed. It was, after all, just a hiccup. With any luck, they'd name the great man and his acolytes next day. The mystery would merely whet the public's appetite. It would give *The Announcer* two bites at the cherry.

After a couple of slugs of The Macallan, he set about crowning a distinguished career with its defining leading article:

A day of celebration

It has been a long and, at times, bitter struggle. But *The Announcer*'s campaign to uncover state population control by stealth in Britain has finally been vindicated. The clandestine project we have exposed today planned to reduce the population of these islands by a quarter by the middle of next century.

Its perpetrators intended to achieve this monstrous objective through compulsory birth control, abortion, sterilisation and euthanasia inflicted on Social Security claimants, cynically described as the 'underclass'. Women who refused to be sterilised were likely to find themselves herded into detention camps – a grim reminder of eugenics-driven totalitarian regimes long thought consigned to history. But history has a habit of repeating itself. For state population control, read state terrorism.

While our embattled nation was disorientated by the fear of suicide bomb attacks, a more subtle and sophisticated form of terrorism was unfolding under our noses. No bombs or physical violence were involved but it embodied an equal contempt for human life and its consequences were infinitely more deadly in the long term.

Like all political despots, the elitist clique behind the project claimed 'the national interest' transcended the violation of human rights involved. By raiding the welfare budget they would close a £10 billion 'black hole' in the economy discovered by the European Union. And there was a bonus – the cuts would also fund more weapons of mass destruction for our endless foreign wars.

The 'overclass' elitists gave themselves the soubriquet of Tina – There Is No Alternative. But *The Announcer* decided there was an alternative – that it was in the national interest to oppose this grossly misconceived scheme, whatever the cost. When you fight powerful people you cannot expect an easy ride. Determined efforts have been made to silence us and, even now, the group's leader has succeeded with a temporary legal injunction prohibiting us from naming him and his members. However, an application to prevent publication of our substantive news report was refused.

Our exposure is clearly in the public interest and we stand by every word of it. It is all recorded on tape and has been independently verified for authenticity. Our lawyers are confident that the technical restraint on identifying those involved will be lifted in the interests of justice at today's emergency court hearing.

During the course of their investigations, our reporting team – and even members of their families – have come under sustained pressure from a European-financed spy unit acting for the Tina network. Their repugnant, secret police tactics have brought a new meaning to the expression 'dirty tricks', and this newspaper will pursue them unrelentingly in further court actions. Punitive damages will be sought on behalf of our staff who have shown remarkable courage and tenacity in the face of extreme intimidation. *The Announcer* is indeed proud of them.

Today is a day of celebration. The culture of death's hidden agenda has been revealed for all to see; insidious state terror averted, at least for the present. It must be hoped that our campaign may yet signal a more enlightened age of respect for the fundamental human right to life and individual liberty.

It has been a long and extremely difficult struggle. But it has been worth it.

The scoop

As the first edition deadline loomed, picture desk staff blurred the visible faces of Tina's supporters on their double-page spread and Bernard juggled with the splash headlines. But you didn't need to be a star sub-editor to write tomorrow's news:

WORLD EXCLUSIVE

Pill company backs campaign to reduce citizenry by a quarter; 'Internment' threat for dissidents; Court gag on naming eugenicists

STATE POPULATION CONTROL PLOT EXPOSED
Secret project targets poor families

And there it was, scrolling inexorably on Howard's screen, the scoop of his career:

by Howard Mitchell,
Announcer Chief Investigative Reporter

A top-secret project to stop Britain's poor from breeding was launched yesterday as part of an official drive to reduce the nation's population by up to a quarter and halt the drain on welfare resources.

Proposals for a 'Health of the Nation Bill', intended to be fast-tracked under the government's emergency powers, were approved at a closely-guarded secret seminar chaired by a well-known public figure. Delegates included MPs, peers, international political leaders, TV celebrities, representatives of non-governmental organisations and the contraceptive pill manufacturer, IPI UK.

The High Court has banned *The Announcer* from naming individuals pending the hearing of an injunction later today but a separate injunction to prevent publication of this news story was refused.

The full text of the seminar's proceedings is published on Pages XX [the chief sub-editor would insert the appropriate numbers when he had decided where to put the transcript]. This unedited record of the secret conference was recorded and verified by independent electronics consultants.

Delegates unanimously approved a seven-point agenda 'in the national interest' targeting members of socio-economic groups D and E, described as the 'underclass'. It called for:

ONE CHILD per couple;

COMPULSORY contraception;

ABORTION and sterilisation grants;

DETENTION centres for non-compliant mothers;

WITHDRAWAL of benefit for dissidents;

COMPULSORY euthanasia in terminal cases;

COMPULSORY sex education from age five.

Delegates from China attended the meeting and their national population control policy, incorporating mandatory abortion and sterilisation, was adopted as a model for the United Kingdom. The Chinese one-child-per-couple system employs coercive methods and has been widely condemned by pro-life groups. But it is supported by the United Nations Population Fund (UNFPA). The European Union recently approved £350 million in aid to the UNFPA.

As full details, pictures, background and analysis of all Tina's proposals appeared on nine inside pages, Howard's splash then picked up on a series of quotes from opponents and supporters of the proposed social upheaval. These had been collected by reporters organised by Kath Benson on the desk and ranged from: "The politics of despair", (Tory official spokesman) to "A crime against humanity", (SPUC).

A spokesman for the Medical Ethics Institute commented: "They have lost all understanding of human dignity". A Catholic bishop called on the nation to take an uncompromising stand on "this violation of God's law" and the Anglican church returned a "No comment".

Praise for the so-called reforms came from fairly predictable quarters. The leading UK eugenics apologist, speaking on BBC TV, welcomed "this caring, humane and far-sighted project" while the BBC's resident animal rights activist saw it as "a timely intervention to save the planet".

Women's rights groups found themselves in some difficulty. After decades demanding abortion and sterilisation on demand, they now found themselves opposing compulsory implementation of the procedures. But a spokeswoman for the Lesbian Alliance, had no such reservations. She welcomed China's enforced abortion policy as a template for the United Kingdom and a final blow to "the iniquitous family unit".

The BNP described Tina's agenda as an "imaginative step forward" and "a welcome break from the straitjacket of conventional politics".

*   *   *

A November chill suffused the air, heavy with the fermentation of fallen leaves, when Howard met Dominic Greaves in the neat little churchyard where Sir William was buried. Although still early afternoon, the sky was already darkening around the bare branches of the trees surrounding the ancient church. Both men wore overcoats and Howard carried a wreath of red roses.

"Congratulations on your masterpiece," Dominic said generously as they shook hands.

"Not my masterpiece...your father's," Howard corrected. "Without him, not a word of it would have been written."

"All the same, you did the dirty work."

Howard smiled at the adjective. It was spot on. "I just carried on where your father left off. It was important to finish the job."

There were already fresh flowers on the grave when the two men reached it. Howard bent and gently laid the wreath against the grey marble headstone. He stepped back and stood briefly to attention. "Mission accomplished, William," he said quietly.

"We're still waiting for a date for the inquest," Dominic said as they returned to their parked cars."

"You may not have to wait much longer, Dominic. I think you'll find our story will have disturbed the coroner's slumbers."

"The family decided not to pursue the policeman, after all. You were right – there was no way he was going to tell us the truth. Pity you couldn't use him in your story though."

"Our lawyers killed it. There was no direct evidence of collusion."

"No, they got rid of that fast enough. But what about your pictures?"

"Inconclusive without Inspector Scott's testimony."

"I understand the legal restraints but it would finally have given us a sense of closure. Okay, we'll never know the truth. The legal experts say the most we could expect from an inquest, if it ever happens, would be an open verdict…but even that would draw a line under the whole traumatic business…"

Howard felt a rush of sympathy for his friend. "I know how you must feel, Dominic. But your father achieved his objective. He can rest in peace now." He reached into his pocket and took out Sir William's letter. "Let me give you this. It's your father's letter to me – the one you gave me at the funeral. Show it to your mother. She'll see his mission's been fulfilled. Maybe she'll draw some comfort from that. Perhaps you will too."

Dominic took the letter. "Thanks very much, Howard. Thanks for everything. You've done a great job. My father would be proud of you."

Normality

What a precious thing normality was, Howard thought as the family sat down to lunch the following Sunday. It was almost a physical sensation. Like so many things, you didn't value it until you lost it. Now the pressure was off, he and Barbara could finally relax. They could taste the wine again, savour Barbara's secret recipe gravy and actually notice Christopher furtively hiding sprouts in his napkin when he thought nobody was looking.

The assignment had been distinctly hairy at times but now that the whole Tina scandal was out in the open, they were safe. The spooks had disappeared back into the Belgian bush. Howard's lawsuits against the police, supported by *The Announcer*, claiming punitive damages for their harassment of himself and his mother, seemed to have concentrated minds wonderfully. It was true what they said: the best form of defence was attack.

The legal actions would obviously be settled out of court although you had to take them all the way to the courtroom door first. It would take months, if not years, but when the cheque came through he planned to buy Barbara a new car and take the family on an extended Caribbean cruise. They'd never been to the Caribbean. It would make a change from Mijas.

Then he'd ask for a transfer to sub-editing. He was serious. He'd done his bit in the relentless pursuit of truth regardless of personal cost. Let some of the fresh-faced university graduates on the news desk try their hand at it…if they'd got the bottle.

When their new son arrived, they'd name him William Edgar, after two men who had plenty of it. Barbara didn't know yet. There could be an element of dissension, especially over the 'Edgar' bit, but he'd talk her round. He always did.

*   *   *

Howard and Edgar were playing a black ball game in the snooker room when Howard's mobile squeaked. It was annoying because he was just about to pot a difficult final black to win the frame. He straightened up, put down his cue and picked up the instrument. "Hello."

"Is this Mr Howard Mitchell?"

"Yes." He was still studying the pot.

"Marcus Quinn here, Mr Mitchell. I just wanted to congratulate you on your success."

"Thanks, I'll take that as a compliment, even coming from you." The guy had a nerve after all the damage he'd caused.

"It's a tough deal...I've been trying to work out how you did it."

"I'll bet."

"We took every precaution."

"Obviously not."

"It can't have been a bug, we swept the place before and after. The chamber is totally soundproof...so how did you do it?"

The guy was obviously a bad loser. The thought of being outwitted by a stroke he hadn't thought of – and by an Englishman at that – was deeply humiliating. He desperately needed to know how such a bizarre defeat had been allowed to happen...just so it didn't happen again. As a captain of industry he always got his own way. Not this time, buster...

"Closely guarded secret, Marcus. You'd never get your head round it." That was a pretty good one-liner, Howard thought. Even if he did say so himself. "You're a Royal Arch Mason, OK?"

"Maybe."

"And you have secrets that will never be revealed, right?"

"You could say that, sure."

"Well, so do we."

"It was a leak that put you on to us, wasn't it...you paid one of our profane guests? It couldn't be a Mason. But I still don't understand how you got the transcript."

"A tough one, as you say."

"If there's a lesson here, I'm ready to learn..."

"The lesson is you don't mess with the Press, Marcus. So get lost. This correspondence is now closed."

Howard snapped off the phone connection and retrieved his cue. His face was slightly flushed.

"Problems?" his snooker opponent asked.

"None at all, Edgar."

He studied the crucial pot again. Just this ball to win the frame…a difficult, quarter-ball cut into the corner but he'd played it hundreds of times. It was the sort of shot which, if you missed, you'd leave an easy pot for your opponent.

There were opponents and opponents, of course. The arch villain he'd just seen off was one it was always vital to beat. But Edgar…the balding, mild-mannered hero who'd risked his neck to provide him with the scoop of his life? Edgar…whose mastoid cavity had confounded a network of dangerous fanatics…who so badly wanted to beat him just once at snooker?

He bent into his stance. Sometimes even a winner knew when he had to lose. Deliberately, he overcut the pot and the black ball rolled invitingly over the pocket. Even Edgar couldn't miss *that*.

*   *   *

They never did name Tina's elitists. The Powers that be made sure of that. After a lengthy delay, the High Court made the temporary injunction permanent. But word gets around. Most people now reckon they know the identity of Mr Big – though they'd rather not say.

Speculation ran riot for a time about his cronies, but then died down. Other running stories came along, like the entire Premiership football team accused of raping a waitress. The Health of the Nation Bill fell terminally ill and, by way of poetic irony, suffered the fate it prescribed in such cases. Its supporters lay low for a long time, licking their wounds. But they're still alive. You may have noticed.

And as for Julian's knighthood…

*   *   *

All is quiet on The Meadow these days. The sound of mechanical diggers and concrete mixers has long faded. The surveyors and the workmen have all departed. Apart from a few half-dug trenches and a rusting, broken-down JCB, it's still the same rough wilderness it always was.

Tragically for Brother Quinn, Tina's demise and the ensuing national outcry had a catastrophic effect on sales. Women's rights groups urged a boycott of all IPI pharmaceuticals, including the Pill. Chemists in working class areas refused to stock anything from the IPI range. The company's share price went into permanent meltdown. The bigger they are, the harder they fall.

Faced with a disastrous drop in demand for their products rather than the dramatic surge their chief executive had confidently predicted, IPI's directors were forced to revise their new buildings programme. The factory about to be built at Brawton was clearly redundant. They decided to cut their losses and abandon it.

The only reminder of the grandiose project is the building's foundation stone, now overgrown and moss-covered. Sometimes, when Edgar takes his walk through the surviving elms to inspect his secret colony of wild primroses or pick bluebells for Janice, he stops and looks round to make sure no-one's watching.

Then he jumps up on his vanquished enemy's grave and breaks into a little jig.

The End